APOCALYPSE
IN PIECES

MARK SIBLEY ✳ BLAINE L. PARDOE ✳ PETER NEALEN

JOEL GAINES ✳ PHILIP VOODOO ✳ SHIRLEY JOHNSON

DOC SPEARS ✳ STEVE STRATTON ✳ MIKE BENNETT

JIM KIERNAN ✳ BRETT ALLEN

EDITED BY MARK SIBLEY

ISBN: 979-8-88922-084-8

Edited by David Gatewood

Published by WarGate Books, an imprint of Galaxy's Edge, LLC.

Cover Design: M.S. Corely

Website: **www.wargatebooks.com**

CONTENTS

Foreword   1

1. VFW   3

Author: Blaine L. Pardoe

2. Echoes from the Silent Front   39

Author: Joel Gaines

3. GONE NATIVE   68

Author: Steve Stratton

4. Remember the Drift   99

Author: Mark Sibley

5. The Spare Parts Club   128

Author: Brett Allen

6. Hudson Hay   165

Author: Shirley Johnson

7. The CHERENKOV Protocol   197

Author: COL Mike Bennett

8. The Worst Case Was His Job   225

Author: Doc Spears

9. The "Battle" of Diego Garcia   262

Author: Mark Sibley

10. Libreville   292

Author: Philip Voodoo

FOREWORD

I realized early on from readers and my own thought process that there was a key aspect missing from the Mongol Moon world. My characters only went so many places. Many readers asked me about other regions. What was happening in Europe or Asia? What was, indeed... So, I decided to write several short stories within the Mongol Moon world that were stand-alone in nature in order to explore different settings around the world. These short stories would linkback to the third book (forthcoming), but readers could enjoy both without having to read both.

That led to a conversation with Jason Anspach at WarGate Books. Jason, in his infinite wisdom, suggested an anthology of short stories written by the WarGate author and Twitter (X) communities. I enthusiastically agreed, and in a couple of days, we had over a dozen authors signed up and writing. I was completely floored that other writers wanted to jump into the world I created and be part of the journey with me.

Jason reached out to some writers, and I did as well. The response over whelmed me. Every author included in this anthology (two volumes!) is a wordsmith—whether they are fully established authors or first-time writers whose unique viewpoint we wanted represented.

Where have these authors taken the Mongol Moon world?

From the Demilitarized Zone on the Korean Peninsula to the dark north of it. The Hoover Dam makes an appearance along with other critical infrastructure sites. Veterans on Christmas Eve having a drink at a VFW, and secret caches deep in the West Virginian hollers. Out in the Bering Sea with the Coasties, all the way to many different locations in Africa, a gun shop in flyover country, to Texas farmland. That's not all, folks, and some may not even be what you think they are. I haven't yet mentioned the ones I wrote.

The lights haven't gone out everywhere in the world, but the impact is certainly felt everywhere, and now you'll get to experience the life-or-death struggles of common men and women banding together to survive and even strike back. I hope you dive in and enjoy thesestories as much as I have as you experience the wider Mongol Moon world.

And just in case you were wondering, there's still no tacos in the apocalypse.

VFW

Blaine L. Pardoe

Former Staff Sergeant Jason Murdoch sat at the bar of the Addis, Louisiana, Veterans of Foreign Wars, Post 3785, cradling his bourbon and ginger ale. The small gathering there didn't necessarily want to be there on Christmas Eve. They were there because there wasn't any other place for them to go. Josh Jackson, the bartender, sat on a stool next to the register and watched the TV hanging over the far corner of the bar as *It's a Wonderful Life* played for the third time that night. Seeing the show was nostalgic, and it helped drown out the realization that Jason, Josh, and the others were in a bar rather than with family.

When he was younger, Christmas Eve was spent with his mother. She had died three years before, preceded by his older brother Martin, the great war hero of the family. Martin's death had broken his mother's heart; Jason had seen that in real time. Martin had always been the favored son, no matter how much she had tried to deny it. Her death left him alone in the world, the second son that never could outshine the first. Now, for him, the VFW was the only place to go. In some respects, the patrons there were his only remaining kin, and he was comfortable with that.

The VFW was more than a place to go to be with others who understood who you were and what experiences a vet had endured. It was a last refuge of sorts. There, it was more judgment about what you drank than for your military experience. For some, it was a home and family. Jason didn't go for the alcohol; he usually just had a Diet Pepsi. This was different though, a holiday. The people that came in on Christmas Eve were there because, like him, they had no other place to go. Josh fired up the grill and made a full BBQ chicken dinner which was one of the best Jason had enjoyed in years.

"This movie always makes me cry at the end," Silvia Klein said from the bar as she side-eyed the movie. Jason found that hard to believe. Silvia was a hard-ass biker. The former Air Force Security officer may have put on some weight, but she was every bit the brawler still. One former Marine commented that she looked like Melissa McCarthy. While Jason thought the description fairly accurate, he saw what she did to the poor Marine in response. She had his chipped tooth made into an earring that she still wore. Picturing her crying about anything was difficult to imagine.

Suddenly, the VFW plunged into darkness. Even the emergency exit lights went black. "What the fuck?" muttered Marine Steve Strayer from his seat further down the bar. "Someone not pay the electric bill?"

Josh fumbled in the dark, opening an electric panel, holding a lighter up and throwing the breaker. It garnered no effect.

Rudy, the Desert War vet that was at the far end of the bar, managed to find, then open the door. It didn't help much. The blackness was everywhere. Jason pulled out his Samsung to turn on the light, but it was dead. "Merry fucking Christmas. My phone is dead."

"Mine too," Silvia said. "Aw shit, it figures, I just upgraded."

Jason slammed back his drink and walked to the door. Normally, the parking lot was illuminated by a pair of streetlights. Tonight, though, even the lights were out. He could smell the Mississippi River just a short distance away.

"It couldn't be a power outage," Rudy said, standing next to him. "If it was, our phones would work."

"What is it then?" Steve asked as he joined them outside, looking into the distance.

"Something bad," Rudy said in a lower octave. He went to his truck, a battered F-series Ford, got inside and fidgeted with his keys. "Just like I thought," he grumbled as he got out.

"What is it?" Silvia asked.

"EMP. It fries the electronics. That's the only thing that could take out my truck, the lights, and the phones."

Steve hurried to his bike, but like Rudy's truck, it refused to start. "Damn it."

Jason knew what an EMP was, and it was a sobering thought. "We got nuked."

For a few moments, none of them spoke. They looked north, towards Baton Rouge. Usually, the ambient light from the city marked the clouds. Now the only light was from the stars. Jason heard the sound of an explosion in the distance, almost like thunder. Josh acknowledged that. "What was that?"

Rudy stood with them. "Could have been anything. Probably a plane."

The warm joy and relaxation that the bourbon gave Jason evaporated in that instance. "We need a plan."

Rudy spoke up, his gravelly voice sounding firm, almost like the officer he had once been. "My place is about three miles north of here. I have a 1960 Dodge I've restored. It wouldn't be affected by an EMP. I've got guns there and provisions. We can go there and see if we can figure out how bad this really is."

***

Guo Huang led the other three members of his team under the Horace Wilkinson Bridge as he had during their trial runs. This night was markedly different. There was no rumble from semis and cars above. Baton Rouge was silent and dark, except for a lone building fire in the distance across the Mississippi. No cars were about either, silenced by the invisible pulse of electromagnetic energy.

His team had come across the southern US border three years earlier. He remembered that night distinctly since it involved a river crossing, albeit different. That night he had been afraid, which was laughable in retrospect. The Americans did nothing to stop his crossing. If anything, they helped with clothing, shelter, food, and even a new phone.

He barked out crisp orders and his team placed the explosives, just as they had rehearsed. Earlier, they had set similar charges on the Huey P. Long – O. K. Allen Bridge. They would be going off almost at the same time as these. Once they did, they would sever traffic from crossing out of Baton Rouge to the west. Then he and his team would travel north along the river, repeating the actions.

As he moved up to where his team worked, Chao Yuán spoke out. "What is the point of this again, Commander? I am sure we can put these explosives to far more productive use." Chao always enjoyed his little jokes, but on this night, Guo was far from amused.

"Eventually, the Americans will realize that they lack food and supplies to make it through the winter. They will head west, hoping that the farmers there will be able to feed them. We will remove their crossings, restrict their movement, and speed up their starvation."

"Most will die on such a march," Chao countered. "You have seen them as we all have. They are fat and complacent. Most will sit and wait for their government to come to their rescue. Besides, our troops will be in position in their heartland. Those that might make it will be slaughtered." He struggled to secure the last charge, finally getting it in place, assisted by Jia Hao Peng.

Peng talked little, and when he did, his comments were grim. "These people deserve to starve. They live in such opulence and complain that it is never enough. Let them wither slowly, suffering what our people do."

Guo ignored Peng and concentrated on Chao's comments. His comrade's thinking was far too familiar to Guo. It was the product of a lifetime of propaganda. He had been in the United States before his assignment. He had come to know the Americans. Underestimating them was dangerous and foolhardy. "You have been there three years, Chao. You've seen the American obsession with guns. While you may prefer to think of them as a starving weak mob marching out to the plains to die, I see them as a desperate and well-armed army. There are millions of veterans in this nation too, compliments of American imperialism. They would not meekly saunter towards us begging for food. They will come to fight for their lives. That is why our mission is so important."

Chao nodded. "Your point, as always, is well taken."

"Sir," Chun Cai spoke up. "Sir, I have double checked the connections. I am ready to set the timer."

"Proceed," Guo commanded. In a matter of days, the Americans would have their nation cut in two, thanks to the chilly waters of the Mississippi River.

***

Retired Lieutenant Rudolph "Rudy" James's house was a tiny bungalow. The garage behind it was twice the size of the home. His small home was not on the best piece of property. It was only a half mile or so from the bridge that carried the I-10 over the Mississippi. Rudy unlocked the door and ushered them in. It took him a few minutes to find a flashlight, and as he swept it around the room, Jason saw that the room's only decoration, other than a cross on one wall, was a captured Iraqi flag from Rudy's time in Operation Desert Storm. This one was signed by his brothers... comrades-in-arms.

"Come with me," he said, leading them to one of the two bedrooms. Inside, there was radio gear on shelves and on a large table that was clearly used as a workbench. Some of the sets were genuine antiques, others were from different eras. "An EMP is going to knock out a lot of this stuff," Rudy bemoaned as he hooked up batteries to one of the larger sets, a 1950s ham radio. "I'm counting on old Bessie here to pick up some sort of chatter."

Turning it on, Jason found himself strangely enticed by the glow of lights coming from the various controls. It was reassuring that not everything was rendered useless. Rudy pulled up a stool and went to several channels, signaling his call sign, N5BZC. After the first dozen times, Jason's morale started to sink.

Suddenly, a voice did come on. "This is N2ZUB."

Rudy shifted on the stool. "We are in West Baton Rouge. We apparently got hit with an EMP, can you confirm?"

"I'm outside of Albany and the situation is the same here. No juice, nothing electronic working except the old-school stuff."

"Any idea of who is behind it?"

"I'm getting chatter from all over the place. Some are pointing the fingers at the Russians and the Iranians. Apparently there's been some shooting between Pakistan and India too. The current thinking is the Chinese."

"Any word from DC?"

"Mixed reports of a nuke going off there," the voice replied. Jason felt his stomach knot at that thought. Was it really that bad?

"Any idea of who is in charge?"

"Zip. Right now, everything is a hot mess."

Rudy dipped his head low in thought, saying nothing for a few seconds. "Thanks, brother. I will come on this channel in two days at 1700 hours with an update."

"Copy that. Good luck, buddy!" Rudy reached up and shut off the set.

"Damn," Silvia muttered. "I'm all about getting the Swamp cleaned out, but not with a nuke."

Rudy raised his head and even in the dim light of the room, Jason could feel his gaze. "They hit us when we were our weakest. Most of the military is on leave."

Jason waited a moment before speaking up. "We need to get our shit together. With no electricity, food and drinkable water are going to be at a premium. People are going to panic and are probably already starting to loot the big box stores."

"Morons will probably grab big screen TVs," quipped Steve. Jason thought he was probably right.

"I've got guns and some prepper buckets of food at my place," Silvia stated.

Steve spoke up. "I have a shitload of camping gear and enough ammo to hold off a battalion of baddies if we are pressed."

Jason nodded. He didn't have a lot of guns; he didn't need a lot. What he did have was high-end gear, and he had plenty of ammunition. This wasn't the apocalypse scenario he had envisioned, but he hadn't planned for one particular disaster. He had built up skills and gears that would apply for all of them.

Rudy rose to his feet. "I'll get the truck. I can get you all home to grab your gear. The party store two blocks from here is closed for the holiday; we can pry open the door and take what we need. Not exactly health food, but if this is as bad as it sounds, any food is going to be better than none. And if this is what I think, none may be on the menu for some time to come."

Jason nodded. "We need to look at this for what it is, a survival situation."

"We have to assume that anyone approaching you is armed and dangerous," Rudy added. "I learned a lot being in intelligence in the Army. One of the key things is that fear breeds stupidity. A lot of people are shitting themselves right now. Their precious little lives were all based on technology that is now worthless. Most of them have never had to function without it and that will frighten them."

Rudy's truck was painted flat black and was a pristine restoration Dodge D-Series. It fired right up when he turned the key and the ad hoc crew climbed in the back, sans Josh Jackson. With his prosthetic lower left leg, they offered him the passenger seat. They stopped at Steve's netted guns, ammo sleeping bags, and a lot of camping gear. Sylvia came out with four handguns, food, and a big ass Rock River Arms Predator. Jason looked at the huge hunting rifle with a bit of surprise.

"Hey, go big or go home," she replied.

Josh's house netted them a crossbow, bolts, a .44 Desert Eagle, and a garbage bag of clothing and food.

They loaded up at Jason's home as well, then stopped at the party store. Sylvia was less than subtle, using her Predator to destroy the lock. The ransacking of the tiny store took less than twenty minutes.

Rudy was the smartest, focusing on protein sources like SPAM and canned Vienna sausages. Josh took two cartoons of eggs which would have to be eaten soon or they would spoil. Josh loaded up on every bit of coffee and Mountain Dew he could, no doubt worried about their caffeine needs. He secured several cartons of cigarettes, despite not being a smoker. "Hey, people will trade anything for a fix once they run out of these babies." Steve was more random in his selections, grabbing a lot of liquor and bags of chips and other junk food. They moved fast, which Jason realized wasn't necessary. The police were as stranded as the rest of the population. Still, there was a nervousness about being in the open.

The group of VFW members pulled into Rudy's when a loud explosion caught their attention. All of them had heard the sound before. This wasn't thunder, it was explosives.

Glancing up the road to the Horace Wilkinson Bridge, Jason watched in amazement as an entire section of it fell onto the bank and into the Mississippi, bringing down six vehicles that had died on the bridge as a result. The metal of the collapsed section groaned loudly and the cars banged and boomed as they splashed into the water and crunched on the muddy bank. Only one section of the bridge had collapsed, but the effect was clear in the starlight: the bridge was closed for business.

"What the hell?" Josh muttered.

"That was no accident," Rudy growled through his gray beard.

"No shit," Steve replied. "With everything knocked out, why would you want to blow up a bridge? It's not like anyone would be using it."

Rudy's gaze narrowed. "Maybe there's more going on here than just us getting nuked."

Jason understood his logic all too well. "You're thinking there might be boots on the ground."

Another more distant boom of an explosion echoed down the river from further upstream. They couldn't see the source, but Jason knew what it was instinctively. "They just blew up the Huey Long."

Rudy was still stroking his beard as he spoke, "I was going to suggest us hunkering down for the night. Let's drop off most of our food and non-combat gear and head up there. We need to find out who is fiddle-fucking with us."

"And if we find them, kill them, right?" Silvia asked, with a hint of excitement in her voice.

"Damn straight," Josh replied.

An hour later, they stood in the darkness under the bridge. Each of them was carrying a weapon. A few hours ago, it wouldn't have been even a remote consideration. From Jason's view, it was a Christmas Eve no one would ever forget.

One entire section of road had been brought down by the blast. Josh marveled at how precise it was. The twenty-five-foot section looked as if it had been cut out. The lines of fracture were perfectly straight. The smell of the river commingled with gasoline from cars and the hint of explosives that lingered in the still air. Josh stood where the fallen section had crashed down some fifty feet into the embankment and the edge of the river. "This was done very deliberately, by people with engineering background."

"How do you know?" Rudy asked.

Josh patted his titanium alloy prosthetic leg. Even through his pants, his ring hitting the leg made a tinging sound. "I was a combat engineer in the Army. That's how I lost this." He turned his attention back to the bridge. "Inexperienced people would have done too much damage or not enough. This was precise. They probably used some shaped charges just for this job. They didn't overdo it and take out the whole bridge, they took out just a section."

"Why not take it all out?" Steve asked.

Jason responded. "There are two possibilities. One, they didn't have to. Two, they wanted the bridge unusable but something that could be repaired sometime in the future." As he spoke the words, he cringed at the implications.

"Why take out the bridge at all?" Silvia queried.

"I have no idea," Josh said. "I would guess to either keep people in, or out. Taking this out here, they have cut off Baton Rouge from reaching the west side of the river."

Steve weighed in. "This leaves us with more questions than answers."

Rude spoke up. "Actually, this does tell us a few things. Whoever set off that EMP has agents already in our country. A fifth column. They were already in position, with their gear, when the bomb went off. They had a target list and got to work fast. Hell, they may have had this bridge wired and a timer set on it before the EMP happened. We can also assume that these saboteurs are on this side of the river." He walked around the area of the crashed section, pulling out a flashlight and checking the muddy bank. "There's at least two sets of boot prints here."

"How do you know those belong to them?" Steve asked.

"They're fresh, for one. I've lived along the river most of my life. Footprints fade fast here. Also, nobody would be down here fishing or anything, not on Christmas Eve."

Jason grinned slightly. "Spoken like an intel officer."

"I can neither confirm nor deny that." Rudy grinned back, stroking his beard. They all knew that much about Rudy's past but he rarely spoke of it out loud. "I suggest that we check out the Horace Wilkinson Bridge upriver. We heard a second blast, I bet it was there. If it is damaged like this one, my hypothesis holds water."

"Then what do we do?" Josh asked.

Jason responded first. "We hunt these asshats down and kill them before they do any more damage."

***

As they packed up the 1970 Ford Econoline van, Guo Huang surveyed the damage done to the Huey P. Long – O.K. Allen Bridge. The explosion had been less precise than the first one. Part of the bridge deck had managed to stay attached. The explosion had shifted the entire bridge violently enough to make some of the guard rails pop off and hang down over the river. Despite the lesser damage, it would be impossible for people to cross it in any numbers.

Chun Cai packed up their protective blast mats in the back of the dull red van. "This bridge was much tougher than we expected," he said, glancing up and off into the distance.

Guo took one final look at the hole in the structure. "The entire bridge shook. I heard the rivets hit the water. While the hole we made wasn't nearly as a large as the previous target, this one has been significantly weakened for years to come." There was a sense of pride in his words.

He heard something unexpected in the distance, the sound of a running engine. When it stopped, he moved back to the open van door and grabbed his rifle. "What is it?" Chao Yuán asked. Seeing Guo's action, he reached into the van and pulled out his pistol. Guo heard a *thunking* sound, like someone closing a vehicle door. His senses were instantly heightened and the rest of the team seemed to sense the change of his mental posture.

"I don't know," Guo confessed. "Get our gear into the van."

"Hold it right there!" a voice boomed out of the darkness.

Guo's eyes narrowed, and he lowered his stance.

***

Jason had called out, "Hold it right there!" as soon as he got eyes on the figures huddled around an old van. He wasn't sure that these people had anything to do with the explosion of the bridges, but he also wasn't taking any chances. Dense brush nearby gave them some concealment, but would be worthless once the bullets started flying.

They had come upon the van, barely spotting it because of its own running lights when Rudy had shut off his truck. Their deployment was sloppy and uncoordinated. Jason understood; it had been a long night. Jason was armed with his Sig, and he crouched low as he moved towards the river and the unknown's flank. Almost immediately he wished he had grabbed the AR out of the truck bed.

Gunfire came back at them. *That's my fault. I shouldn't have called out so soon.* He saw Josh move further upstream, with Rudy, Steve, and Silvia taking the center. They fired back. Someone hit the van; he heard the distinctive metallic *tunking* sound, giving him a fleeting moment of joy.

Then came a burst of automatic fire that tore through the brush, showering them with little bits of broken branches and dead leaves. Silvia's big gun boomed, the echoes thundering from the remains of the bridge above them.

Another burst of automatic fire came dangerously close to him, forcing him to lie flat on the wet muddy ground. It had been a long time since someone fired at him in anger, and the memories flooded back. Jason remembered why he had hated it. It was the randomness, the indiscriminate shots, any of which could kill him.

Crawling flat, he continued down the bank towards the river, hoping to get a better angle on who was shooting them. A trio of shotgun blasts went off, probably from Rudy, given the source of the booms. Shotguns knew no friends. He wouldn't likely be hitting them with anything lethal, but he would get their attention. His blasts gave Jason a chance to better position.

Poking his head up, he saw the top of an old Ford van and two people seeming to throw things in the open side door. Raising his Sig, he took careful aim at one of the men and fired two rounds. He knew he missed his target with one, mostly because he heard it *thunk* into the van. The other shot, he was unsure.

What was evident was that they jumped into the van and its engine started. From the passenger window, an automatic weapon sprayed the brush again. His mind classified the sound's source, an AK-47. It was a noise tattooed on the inside of his brain. The van tore off, getting onto the access road and taking off into the darkness.

Jason rose up slowly. His heartbeat was thundering in his ears. There were muscles and joints that protested and he noticed he was shaking a little. Walking towards the truck, he saw everyone still alive, which was positive. Josh, however, was holding a wound on his left shoulder, pressing it hard as blood oozed from it.

"Shit," Steve said, running to the truck, having seen Josh's wound. He came back with a medical kit.

"Hurts like a bitch," Josh muttered, taking, moving to the truck and sitting down on the bumper so that Steve could check his wound.

"You got creased. You were lucky," Steve said.

"I don't feel damn lucky," the big bartender snarled.

Rudy moved around the truck and cursed, "God damn it!"

"What is it?"

"We've got a flat tire."

"You got a spare?" Silvia asked.

"Yes," he snapped.

"So what's the problem?"

"They have a lead on us," Rudy replied to her. From the bumper, Josh let out an audible moan and Steve told him he was sorry.

Jason holstered his weapon and started to help Rudy get the spare out. Silvia scrounged a piece of wood for the jack.

"Did anybody get a good look at those guys?" Jason asked as they wrestled the jack into place.

"I saw three of them," Rudy said. "There could have been another, I'm not sure. They were short. Urban camouflage, probably surplus from the pattern. Those AKs they had were full auto. I heard only one pistol."

"You got all of that in the dark?" Silvia asked with a hint of astonishment. Jason too was impressed with what the intelligence officer had picked up on.

He grinned as he worked the jack. "Imagine what I could have done if we had lights on them."

Josh and Steve joined them. Josh's shoulder was wrapped in gauze, the blood was already seeping through. Jason rose and looked at the bartender. "You going to be okay?"

"Steve here gave me two stitches... says that it's looks worse than it is."

Steve gave a reassuring nod. "It did screw up your tattoo, bro."

Josh glanced over at his arm where the bandage was. "Then those bastards have a lot to answer for."

***

Guo Huang drove the Ford Econoline van towards Lucky Louie's Casino poised at a bend in the Mississippi. That was his planned turnoff point. He had purchased the Ford for its lack of circuits that could be destroyed in the EMP. The van had been rebuilt some ten years ago as a camper, complete with new shag carpeting. To Guo, it was a beast to drive, but it held all of them and their equipment. More importantly, it worked. He was going fast, only slowing to swerve around cars that had died during the EMP attack. The van now smelled of their sweat from the unexpected gunfight.

Exchanging gunfire was something his little team had prepared for. What surprised him was how fast things had gone that way. They had been fortunate. The van had been hit by several bullets, but not seriously damaged. Chun Cai had been nicked by a round that may have been a ricochet. It had not bled much, but now he was nursing a limp with his right leg.

"Who were those people?" Chao Yuán asked.

"I have no idea," Guo replied. "It may have been nothing more than a few armed civilians coming to see what happened at the bridge."

"They didn't react like civilians. I saw their headlights, they had a vehicle that was operable," Jia Hao Peng said from the dark back of the van.

It shouldn't have been possible—the EMP was an indiscriminate auto killer. "Is it possible that they were Homeland Security? They were on us so fast. Perhaps our security at the operational level has been compromised."

Guo had considered that as he dodged another car on the road, its occupants waving for his attention from the shoulder where they walked.

19

"I don't think so. If the Americans' intelligence services knew about us, they would have intercepted us before we did any damage. Or they would have prevented the EMP. No... these people were something different."

"Police?" Cai asked from the bed of the van.

"American police have rules. They would have identified themselves before returning fire. They would have talked. These were not police."

"Have we lost them?" Yuán asked.

Once more, he checked the rearview mirror. Only the blackness of the early morning hours of Christmas day was behind them. "I see no sign of them. If they are following us, they are doing it with their headlights off—suicidal with the abandoned vehicles out here."

A few minutes later, he was forced to slow down dramatically thanks to the clogged traffic on the road. At one point, the road was blocked completely and with a deep ditch on either side, they had to get out and push one of the blocking cars out of the way just so they could pass. Glancing south, Guo still saw no sign of pursuit.

A quarter mile up, they approached Lucky Louie's. Like everything else, the casino was dark. The parking lot was full of dead cars and people wandering aimlessly—some holding their phones in the air as if somehow they might get power.

"Behold the truth of America," he said as they got closer. "Here it is, a holy holiday, and these people chose to spend it at a casino, gambling. This is the misplaced allure of capitalism."

A few people saw the van approach and started towards the road. That only made Guo hit the accelerator. "You should drive into them," Peng muttered from the back of the van. "Then again, that might be merciful for them, given they will starve to death."

Guo rolled his eyes for a moment as he angled around the tight bend in the road, driving past the people as they called for him to stop. Their pleas were strangely rewarding. Having lived in the United States, his contempt for the nation had grown. Seeing people trying to get him to stop, hoping that he might give them a ride or offer help, gave him a sense of power. It felt good.

Turning on River Road, which ran parallel to the levee, the van continued past trailer parks and run-down hovels.

"How far to the next target?" Chao asked from the passenger seat.

The target was the John James Audubon Bridge. "Getting near the bridge will take us about twenty minutes. Getting to where we can do damage, that will take some time. If you recall, this bridge is flanked with a pretty dense growth of trees and brush."

"Oh, I remember this one. It was a good half-hour walk to reach the pylon we need to climb to plant the explosives," Peng moaned.

"We could drive up on the bridge and go over the sides to plant the charges," Chao offered. "It would be easier than carrying our gear through the woods in the dark, then climbing up.

Guo thought for a moment. There were some challenges. There were bound to be some vehicles on the bridge, even on Christmas Eve. That meant there might be people still there as well. It would be faster than lugging gear through the woods. After the encounter with the Americans, speed might be a factor.

"Very well, we'll do this top-down. Once we take this one down, we'll head north and find a place to get some rest." His decision was met with silent nods in the van.

Three bridges in one night were more than they had been expected. Taking out this bridge would sever Louisiana from the west. The next one was miles away in Natchez, Mississippi. They would address that one tomorrow.

In just five nights, we will cut the United States in half!

***

It took them close to fifteen minutes to put on the spare tire, far too long in Jason's mind. Rudy paced as the younger vets did the work, clearly frustrated. All of them knew that each passing minute put them further from the team that had blown the two bridges. As soon as they were done, everyone piled into the truck.

As Rudy drove, Josh took the passenger position, still nursing his wound. The old Dodge didn't have separate seats, but instead had a single bench seat for both the driver and the passenger. In the back of the old truck, Steve produced one of his liberated bottles of whiskey from the store they had plundered. He took a double gulp and passed the bottle to Jason, who eyed it with contempt. "I'm not sure we should be drinking right now," he said over the roar of the engine and the cold wind hitting him.

"I sure as hell don't want to kill people sober," Steve replied, taking another hit. Silvia reached over and grabbed the bottle from him, taking a gulp herself.

"I take it you don't want to kill sober either," Jason asked.

She handed him the bottle. "No. I was in Air Force Security. I never got much chance to shoot at people. No, I just wanted a drink because this is the worst damn Christmas I've ever had. I figured the booze might help. It sure as hell couldn't make things worse."

Jason understood her comment all too well, and it was a far more compelling argument than Steve had made. Silvia's dark sense of humor was strangely welcomed on a night when everything had gone so horribly wrong. He took a long burning sip of the whiskey and felt the warmth surge through his chest and rise to his cheeks. Handing the bottle back to Steve, the former Army Engineer took another sip, then put the cap back on.

Rudy swerved around now-dead cars several times, jostling the passengers in the bed. Jason's butt ached already from the wood bed of the truck. As they approached Lucky Louie's Casino, Rudy slowed the truck to a stop. A small gathering of casino patrons, wandering like zombies from the parking lot, approached. Jason's hand went to his gun, as did Silvia's. Steve pulled his Desert Eagle out as well, giving Jason a nod. People were afraid and frightened people sometimes did stupid things.

One woman, easily near sixty, with a cigarette in hand, came up alongside the bed of the truck. "Hey, can you give me a ride? All our cars had something happen to them. The casino is dark and they kicked us out. Now we can't get home."

Jason shook his head as Josh manually cranked down the truck's passenger window. "We can't right now," he said in a deep tone of voice that demanded instant respect.

"Do you know what happened?" another younger man, so skinny that Jason wondered if he was starving to death.

Jason's mind raced to find the right answer, one that would not completely demoralize the people, nor tie them up there any longer. "We aren't sure. We were lucky to get this truck running," he said, lying with perfect precision.

"We are stuck here," another woman called out. "You have to give us a lift."

"We're already full up," Josh said. No one seemed to doubt his word. Jason and Silvia were on their knees in the truck, watching as the crowd started to gather. Silvia whispered, "We need to get going before this gets ugly." Jason gave her a slow nod in response.

Josh seemed to sense it too. "Did you see an old Ford van drive through here?"

"I did," called a man in bib overalls from behind the smoking woman. "They tore right past us a few minutes ago."

Rudy yelled past Josh. "Were they heading north?"

The man nodded. "I reckon they were. They barely slowed down. They sure as hell was in a hurry."

Rudy thanked him. "If you see them coming back, stay out of their way. They are armed and dangerous."

"Thank you, buddy!" the man replied. Where the others seemed nervous on the edge of panic, the man in the overalls seemed strangely content.

Rudy accelerated slowly, dodging around a man that stepped out in a vain attempt to block the truck. As soon as the Dodge started moving, the crowd seemed to close in. They got clear and Jason relaxed his grip on the gun, which he realized was so tight, his fingers ached from his grasp. That hadn't happened to him since Iraq, and with that realization, memories surged back to the forefront of his mind. Thoughts went to friends, now long dead and gone. Even with the cold air hitting him, he felt warm, not from the whiskey, but from sweat.

It took another twenty minutes before they could make out the dark outline of the Audubon Bridge. It was long, running over the road they were on before gently rising over the Mississippi River. Rudy slowed at the sight of it, then pulled off the road. It was a gesture entirely based on driving when there were functional cars. In a weird way, Jason liked it.

Rudy got out, followed by Josh. They both moved near the bed. Rudy's eyes never left the bridge in the distance, barely visible in the starlight. "I've driven under and over this bridge a hundred times in my life. This is the first time I realized just how big it is."

"Where do you think they are?" Silvia asked.

Rudy's gaze shifted from the bridge to Steve. "Damned if I know. Steve, you're an engineer. Where would you be?"

All eyes fell on Josh who looked at the bridge. "It's long and spread out, but if you want to cripple it, you need to do it over the river or close to that. Based on the other two bridges, they aren't dropping them entirely, just making them impassable. So, you have to do that in a place where people walking across can't just climb or drop down." His eyes were fixed on the bridge, drinking in the details.

Rudy nodded. "So, would they try to do it from on top, or the bottom?"

"You need to do it underneath. Otherwise, the force of the blast gets reduced by the road surface. From the underside, you can take out key joints on the cross supports and drop an entire section with a minimal amount of explosives."

"There's a lot of underneath with this bridge," Steve noted. "This thing runs just above the treetop for a half mile, at least before it gets to the river."

"Yeah," Josh replied. "I'm pretty sure they will drive out on top of the bridge and then climb down and under to plant the charges."

Jason was surprised at his comment. "What make you so sure?"

Josh pointed in the distance. "Because their van is driving up there right now."

Looking up, they could make out the running lights on the Ford Econoline as it maneuvered around an abandoned semi tanker truck. Rudy reached in and hit the knob on the Dodge's headlights, plunging the street in front of them into darkness. They all stared as the Ford slowly moved out onto the bridge.

"How long for them to plant the charges, Josh?" Rudy asked.

"Twenty, maybe thirty minutes, at least to do them right."

Rudy cracked his neck, then stroked his beard. "Last time we rushed in all willy-nilly. Not this time. We do this like we were trained to do it, slow and steady. These ass-munchers are playing for keeps. They have full auto weapons and explosives. They are clearly working their way upriver, taking out every bridge along the way. On top of that, they are hitting us when we are down, they are attacking on Christmas Eve... that's our thing to do!"

Jason got the reference to Washington crossing the Delaware and he couldn't help but smile. "Agreed. We need to drive up there, park where they can't see us, approach on foot."

"They probably think they shook us after that shootout," Silvia said. "I say we creep up on these bastards and give them a full metal jack enema."

For the first time since the power and their normal lives disappeared into the night, the members of VFW 3785 actually smiled.

***

Guo helped break out the harnesses and thick nylon roping they would be using to get under the bridge. They had rehearsed similar maneuvers prior to this night on smaller bridges, but this would be their first time on a bridge this size. They were all aware they were likely to encounter problems they hadn't anticipated. Training helped take the edge off that. The rest would have to be dealt with creatively.

Part of the challenge they would be facing was that one of the explosive experts, Chun Cai, had been wounded... hit by what appeared to be three shotgun pellets. Two weren't deep. They had popped out the pellets. One bit of buckshot did go deeper and would have to be dealt with by more than mere field medical expertise. He walked with a limp and when he tried to put on the harness, it was clear that the pain was going to interfere with his work. That meant that Guo was going to have to take his role under the bridge. He was confident that he could do the task, but he preferred to remain topside.

For a moment, he paused, freeing in place. Guo thought he heard the sound of an automobile engine echoing from the dense foliage below the bridge. It had only been for a split-second, then disappeared. What it had done is reignite his concerns that they might be followed. His team would be most vulnerable with two of them hanging under the bridge with the explosives and detonator packages. Looking out under the starlit treetops, he wondered if his unexpected guests from the previous bridge were down there, lurking in the shadows, waiting to come up on them.

His options were limited. If he waited much longer, they might be fighting the rising sun and even greater exposure. If they went ahead and got attacked while half of his team was under the bridge, with the other two helping with the ropes, they could be slaughtered. Such choices were not new to Guo. Several years earlier he had been on a convert team that had sneaked into Vietnam for a sabotage mission. Their extraction point became compromised by a Vietnamese patrol and, with his team leader injured, he had been forced to make a tricky call to cross the border at a different point. It had not been easy then, nor was it easy now.

"What is it?" Yuán asked, seeing Guo's stare out over the treetops.

"I thought I heard something." Just saying those words seemed to generate an air of tension... he could feel it all around him.

"Sounds are funny out here. They bounce off of the river."

"It might have been a car motor."

"You think it might be the ones we encountered earlier?"

"Perhaps. Then again, it may be nothing."

His team stopped putting on their gear and looked to him for his decision. "We continue. Chun, you and Yuán will be up here, topside. Use your eyes and ears while Peng and I attach the explosives. If you even remotely think there's a problem, pull us back up."

Everyone nodded in response.

***

Jason's knees screamed at him in protest as he silently moved behind an abandoned car, using it for concealment. He could make out the figures in the distance, standing behind the old Ford van, apparently putting on some sort of gear. They were a good hundred yards ahead, and with the rise of the bridge, he knew he'd have to adjust his scope accordingly. He had pulled out his AR-15 and adjusted the scope. With darkness, attacking at this range was going to be a challenge. Even if they had night vision gear, it wasn't going to work. Rudy had even quietly complained that laser sights were now worthless thanks to the EMP.

He was slightly concerned by the abandoned tanker truck on the bridge. The Ford van was poised to use it to block visibility from below. It could be loaded with anything. While it was far enough away that if it exploded, they might be safe, it could damage the bridge deck. Rudy had prepped them by saying to avoid shooting at it if practical.

They had parked at the base of the bridge, nearly a mile back. Two civilians passed them, walking back. They confirmed that their target van had driven out on the bridge and appeared to have stopped. Knowing they were ahead meant moving on foot to close with their targets. Glancing down, he realized it was the first time he had gone into battle wearing New Balance running shoes. He was tempted to chuckle, but instead maintained his focus on the task at hand.

Silvia moved up beside him, her Predator in her arms, panting heavily. She peered around the side of the vehicle, then pulled back. "That's the assholes that shot at us."

"Who else would be up here?"

"Are we going to kill them, or what?" she whispered.

Jason peered off towards Rudy, who was moving along the far guard rail, creeping along at a steady pace to close up with him. Off to Jason's left, Josh and Steve were so low, it looked like they were going to crawl. They were already doing better than they had in their first encounter. They had good coverage of the flanks, with he and Silvia taking the center.

Rudy stopped, looking at his scope, making adjustments just as Jason had done. Then he looked over at Josh and Steve, who were now lying on their stomachs, taking aim.

Rudy remained kneeling, holding his arm extended, and made a horizontal arc. *Fire.* Rudy held up three fingers, then two, then one.

Jason rose, aiming over the roof of the vehicle and the moment he heard the first gunshot, he fired. The flashes were brilliant in the darkness. Silvia leaned out with her Predator and joined. Their targets dove for cover or fell from being hit. The van that was behind was riddled with missed rounds. The sound of breaking glass was barely heard through the cracks of fire.

It took a few moments for the enemy to start shooting back. One of them rose to the vehicle and looked as if he were pulling out weapons. He got two weapons for his comrades, then twitched, collapsing straight down.

Two AK-47s fired controlled bursts down the bridge. Jason ducked down as bullets tore into the car he was hiding behind. The rear window of the vehicle blew out, raining chucks of glass down on him and Silvia. Sparks flicked off the pavement as bullets seemed to inch closer to his position.

"I hope this guy's insurance is paid up," she muttered, lying flat on her stomach and firing under the car, using a rear wheel for cover.

Glancing off to his right, he saw Steve rush forward about ten yards, then once more fall flat and fire. Josh emptied his magazine. Rudy blazed away with his own AR-15, emptying his first magazine and slamming in a fresh one. Suddenly, both front tires of the car he was behind were hit. The bang and sudden shift of their cover was startling. Rounds thunked, devouring the metal and plastic around him.

"Well, this sucks," he muttered.

"You ain't kidding!" Silvia replied.

Glancing over at Rudy, he saw him motioning for them to advance. He cringed at the thought, but he knew it was the right thing to do. "We're going to advance."

Silvia fired another round. "Wonderful."

His eyes surveyed the ground. There was a good fifteen yards of openness to the next car they might use for cover. "That Honda," he said nodding towards it. "That's where we are going to go."

Silvia nodded.

"You go on three, I'll put out some suppression fire. Once you get over, give me a signal, then you cover for me."

"Alright. Call it."

He drew a deep breath, then angled out above her, firing. "Go!"

Silvia jumped out as best she could, almost tripping in the process as he fired off half a magazine in rapid succession at the van. Just as she reached the Honda, she fell, then rolled behind the car, gripping her left shin.

"I got hit!" she called out, her voice in a slightly higher octave than before. She made a low moan followed with the words, "I'm going to cut that guy's balls off."

Jason had no way of knowing how bad it was, other than she got on her knees and brought up her Predator. "Alright, when I say three," she called.

Jason readied himself, then she called out, "Three." Silvia rose, firing away with her Predator as he hunched low and moved fast, faster than he had in years. Bullets cut the air around him, he could hear them, and he lunged the moment he got close to the Honda, landing behind her.

"How bad are you hit?"

She fired another few rounds, then lowered herself, pulling at her pant leg. "You tell me."

The bloody hole was small. It was impossible to see how deep it went. Pulling off his elastic belt, he wrapped it around her leg as she moaned in pain. It wasn't a great bandage by any means, but it would have to do. "Sorry about the hurt."

He looked over and saw Rudy had used their advance to elbow his way closer as well. "We need to end this, and pretty soon," Jason said as a spray of automatic fire savaged the Honda between him and the enemy.

"No shit, Sherlock," she replied, coming up on her knees and firing a trio of shots.

Jason popped up again, and fired. This time he noticed light, from a flicker of flame, near the rear of the van. Emptying his magazine, he dropped back down. Something was burning... and he was thankful it wasn't the car he was hiding behind.

***

Guo lay in a slowly growing puddle of his own blood. The two wounds were not bad, or so he hoped. One was in his upper chest, the other was a flesh wound to his right leg. Near him was Chao, who was close to death. The only sign of life coming from him was a gurgling noise.

Peng called out from under the van, hiding behind one of the tires. "We need to fall back."

"Our gear is in the van. No gear, no mission," he replied between volleys of gunfire.

Suddenly he smelled something, smoke. "Is something burning?"

Chun, who was near the front of the vehicle, called out, "The van's on fire!"

"Move, move, move!" Guo called as he started to rise next to the vehicle.

There was an explosion and the side of the van, old-school Detroit steel, hit him like a flyswatter, throwing him hard a good fifteen feet into the guardrail for the bridge. He heard bones crunch on the impact, a sickening sound. Vertigo devoured him as a brilliant ball of orange flame rolled in on itself as it loomed skyward over the bridge.

Guo tried to move, find his weapon, anything... but darkness swept over him.

***

The explosion was huge, turning the Ford van into shrapnel that riddled the bridge and rained down all around Jason and Silvia. He had no idea what they had hit, and he didn't care. The gunfire ceased immediately as a massive ball of flame soared skyward, lighting up everything on the bridge. For a fleeting moment, he worried that the nearby tanker truck might explode, but there didn't seem to be an indication of it leaking.

"Fucking yeah!" Silvia called out.

Jason got up slowly, raising his weapon in case there were survivors. Rudy came up alongside him, now on his feet. "That was spectacular."

Josh came up to the Honda. "Now what?"

"Where's Steve?" Rudy asked.

Josh's head hung low. "He got hit between the eyes."

Dying on Christmas was horrible. Dying stopping terrorists, that was heroic... that was how Jason mentally processed Steve's death. Silvia hobbled to her feet, clearly in pain. Rudy surveyed them and what little was left of the van, now fully ablaze. "We'll take care of Steve when we're done. Josh, get up on the flank. Go slow. These bastards might still be alive."

They moved cautiously toward the van, checking around and under vehicles. In the flame's flickering light, they saw at least two corpses burning. There could be more; it was hard to get close, the flames were pumping out so much heat.

"I've got a live one!" Rudy called from the guardrail.

Jason and Silvia converged on Rudy's voice. When they got there, they saw a man crumbled against the guardrail. Blood trickled down the curb onto the bridge surface. In his leg was a jagged piece of metal, no doubt from the exploding van.

The man's breath was ragged as he glanced up at them. There was no fear in his eyes, only pain. Josh joined them. For a full minute, none of them spoke. What Jason saw was a man in agony, a man who was attacking his country.

Rudy gave the man a nudge with his boot. "Who are you? What country are you from?" Rudy demanded.

The man coughed, spraying a spittle of blood. "You are so arrogant—all of you. Your fragile nation doesn't deserve the riches it possesses. Taking them from you is not war, it is justice." His English was remarkably good.

"I don't give a flying fuck at a rolling donut about your justification," Rudy said, kicking him a little harder with the boot. "Who are you? Who are you working for?"

"I am Guo Huang," he said proudly. "I proudly serve the People's Republic."

"The Chinese," Josh said. "It figures."

Guo moaned, struggling with his breath. Jason was under no compulsion to help the wounded man. In fact, watching him suffer made some of his own pain fade.

"How many other teams are out there like yours?"

"I do not know," he said. "Dozens... hundreds... the number doesn't matter. Cutting your hamstring is what counts. All you did is stop us... others will pick up where we left off."

Josh shook his head. "That may be, but you will never see it."

Guo's eyes met the gazes of each one of them, in succession. "Who are you?"

"We're the V F freaking W!" she fired back.

Jason actually smiled. Guo heard her words but looked confused. It was an expression that stayed with him as he died.

***

They wrapped Steve in a tarp and recovered one of the AK-47s. There had been talk of bringing the dead terrorists off the bridge, but Rudy shot that down. "Let 'em rot." Jason understood the logic. These were not combatants, they were saboteurs. They didn't deserve to be treated honorably. As they finished, sunrise started on a Christmas day that none of them would forget.

Driving back to Rudy's, they did pick up four people from the casino and drive them down the road, letting them off not far from Rudy's.

While Rudy had two old generators, his refrigerators had too much circuitry and couldn't be revived. So they cooked what meat and food they thought would go bad for a small feast. While Silvia nursed her injuries, Rudy and Jason dug a grave out behind Rudy's house for Steve.

Jason felt he deserved better, but things being what they were, he was getting a small ceremony. Rudy produced a flag which they folded over his body, and despite the older man's objections, they did fire a twenty-one gun salute. They all drank a toast to Steve with the bottle of whiskey he had brought with them. It all seemed weirdly fitting and was the best they could do.

Their Christmas feast was consumed in silence. They were all exhausted and ached from their ordeal. Josh's talents at the stove were deeply appreciated as they stuffed themselves on food. Silvia actually teared up for a few moments at the end of the meal.

"What's wrong?" Rudy asked.

She wiped away her tears. "I lost my damned earring," she said, touching her ear where the tooth had once hung.

There was a full second of silence, followed by laughter. This wasn't the end; Jason understood that much. This was a beginning. The world had changed, and with it, so had the once lonely members of VFW 3785.

And for that, he was strangely thankful.

ABOUT THE AUTHOR

Blaine L. Pardoe

Serious Version:

Blaine Pardoe is a New York Times Bestselling author who writes military sci-fi, true crime, military history, and political thrillers. He wrote for the BattleTech franchise for over three decades before being canceled by the woke. He has been a guest speaker about his nonfiction works at the US Naval Academy, the Smithsonian, and the National Archives. As of late, he has written novels for Galaxy's Edge, the new Tenure series, and is the primary author of the bestselling Land&Sea series.

Funny Version:

The son of mercenaries from the Trivon system, Blaine was raised as a Terran. He is a semi-professional astronaut, bounty hunter, licensed tiger castrator, private investigator, registered cat juggler, and has killed fourteen alligators by hand. At sixteen he was on the professional bear wrestling circuit and in one match, killed his opponent, skinned it, then posed for Playgirl magazine on the hide of his foe. He is best known for his work as Tom Cruise's stunt coordinator and Brad Pitt's personal testicle fluffer.

Wanted for the murders of twenty-seven pedophiles, two Nazis, six socialists, and an escaped giraffe, Pardoe resides in seclusion in a special government facility in Virginia. He is currently working on books about his personal exploits during the Napoleonic Wars along with a guide to shaving felines. Secretly married to Taylor Swift, he is the father of sixteen children, two of which he pays child support for. In his spare time, he composes operas for the bagpipes and funeral dirges for the banjo. He is noted for his patenting of the Spanx and the Shake-Weight.

ECHOES FROM THE SILENT FRONT

Joel Gains

Chaos

Pyongyang, North Korea

6 AM

There was only silence. Ko Min-Jee awakened with a start and looked around. Usually, the eerie strains of "Where are you, Dear General?" reverberated from every nook and cranny in Pyongyang at this time, the call to all workers that it was time to start the day. A street orphan, so slight that it looked as if a strong wind could knock her down, she had mastered the art of invisibility amid the capital city's grand monuments and austere buildings. She was far removed from the glorious portrayals of the Hermit Kingdom seen in state media. The towering statues and massive murals that depicted North Korea's eternal leaders in heroic poses were landmarks she used not for admiration but for navigation. In one place, she might find a meal. She avoided other places to stay out of the police cadre's grasp.

Ko Min-Jee knew every alley and shortcut, every hidden nook where she might find shelter or scraps of food. Standing tall and illuminated, the Juche Tower did not serve as a beacon of ideology but as a means to navigate the darker, less welcoming parts of the city where she could go unnoticed.

The city was always silent at night, but at 6 AM, every day except Sunday, those eerie tones from loudspeakers echoed through the streets. Yet, it was already past six, and it wasn't Sunday. She was reasonably sure.

"This never happens," Ko Min-Jee muttered.

As she wondered about this most unusual occurrence, the stillness of the morning was shattered as an explosion rocked the streets and shuddered the ground beneath her. Ko Min-Jee dropped low and covered her ears in terror, her heart pounding. Then air raid horns blared, slicing through the city like a knife. More explosions followed, each one further away than the last, but that did nothing to soothe the fear that had taken hold.

"Is it the Americans?" she thought in panic. "They always tell us to prepare for the worst and that the Imperialists will come to destroy us."

As her first dose of fear subsided, Ko Min-Jee's survival instincts kicked in. She rounded a corner and saw that the next street over was in chaos. Wounded and unwounded alike were running in every direction. Children cried. Large army trucks pulled up and soldiers spilled out, trying to restore order. The propaganda posters that usually lined the streets now fluttered helplessly in the morning breeze as if they were uncertain of their own messages.

***

Across the city, in a military barracks in the fortified sector of Pyongyang, Myung Jin-Ho was abruptly awakened by the same series of explosions that startled the young orphan girl. However, the blasts were deafening, closer, almost personal for him, as though the city's core was under siege. He had been looking forward to a solid rest after a long night of guard duty, but now, his thoughts of sleep were violently shaken.

Disoriented, Myung Jin-Ho leaped from his narrow bunk and quickly dressed as others were doing—all of them wide eyed with fear.

"Outside! We are under attack! To the armory!" he heard the captain shouting between blasts from his whistle.

Outside, Myung Jin-Ho found a city in surreal chaos. The streets were filled with panicked people scattering away from burning buildings that were once imposing government offices and military centers. He saw civilians and soldiers alike stumbling and falling, bleeding from wounds inflicted by the explosive devices and the secondary projectiles they had created. It was a scene of utter carnage.

***

Nurse Lee Hye-Rin's home starkly contrasted with Pyongyang's bustling epicenter. She lived on the outskirts, in an area reserved for those without full city privileges, known as "410-ers." To get her status, she had to make a large donation to the Pyongyang party leaders. But it was worth it, as at least food existed in the shops—unlike in her village, which was far from the capital.

Her daily life was a far cry from the luxuries enjoyed by the elite. Instead, she spent her time in a local hospital, primarily serving the farmers and townspeople outside the city center. For them, this was "going to town." They did not know how different it was for the privileged; most did not even have television sets. They consumed all their news from the political officers and the state-run radio broadcasts.

Lee Hye-Rin often saw the stark despair in her patients' eyes when they realized that the medical aid the Dear Leader had for them was barely a notch above none. But it was always the fault of the Westerners, according to those who knew better than she. The Americans, with their greedy imperialist hunger for power, kept the North from being prosperous.

Her thoughts were abruptly interrupted by the blare of loudspeakers, not with the customary strains of propaganda. But instead, a shocking call to arms: "The Americans are attacking! Report to your assigned places!"

Despite years of indoctrination painting the Americans as villains, Lee Hye-Rin's heart surged with an unexpected sense of curiosity. Perhaps this was the moment of change, the chance for liberation from the tyrannical grip that had long suffocated her and her country.

***

A hidden bunker lay deep beneath layers of concrete and steel in the heart of the capital city—a fortress where Kim Jong-un sat isolated but not uninformed as the Western world had cast their final judgment through relentless metal and fire. This was retaliation. There was no doubt—but how?

North Korea had extended a covert hand to China, not with traditional military assets, but through a collaboration between North Korea's Bureau 121 and China's People's Liberation Army Unit 61398. Bureau 121 was the covert unit within the Reconnaissance General Bureau of the Korean People's Army. It was notorious for its advanced cyber warfare capabilities.

Throughout the last decade, Bureau 121 was responsible for numerous cyberattacks globally. However, this time, they were not acting alone. They had extended their reach by forming a covert alliance with China, leveraging resources, and sharing intelligence to launch a sophisticated cyber warfare campaign against the United States.

They were able to weaken American defenses and sowing confusion. North Korean hackers, working in tandem with Chinese military strategists, targeted critical infrastructure in the United States, from power grids to communication networks, crippling their functionality and creating chaos ahead of the planned physical invasion. But how had the West uncovered this treacherous alliance?

Of course, Kim Jung-un would retaliate. He would strike back at the United States as he had threatened to do for many years. And he smiled, knowing he could say he had done it to defend his people.

He picked up a phone, not needing even to dial a number. "Launch a nuclear strike against the American west coast. Immediately," he ordered. He smiled again and thought, *I will be remembered in history as the Defender of the People. And I will rebuild his nation, but the Americans will remain doomed. Nothing can save them.*

"General, launch phase two," Kim ordered.

***

Born to humble farming parents in a small village near Taegu, South Korea, Lee Jung Ah's early life was steeped in the hardworking ethos of a rustic existence. They farmed a bit of land, and his days were filled with the rhythms of the seasons, helping his family in the fields. For some years, he attended the local school, where he learned the basics of education, his homeland's often chaotic history, and the complex realities of his divided nation.

Like nearly all young South Korean men, Lee was conscripted into the military upon reaching adulthood. Mandatory military service was a crucial aspect of South Korea's defense posture. His service eventually led him to one of the most fraught frontiers in the world: the DMZ, a strip of land running across the Korean Peninsula at the 38th parallel that serves as a buffer zone between the two Koreas.

Tonight, he was peering through binoculars at the North Korean soldiers stationed across the border while they peered through their binoculars at him. It was so odd. Why was it so hard to unify the two Koreas?

Lee could not fathom the history of hate and resentment that had driven the two countries to remain divided for so long. He knew enough to understand that the Kim family held an iron grip on power in the North, but how hard would it be to revolt against such a regime? Especially when most of them were starving over there. Is that how the regime kept them subjugated? How much could those people take?

Suddenly, Lee heard the sound of artillery fire. *Is that outgoing?* he wondered, still looking through the binoculars. Oddly, the lights on the other side of the DMZ had suddenly extinguished. Now, he could hear artillery rounds as they passed overhead.

"INCOMING!" he shouted.

The reality of the situation began to dawn on everyone when the ground shuddered violently, a clear sign that the artillery rounds were not friendly and certainly not far off. Confusion turned to chaos among the troops as they scrambled for cover, their training now a scramble for survival.

With his heart in his throat, Lee grabbed a nearby bunkmate by the arm, pulling him toward the nearest bunker. "We need to move now!" Lee shouted over the noise, his voice filled with the urgency of imminent danger. Lee and his bunkmate stumbled into the safety of the bunker. The clamor of the outside world seemed to muffle. Then he heard another sound, and it turned his bowels liquid with fear. It was a deep, resonant rumbling growing louder by the second. Tanks! They were being invaded!

"Out of the bunkers! To your positions! We must hold our ground!" The order came from just outside the bunker. Lee grabbed his gear and ran toward the bunker exit, his eyes fixed on his captain framed in the doorway opening. Then, in a flash, the bunker was filled with smoke, and his captain was no longer there. Seconds later, Lee was in the open air, running as fast as he could. Artillery rounds thundered, exploding just meters away. His fellow soldiers shouted and screamed in the smoke. Tanks fired rounds, their tracks rumbling closer.

Lee turned a corner in the bunker system and saw soldiers appearing from the smoke, and they were wearing gas masks. His heart seized, and his instincts screamed in silent terror as he realized too late that they were the enemy. A burst of machine-gun fire cut through the haze and tore into his body. Lee jolted with the impact and fell to the ground. Lying there, his vision blurred with pain and disbelief: he saw the muddy boots of the enemy soldiers as they moved past him, indifferent to the life ebbing away beneath their heavy, soiled steps.

"I'm dead. There is no doubt," he whispered to himself.

As his world faded, Lee thought he heard his mother's voice. That couldn't be. She died years ago. That couldn't be...

Allegiances

Night descended on Pyongyang. The city lay under a blanket of darkness, broken only by the sporadic glow of fires that had fiercely burned in the wake of the missile strikes. Her heart pounding, Lee Hye-Rin navigated the shadowed streets, moving toward the heart of the destruction.

The air was thick with dust and acrid smoke. Once proud symbols of the regime's might, most of the surrounding buildings were now fractured skeletons, their facades crumbling. Lee Hye-Rin's senses were assailed by the plight of the wounded and the homeless, the innocent souls caught in the crossfire of a conflict they had no hand in creating.

She understood the risks; entering Pyongyang as a 410-er was practically begging for a short life of severe punishment, torture, and then a death sentence. Yet the thought of turning back, of abandoning those in need, was unfathomable.

Her steps quickened as she approached the city center, the devastation growing more pronounced with every block. The once orderly streets were now disheveled, littered with debris, the remnants of lives destroyed. She moved past vehicles abandoned mid-escape, their doors ajar, many burning in speechless testimony to the panic and destruction that had swept through the city.

The sound of crying drew her to a collapsed building. It was a residential block, or what was left of it, now just a heap of rubble under which Lee Hye-Rin could hear the faint cries of someone trapped—a child!

Adrenaline coursed through her veins as she dug through the debris, her hands quickly becoming bloodied and raw from the effort. Time lost meaning as she worked, removing chunks of concrete, furniture, and twisted metal. Around her, other volunteers gathered, drawn by the same purpose. Soon, a hand appeared. It was opening and closing.

"Here! Someone is alive! Help me!" Lee Hye-Rin yelled to the others. They began to uncover this helpless soul from the wreckage. Finally, beneath a shattered beam in the rubble of what had been someone's home, they found a young girl barely clinging to life.

Ko Min-Jee's frail body, now marred with wounds and caked in dust, trembled with shallow breaths. Lee Hye-Rin gently lifted her from the debris, whispering words of comfort, though she knew the child was too far gone to understand.

Many hands tried to relieve her of the battered body she carried, but Lee Hye-Rin ignored them as she spoke softly to the child in her arms. She carried the girl to an improvised clinic set up in the remains of a nearby building, its walls echoing with the moans and cries of many wounded. The space was crude, with makeshift pallets for beds and medical supplies scavenged from the debris.

A doctor looked at the girl's wounds and told Lee Hye-Rin and the others to take her to the back room. There was nothing he could do for her here with their limited means.

"We can save her," Lee Hye-Rin, crying but resolute.

"We cannot begin to treat the wounds she has suffered. I am sorry," the doctor said grimly. He was sympathetic to the plight of the poor child, but they had to prioritize those who had a chance of survival.

"I will stay with her then. One so young should not die alone," Lee Hye-Rin said.

The finality of the decision weighed heavily on her. Lee Hye-Rin fought back more tears as she gently touched Ko Min-Jee's forehead, brushing away the dirt, blood, and sweat.

In our country, human life seems always so cheaply regarded, she thought.

This felt like a personal failure, although Lee Hye-Rin knew in her heart it was more a failure of the Dear Leader and his terrible regime. So many times, he, his father, and his grandfather before him had promised the people that they would be protected from the Imperialists. They lived such austere lives, most of them. Many starving to sacrifice for in the spirit of Juje and the strength of their nation.

As Ko Min-Jee expelled her last breath, Lee Hye-Rin held her close and rocked her like a mother would a toddler. She was so small, this child. Whispering words of reassurance and comfort to the small girl until she finally conceded that the girl's life had departed, Lee Hye-Rin cried silently for a moment. As she left, she placed a small flickering lantern by Ko Min-Jee's side, a feeble symbol of light in a dark world.

Returning to the central area of the clinic, Lee Hye-Rin threw herself into efforts to care for the wounded.

But someone would pay for this. Someone.

***

Myung Jin-Ho spent much of the night carrying the wounded to the clinic on a litter and then running back into the chaos to collect more. There were always more. He was exhausted and hungry, but what else could he do? He was arriving again at the clinic when a young nurse stopped him. "Bring this one here," she said, looking at him with concern. "You are hurt. Let me take care of you."

Embarrassed, Jin Ho looked at his arm. "It is nothing. A piece of shrapnel. Nothing more."

"It will become infected. Let me clean and bandage it. Your valiant efforts can wait for a moment. Here, drink this. It's cold tea, but it will help." She handed him a cup of tea and helped him sit down.

"Do you have any news, miss?" he asked. "Who has done this?"

"We have heard nothing about the attacks. But who has done it is less important than why it has been done," she spat bitterly.

"Certainly, it is the work of the Americans."

"Sir, why would the Americans attack us after so many decades of a silent war? We are a small country. What could the Americans want with us?"

Myung Jin-Ho looked around quickly, grimacing as he surveyed the room to see if anyone had heard Lee Hye-Rin's words. "Miss, you cannot speak like this. We will both be punished for such words."

"Who is here to punish us? Look around. Do you see what we have become? Look at how meager our efforts to save these people are. Look at how little we have day-to-day. Is this the fault of the Americans?"

"Miss, I uh..." Myung Jin-Ho tried to calm her, more so that she would lower her voice. But, looking around, he could see everyone was worried about their own plight—those who were dying and those who were trying to prevent it.

"You have been in Pyongyang. Look at what they have and then look here and tell me not to speak these words."

Myung Jin-Ho listened to Lee Hye-Rin. He couldn't help but feel the weight of truth in her indictments. The opulence and abundance seen in Pyongyang were a bitter pill to swallow against the austere life of nearly everyone else in the country. Some people ate tree bark in the winter with vile digestive results.

"Miss, you speak the truth," Myung Jin-Ho began, his voice low, his gaze meeting Lee Hye-Rin's with a solemn understanding.

But before he could continue, a deafening explosion ripped through the air, shaking the very foundation of their small makeshift clinic. In an instant, chaos descended upon them as the missile struck. The last thing Myung Jin-Ho heard were his own screams piercing the air.

Rebellion

Min-Sung Kim, dressed in a tailored black suit, sat motionless in the backseat of his Mercedes, eyes fixated with curiosity on the horizon where a dull orange glow tainted the dusk. The car, a symbol of his accumulated wealth and enormous political power, sped through the outskirts of Pyongyang, starkly contrasting against the bleak landscapes flanking the lonely road.

As they edged closer to the city's heart, the driver—a man of few words yet unwavering loyalty—suddenly veered off the main road, bringing the car to an abrupt, jolting halt. The reason for this unexpected detour soon became distressingly clear. The entire skyline of Pyongyang was now a chaotic tapestry of destruction, with missiles relentlessly carving arcs of devastation through the sky as they crashed again and again into the city.

At first, he was frightened, but soon the ramifications exposed themselves. "This is the opportunity," Min-Sung whispered, a cold resolve settling over his features. The chaos unfolding before him was not just a display of aggression—it was the moment they had been preparing for, the chance to change the fate of his oppressed nation.

"Sir, where shall we go?" the driver asked, his voice betraying a hint of urgency.

"Take me to the meeting place," he responded. "The others who are able will go there as well." As he settled back into the car, he tried to use his phone, only to find no signal.

The designated rendezvous was an abandoned warehouse on the city's fringes, a relic now serving as the nexus for their clandestine rebellion. As he stepped into the shadowy interior, the dim light showed silhouettes of his fellow conspirators, all influential figures within the crumbling Kim regime.

Among them stood Jin-Ro Jin, the Deputy Minister of Defense, and the unofficial leader of their insurrection. "Initiate the calls," he commanded, his voice cutting through the silence with decisive clarity. One by one, they contacted their allies within the military, those who had sworn their support to the cause. Encrypted messages flew across hidden networks, rallying their secret supporters to initiate the uprising.

Min-Sung then made the most critical call to the unit leader assigned to detain Kim Jong Un and his closest associates. The voice on the other end was unwavering: "It will be done." The plan was simple yet audacious. While the city reeled from the missile attack and their army units took control of strategic locations, a select team would infiltrate the leader's residence. There would be no negotiations, no trials. The tyranny of Kim Jong Un and his lineage would end tonight.

The wait that followed was torturous, each passing minute amplifying the heavy tension in the air. Hope and fear waged a silent war in the hearts of the conspirators as they awaited the signal of their success. However, the stillness was suddenly shattered by the ominous rumble of approaching vehicles. A sense of foreboding descended upon the room as the reality of their situation set in. This was not the triumphant arrival of their allies but the arrival of their betrayal. The doors were flung open with violent force as soldiers stormed the warehouse, their rifles ready, their commands filled with lethal intent.

Min-Sung and the others were placed in the backs of canvas-covered military trucks. They trundled down back roads, the only illumination coming from the dim, eerie glow of the blackout lights. The smell of the canvas covering the back of the trucks was pungent, a mix of must and oil, a scent so tied to Min-Sung's past as a conscript that it transported him back to those days of rigid discipline and relentless fear. Finally, they came to a halt. The back flaps were thrown open, and the conspirators were manhandled out of the trucks.

Upon entering, the chill from the warehouse's concrete floor seeped through Min-Sung's suit jacket, and dread clutched his heart. The warehouse felt cavernous, echoing with the heavy footsteps of the condemned and the soldier. They were forcibly lined up against one wall before the soldiers took position opposite them. The air crackled with tension as the commander's cold and detached voice ordered the soldiers to ready their weapons.

Min-Sung's fellow conspirators, now confronting their fate, began to plead, their dignity crumbling. But Min-Sung held the soldiers' gazes, accepting the grim reality before him with quiet defiance. As they aimed their weapons, he addressed his executioners, "You will kill me. But you cannot stop the action I have already put into place. You will feel my death far more than I will." His words lingered in the air for only a second before being erased by the sharp cracks of rifles.

Nemesis

General Choi Min-Ho stood silently, observing the Supreme Leader. The tension in this underground sanctuary was palpable, a heavy silence hanging between them until the general stepped forward. He bowed deeply, maintaining the respect demanded in Kim Jung Un's presence, before delivering the news.

"We have captured the leader of the traitors and his closest associates," General Choi announced, his voice no more than a hushed reverence. "Our forces are retaking strategic locations across the city. We are systematically eliminating all remaining resistance, as you have commanded."

Kim stood, but his face remained stoic. His cold eyes gave nothing away as he absorbed the news. "I want no one in those units to be left alive," he said, his voice devoid of emotion. "No one."

General Choi didn't flinch at the command; his face remained impassive, a mask that hid any thoughts or feelings he might have had. "No one will remain from these treacherous units, Dear Leader," he responded, his loyalty unwavering, even as he realized the impact of this decision. He was sure the Dear Leader did not. But the decision had been made.

"There is additional news, Dear Leader," he said, his voice carrying a tone that caught Kim Jung Un's attention. "Although our initial assault on the Imperialists was very successful, they have responded much more quickly than anticipated."

This wasn't the news Km Jung Un expected. It was something arrogantly unprepared for in their carefully laid plans over the long years it had taken to plan Operation Mongol Moon.

"Was not our surprise total? How did this happen?" he demanded, his voice betraying his shock.

"It is possible that the Americans were warned by one of the conspirators." General Choi continued on, trying to keep his composure as he revealed a most significant flaw in their plan.

The news stirred a cold fury in Kim Jung Un. "Feed the conspirators to the dogs. They will share the same fate as my late uncle." But later, General Choi, General Min, and these other useless generals would be held accountable as soon as he no longer needed them to contain the Imperialists. Being held accountable had special meaning in the Hermit Kingdom. "Mobilize our reserves and continue to push through Seoul. We want to destroy them as early as possible."

As the door closed with a resonant thud, Kim Jung Un returned to his seat, staring into the dancing candle flames. "We will not stop at the Chosin reservoir this time," he determined.

Outside, General Choi was in a panic. There were no reserves; those were the units in Pyongyang that the Dear Leader had just ordered eliminated.

It is time to flee the sinking ship, Choi thought as he ran through the corridors to find his driver.

***

The US Eighth Army commander staff huddled around a map in their TOC, their faces etched with fatigue and resolve just as the map was etched with grease pencil lines.

"Taking objectives on Phase Line Rascal," began Major Harrison, his voice steady despite the exhaustion clinging to his bones. "Our Cav elements report almost no resistance as they approach Phase Line Bear. The enemy is in full retreat pretty much along the entire FLOT. However, due to the North's attack, we're pretty much surrounded as well."

General Cartwright, an imposing figure, studied the phase lines marked on the map. "This is one giant Charlie Foxtrot. Hold everyone at PL Bear," he ordered.

Colonel Turner, always one to speak his mind, didn't hold back this time either. "Why are we stopping? How many times do we need to make this mistake throughout history?" His frustration was palpable, mirroring the unspoken concerns of many in the room.

General Cartwright turned to face him. "We're not stopping, Colonel. The ROKs will be the ones to reunify this country—and whatever goes with that. This is a Korean war now. We have to make sure the ROKs have that opportunity though."

"This is *the* Korean War all over again," replied Colonel Turner.

"You said a mouthful there, Colonel."

The implications settled in. It was bold, transferring the mantle of the attack and to the South Korean forces to lead the charge toward reunification.

Major Harrison, however, voiced the eight-hundred-pound elephant that everyone else was thinking. "Passing through is a dangerous maneuver, especially if we are still in contact, sir."

General Cartwright fixed a determined look on his subordinates. "We are going to do more than a passing through, Major. We are going to pivot south and destroy any North Korean forces in Korea, the Republic of," he said with finality.

***

They all heard it, but SSG Lawrence was the first to react. "Incoming indirect!" he shouted over the IC and, with practiced agility, yanked the TC hatch of his M1127 variant Stryker closed and crouched down, making sure everyone else buttoned up. Lawrence keyed up on the intercom. "Driver, let's go! Keep that big freakin' mountain at your twelve o'clock, and you will be right as rain."

"Staff Sarn't. I know you are excited and all, but do you have to yell like that?" asked PFC Thibodeaux in his thick Cajun accent.

"I'm sorry. Did I hurt your delicate auditory system, Private?" asked Sergeant Lawrence with a smile. He couldn't understand about a third of what Thibodeaux said a few months ago, but he had gotten used to it.

It's funny he calls me private. I've been a staff sergeant twice already, Thibodeaux thought and shrugged. "Not delicate, so much, Staff Sarn't. Just your voice is a bit high, like an opera singer, when you get excited. I mean to say like a girl opera singer."

Lawrence's eyes flashed with a cocktail of annoyance and amusement. "I will physically throw you out of this vehicle, Thibodaux. I swear I will."

A cheeky grin spread across Thibodeaux's face as he put an unlit cigarette to his lips. "And deprive this temperamental-ass, 19-ton clown car of its best chances of running for more than a day? You wouldn't dare. Besides, who would save your ass then? Sarn't Lofton?"

"You got a point and don't you dare light that dart."

Thibodaux looked wounded as Sergeant Lofton registered his vexation with his West Texas drawl. "I heard that shit, Tib! Now, piggybacking on our illustrious Staff Sarnt's words, I too am prepared to gift you a closer inspection of this here battlefield—you keep that up."

The indirect arty fire they received ended as quickly as it had begun. But somebody knew they were in the area. "Best to keep moving." He loved these jerks but wondered why the Army needed to assign him a delinquent Cajun and a damned Texan.

"You guys know what the difference is between a jackass and a coonass?" Lawrence asked.

"Screw you, Staff Sarn't. Respectfully. We've heard your Sabine River 'joke' before." PFC Thibodaux said.

The battalion radio net came to life before Sergeant Lofton could add his own remarks. "All elements this net, this is India Tango Six Two. All halt at Papa Lima Bear. Say again, halt at Bear, over."

"India Tango Six Two, this is Lima Echo Seven Niner. Roger, over," Lawrence heard Private Riley acknowledge.

Then Riley keyed the intercom. "Staff Sarn't, umm... unless I am reading this map wrong, and I am not, we're past Phase Line Bear."

"We told Battalion that already, right?"

"We did, Sarn't, but I never got an ACK, and they are not ACKing us now, so maybe they didn't hear us. Hard to tell because whoever is running battalion comms isn't exactly on the ball."

"It's probably that new LT," Lawrence replied. "Alright, let's find some concealment up in that wood line and set up security. We can call it in tonight after we get a better antenna up and wait for everyone to catch up."

Damn. What kind of goat rope is this fixing to be? Lawrence wondered. *Nothing but radio comms since the EMP, and whatever happened in space. Radio comms are a crap shoot, only those that were shielded are operational.*

"Hell of a way to run a war," Sergeant Lawrence said to no one in particular.

"Hell of a way to run a war," echoed his crew.

***

"Captain, is that one of ours?" Corporal Shin asked as he peeked through the driver port of his buttoned-up BTR-80. "See there! Moving to the tree line!"

"That is an American Stryker, you fool," Captain Cho snapped back. They were hidden in the forest west of the area the Stryker was moving toward. "Our turret is very different!"

"Will we attack them?" Corporal Shin asked nervously.

"Yes, but I want to make sure they are not the lead element of a larger force. Call the others and tell them to stay put and to exercise maximum noise discipline."

Corporal Shin nodded and put his headset on. "Immediately, sir."

Private Hyun said softly from the gunner's hatch, "We have movement. Someone has dismounted."

Captain Cho verified the information. "Patience," he said, "is the weapon of the hunter." And so, they waited, camouflaged by nature and stillness. "Wait for my signal," his voice crackled in their helmets.

Captain Cho watched the American Stryker crew as they dismounted, their movements cautious as the Americans began setting up a perimeter, a standard protocol if they would be there for any time. "Steady," Captain Cho's voice was calm, starkly contrasting to the pounding in Private Hyun's chest. "On my mark."

The world seemed to hold its breath, the forest silent, the North Korean reconnaissance crew charged with anticipation. Hyun's thumbs hovered over the trigger buttons for the turret-mounted KPVT 14.5mm heavy machine gun. His eyes fixed on the target through the binocular optic before him.

"Fire." The command was calm and quiet but cut through the silence. Bullets tore a deadly whisper through the foliage, guided by the hands of men engulfed in their own fear, as this was their first battle.

***

The sudden eruption of gunfire shattered Thibodaux and Sergeant Lofton's momentary peace as they set up their security position some distance from their vehicle. "Shit! Shit! Shit!" Thibodaux screamed as he threw himself into a slight depression in the ground, his belly trying to turn itself into a shovel to get him behind more cover. He vaguely remembered Sergeant Lofton judo-rolling behind a large tree and going prone with his chin on his hands, waiting for a chance to move—but move where? Sergeant Lofton always made the worst situations look like no big deal. Thibodaux hated that shit.

From the Stryker's TC hatch, Staff Sergeant Lawrence was the first to pinpoint the direction of the incoming fire. "Contact left!" he bellowed, his voice cutting through the chaos with authority. "Gunner, give me some suppressive fire on that entire wood line! Lofton! We are gonna spray these assholes down, and then I will tell you to mount up!"

"Roger, Sarn't!" Lofton acknowledged before he scooted himself from behind the tree to the M240B and began firing short bursts of 7.62 mm fire to point areas along the wood line that their vehicle-mounted .50 caliber Ma Deuce machine gun was sweeping. Overwhelming violence of action. That was the recipe.

Despite his earlier exclamations, PFC Thibodaux was now all business. He next scrambled to the M240B, ensuring Sergeant Lofton didn't have to worry about the ammo side of the house.

"Watch your rate of fire, Sarn't!" Thibodaux yelled.

Lofton nodded but was a little nonplussed about a mere Private First Class telling him how to use the machine gun. Although having been an NCO twice already, with more deployments than any of them, he was a voice to be listened to on some things. But only some things. He was mostly kind of a dumbass.

"Not today, bitches!" PFC Thibodaux yelled.

Yep, Lofton thought. *Kind of a dumbass.*

***

The North Korean reconnaissance team had to reassess their situation quickly. Captain Cho realized that their initial ambush had been met with a fierce and organized response from the Americans. The overwhelmingly violent reaction forced him to make decisions he didn't think he'd need to just a moment before. They were taking very accurate fire, and their ambush had been foiled despite their superior numbers. Their inexperienced crews were just not up to the task of taking on the Americans.

Recognizing the danger of their circumstances and the American firepower, Captain Cho weighed the simple reality that the Americans stood a good chance of destroying them. He signaled a tactical withdrawal. "Pull back! Regroup!" he hissed into his radio, knowing that lingering in their current position would lead to unnecessary casualties.

He had expected the Americans to run or maneuver in some way that he could take advantage of with his superior force. He had expected the American response to be less violent and precise.

I have another way to deal with this problem, he thought as they melted into the forest.

***

"Cease fire!" SSG Lawrence bellowed into his radio. Then, he repeated the command to those outside the vehicle. "Let's mount up before they change their minds!"

"There he goes with that girly opera shit again," Thibodeaux said wearily.

Lofton nodded and chuckled as they started back to the vehicle, carrying the weapons and ammo cans. His chuckle was cut short by a loud thump that reverberated through the forest. Lofton recognized that sound instantly. The North Koreans had not retired so much as disengaged so they could drop mortars on them.

"Take cover!" PFC Thibodaux barked, recognizing the sound a split second before Lofton did.

Explosions erupted all around them. Lofton and Thibodeaux dropped to the ground, clinging to life and waiting for the barrage to end. Amid the impacts and flying dirt and debris, shrapnel buzzed through the air overhead like angry hornets. Then, just as suddenly, it was over.

Staff Sergeant Lawrence burst out of the rear door of the Stryker and ran toward the last place he had seen Thibodeaux and Lofton. "Are you guys alright?" he yelled as he approached.

There was no answer.

"Hey! Guys! Are you okay?!"

Thibodaux groaned loudly and rolled over onto his back—spread-eagle. "Fucking fuck. We're okay. Stop with the opera girl stuff already."

Sergeant Lofton raised himself on all fours and shook like a wet dog. "Hell of a way to run a war."

***

"I wouldn't interrupt the Supreme Leader now, Comrade General Hyu," General Choi warned, his voice barely a whisper yet carrying a weight of urgency. "The spirit of Juje is not present at the moment." This had become a private code among the Korean People's Army General Staff, signifying when Supreme Leader Kim Jung Un was not to be disturbed—times when his mood was dark and his decisions unfathomable. The last time this had happened, he fed his favorite uncle to a pack of hungry dogs.

"This is critical information from the front, Comrade General. Things are not going as planned," General Hyu persisted, his face etched with worry. "The Americans have countered our attack and are advancing several kilometers north of the DMZ."

Choi's eyes widened in disbelief, the gravity of the situation sinking in. "You had better tell our Dear Leader at once," he replied, urgency replacing his initial hesitation.

As they approached the Supreme Leader's chamber, they were filled with the weight of the news they carried. "Supreme Leader, we have urgent news regarding the frontline," General Hyu announced, his voice betraying a hint of the tension that gripped his heart.

"Speak," was all he said.

General Choi took a deep breath before offering the grim news. "Our defenses have been compromised. The American forces have made an unexpected advance and are now advancing quickly toward Pyongyang."

Kim Jung Un was silent for a long moment. "And what of our attack?"

Both generals were quick to assure the Supreme Leader that the attack was still showing signs of success despite the American breakout. "Our special units are already reporting from the outskirts of Seoul. They have secured several of the strategic avenues for our larger forces."

"So, we are trading territory? Wonderful," Kim said sarcastically. "No matter. There is a better way to deal with the Americans. We will engage them with tactical nuclear weapons and non-persistent biological weapons. Bring a plan to me within the hour."

"My Dear Leader, we must consider the loss of our citizens in even a tactical nuclear attack on the Americans."

"General, we will have no citizens to concern ourselves with if we fail to contain the Americans."

"You are quite correct. We will act immediately."

***

They slowly picked their way through the forest before them and Staff Sergeant Laurence was momentarily lost in thought, wondering how long it would take for the main body—hell, even the rest of the recon elements—to catch up. He was conceding to himself that he might have fucked up. He took a deep breath and changed his thinking to what Idaho would look like this time of year. The snow would be just starting to melt, and there would be a slight chill in the air, but it would definitely be warming up.

Suddenly, he detected, more than he saw, a very bright flash of light coming from the south. His back was to it, but it was unmistakable. "No fucking way," he said to himself. As he turned to look, he saw a second flash and a mushroom cloud rise in the distance. Nearly blinded by the brilliance of the detonation, Lawrence was momentarily disoriented. "Button up! For fuck's sake, button up!"

"What the fuck was that?" Thibodaux asked as the rumbling of the detonation grew louder. "What the fuck was that, Staff Sarn't Lawrence?"

"They just nuked our main body. They nuked our main body in their own fucking country."

***

"There's no way. Who does that," asked Sergeant Lofton, incredulous.

"Fucking Kin Jung Un, apparently," Thibodeaux said.

Staff Sergeant Lawrence's mind raced to figure out what they should do next. He could hear Private Riley trying to raise battalion on comms. "Give it up, Riley," Lofton said. "If anybody back there survived, the EMP killed their radios. We don't have the range to reach anyone who can help us."

Riley was becoming more upset by the moment. "What do we do, now, Sergeant? We're fucking dead, right?" his voice was becoming shriller with each syllable.

"We're not fucking dead, Private. Chill for a second and let me think," Lawrence said, placing his head in his hands. *Don't lose your edge, now,* he thought. "Alright, driver halt."

The Stryker rumbled to a stop in the dense forest. An eerie quiet enveloped them, broken only by the faint hum of its idling engine. Staff Sergeant Lawrence dropped down into the vehicle. The entire crew was watching him closely. He knew that their next move could determine their survival, and it was important that everyone bought in.

"Here's what I think we should do. This isn't a democracy, but I do want your input."

"Just tell us what the fuck to do, Staff Sarn't," Thibodeaux said evenly. "We trust you."

Lawrence looked at each member of the crew and they all nodded in agreement. "Alright, here's the plan then. We can't stay put for long, they'll be looking for us. We can't go east because we will hit impassable mountains or get bottled up between them. We have to go west."

"Bad guys are west, Staff Sergeant," Riley said.

"True, but I doubt they're expecting us, and we have speed. We go west and then south, back toward whatever that first phase line was, not Bear." Lawrence looked at Riley for help.

"Phase Line Rascal."

"Phase Line Rascal. Then we will head generally toward Kaesong, hugging the forest as much as possible so we have a means to escape or hide if we encounter anything. From there we'll figure out next steps. Do we agree?"

Sergeant Lofton was the first to answer. "Roger that. Good plan."

Private Riley quickly agreed. Thibodeaux looked back and forth between the two NCOs, his mind working through the implications of their completely fucked up situation. Finally, he dropped his gaze and slowly nodded his head. "Good as any. Hell of a way to run a war, though."

Everyone agreed with that. It was one hell of a way to run a war.

ABOUT THE AUTHOR

Joel Gaines

Joel Gaines is a small business owner and Army veteran. He also worked for the US government in Russia and the former Soviet satellite countries, whetting his fascination with political intrigue. His experiences inspired him to draw on his knowledge of global conflict and high-stakes environments to write his debut novel, *Chaos Terrain*, the first of several upcoming geopolitical thrillers.

GONE NATIVE

Steve Stratton

For Elle who lit the Fire.

"It's easy to be brave from a distance."

-Omaha Tribe

Medicine Bow – Routt National Forest, Wyoming

It was 1600 after a long day of scouting. Back at the abandon mine that was our base for a winter warfare training evolution we'd finished two days before, we were transitioning to an over Christmas late-season elk hunt on private land. Our camp was near Brown's Peak at 11,200 feet, and the town of Laramie lay off to our west. My wife, our intel nerd Elle Parker, boiled water for her tea and my mocha.

While she took care of priority one, I used my satellite phone to call Kieran Kennedy, commander of our U.K. squadron. The phone picked up and Kennedy started in.

"Brigadier General Lance Bear Wolf, I have you on speaker with Charlie Squadron and the support staff. Shit is about to hit the fan. You can quote me on that. I just left the warning and indications cell. We're seeing strange activity from inactive North Korean satellites and a flurry of flights out of Iran—"

The phone squealed, and I yanked it away from my left ear right as the team channel earbud in my right made it a stereo headache. I ripped it out and turned to see Elle and Team Sergeant Chris Bell, aka Ringer, holding theirs and looking confused.

"You guys have comms?" I asked and restarted the phone. They only shook their heads. I tinkered with my radio, then glanced at my wife, her eyes wide and mouth open, pointing. I spun around. "Shit. Get the rest of the guys out here, now!"

Ringer and Elle stood beside me, as two ICBMs lifted off from their silos north of Cheyenne.

What the hell just happened?

From our southeast, two smaller missiles launched and tracked the ICBMs. Much faster, they destroyed them mid-flight.

I turned to the team. "Not sure what the situation is, but I need to know the who, what, where, and why our ICBMs got shot down."

"Did we just witness the start of world war three?" Elle asked.

I sighed. "It looks like it. Let's huddle up. Ant, break protocol and get me on with the National Command Authority," I said to Jeff "Antenna" Bennett, the best communicator in the unit.

"Roger that, boss," he said and dropped his ruck to unfold his satellite antenna.

I checked the phone, nothing.

"Wolf. I need a couple minutes. SATCOM is acting weird. I'm switching to HF backup," he called out.

SATCOM down, satellite phone down, our team radios down. I closed and rubbed my eyes, as if I could wipe away the reality that struck me. *Electromagnetic pulse.*

"Wolf, my radio works, but there's no one on the other end," Ant said.

"Listen up. I think someone has hit the United States with an EMP, which can only mean we are being attacked."

I let them curse. Elle's hand went to her blade.

"Let's go hot until we figure this out."

We entered the mine and replaced our hunting rifles with our assault carbines and put on our chest rigs and rucks.

Back outside, I faced the team as they exited. "There are lots of unknowns. But Ant's gear that was in the back of the mine appears to be working, yet there's no one on the other end. And that includes our go-to-hell channel, which is monitored—"

"Boss," interrupted Brian "Doc" Hennessy, pointing at two more of the smaller missiles as they screamed west. "They're headed for Warren Air Force Base."

"Sweet Jesus," Ringer said.

"Ant, check our NODs and thermal scopes. If they are working, we'll bring them," I said. "Elle and Doc, get me a bearing to the missile site."

I strapped my compound bow to my pack and growled, "We're going hunting. Let's get in the fight."

***

Medicine Bow – Routt National Forest, Wyoming

"The azimuth to the missile site is near a bump in the road called Harmony. It's to our southwest," Elle said.

"It's going to suck getting down from our 11,700 feet of altitude to 7,300 in the dark, but I'm not waiting until the morning," I told my team. "I want to find these assholes and put a stop to their breathing. Same stuff different day. We'll recon and fix the enemy location. Then we develop a plan of attack and destroy what we can before bugging out. If it's the missile system I think it is, there will be a lot of targets onsite. If this turns out to be a 'War of the Flea' hit-and-run type action, so be it. If we get split up, return here. Questions?"

Ringer smiled. "So, the plan is we flow, find, fix, and smoke some bad guys. Same stuff different day, right?"

"No need for one of Ringer's State-of-the-Union-sized five paragraph op orders, right, boss?" Doc scoffed.

"You chuckleheads done?" Elle asked. "We need to stop the threat, then find transportation to Cheyenne. It's our best bet to gain situational awareness and connect with the NCA."

"Agreed, but let's not get ahead of ourselves. I'm on point," I said, cinching up the sling to my carbine.

I headed south, wanting to stay west of the mountain town of Albany and the Owen Lake resort in case any jumpy locals roamed the roads. Pathfinding through the thick timber and rugged terrain put us behind my internal schedule. I tapped the back of my helmet, covering and uncovering the glint tape. A signal to circle up.

I took a knee. "It'll be next week before we see Harmony at this rate," I whispered, only half joking. "I'm going to switch to the forest service tracks." I turned to Barry Seale, or Boomer, our Navy SEAL sniper. "You're our sweeper, bring up the rear. I'll keep the pace down so we can hear if anyone is coming. Check?"

"What happened to going slow to reduce the risk of detection?" Elle asked.

"I think we're okay out here, but head on a swivel. When we pass Owen Lake, we'll be far enough south that we can turn east. We'll slow down again as we skirt south around Woods Landing. That'll put us at the river south of Harmony. Give me a thumbs-up if you can visualize our movement."

The team responded with thumbs up. I stood and headed off at a 45-degree azimuth to intersect the track we'd been paralleling on our right.

Now we were making time and so far, no one was coming out into the freezing cold. We were between Woods Landing and Jelm Mountain when the sun crested the horizon. As we stayed at the wood line, a small herd of elk cows spooked at our scent, trotting forward then turning to snort at us.

I scanned beyond the elk and the group of cattle staring at us. Then I checked my watch, took a knee and the team closed around.

"Take a minute and make sure you can get to your thermal blanket in a hurry. The terrain between here and the river is sparse. I'll stick to lines of vegetation, so we have overhead protection, but I expect the bad guys to have drone support, roger that?"

Their acknowledgements gave me the confidence to push the envelope like we did on our recent mission to Afghanistan. An hour later, we were less than a mile from the Laramie River when a ferocious battle broke out to our north.

It started with a massive explosion that reminded me of a vehicle-borne improvised explosive. A huge black and brown cloud soared skyward as automatic weapons fire broke out.

I pumped my fist up and down and broke into a run. The volume of gunfire had me thinking the bad guys were busy, so I wanted to take advantage of the distraction. We reached the river in less than ten minutes and pushed across at a narrow point. The water was icy cold, just short of freezing.

The gunfire receded, so I stopped us in the trees on the north side of the river.

"That contact must be a National Guard unit or a good-sized militia," Elle said.

"Someone ran into an improvised explosive. Large, but low-order detonation," Boomer added.

"Agreed. Let's move north along the river while we can and find the missiles," I said.

Doc nodded. "We better hurry—those are fire teams killing the survivors."

Thirty minutes later, we glimpsed the upright containers on the far side of a ranch house. The trees and thick brush around the river concealed our movement.

Boomer and I put on our ghillie suits and crawled to an unobstructed view.

Before us was a working ranch. The sign at the entrance was backwards from our vantage point. It said *River Run Ranch*. To our left front was a modest two-story house. The front faced west and we were looking at a snow-covered patio on the south side. To the right was a hay field where the missiles and radar sat.

It is a Russian S-400 system. A 20ft-long radar container and three 40ft-long missile containers in the upright and ready to fire position. How the hell do you get that into the country? Fricking Sinaloa cartel, I bet.

North of the house was a shed, and a barn sat alongside the ranch access road. I guessed it intersected State Road 230 which led back to Laramie. The property was heavily treed behind the house and up past the barn. Dense woods lined both sides of the access road.

A great choke point.

Two SUVs full of men in civilian clothes pulled up to the ranch house. They carried a mix of AKs and AR-15 rifles. One guy had an RPG. Someone, their commander I suspected, strode out of the ranch house and stood, hands on hips. Dude was a big sucker, six-four, two fifty. Knowing some Russian, I picked up some of what he yelled as he ordered them to reload and prepare for a counterattack.

A lanky kid walked outside holding a rugged controller device, looking to the western sky. With a whirr, a drone swooped down and returned to him just feet away. Picking it up, the kid told the commander he was going to change the battery and ambled back into the house.

The shooters entered the barn, and we used the break while the Russians regrouped to back out to the riverbed and rejoin the team who was setting up an objective rally point.

I reported what we witnessed.

"They outnumber us three to one," Boomer said.

"There might be more in the ranch house, the barn, and the radar trailer. If I remember correctly, S-400 takes at least two people to operate," I said. "They expect a counterattack, and so should we. That's when we'll strike."

"Can we thin the herd before then?" Ant asked.

I chuckled. "I like the way you think, brother."

***

Ranch S-400 Missile Site
Harmony, Wyoming

Ant was watching the ranch from a position at the tree line while we improved our hide site under a dense blackberry thicket. He was experienced enough to know when to back out or take the shot.

Our rifles were Sig Rattlers in 300 Blackout with subsonic ammo and suppressors, so taking the shot wasn't a problem, so long as no one else was within thirty feet.

If this is world war three with a foreign invader, it won't take long until we're out of our specialty ammunition. I have a feeling that by the end of the week, we'll all be carrying AKs.

Boomer's 338 Lapua sniper rifle was our long gun. Not exactly heavy artillery, but it was sometimes confused for that. Beside our knives, which we were all pretty good with, we had Sig 320 Legion pistols with suppressors and my bow, a Hoyt Carbon RX-8. It was undetectable.

It was midnight. Doc took the watch, but not before Ant let us know the single drone the Russians deployed was only good for forty-five minutes. That included the time to and from the surveillance area, which was the road coming in from Laramie. It must have had night vision and possibly IR—it was big enough.

Doc took off and Ant said he was going to sweep his HF and amateur radio bands to see if he find a friendly signal. My plan was to get some shut-eye then hunt at 0200, when the Russians would be on the downside of the ambush adrenaline rush.

I woke thirty-five minutes later and drank till I was full. I left my night vision behind; the Milky Way provided plenty of light. Then I crawled next to my wife, and she whispered an all-quiet report. I squeezed her arm and headed to Doc's position.

Fifty feet out, I tasted Old Spice it was so thick, then detected someone—he or she was breathing heavily. Like from fear. Whoever it was had a long barrel hunting rifle.

I knelt, set my bow down, and let the person walk by. I rose and placed my left hand over their mouth with my knife at their throat. He was young. The guy trembled.

"On your knees. One word and I'll bleed you out. Nod if you understand," I whispered.

He nodded, and I lowered him to the ground.

"Whisper back to me your response. What are you doing here?" I asked.

"Trying to figure who this is. Some of my friends died today."

"National Guard?"

"Yeah."

"You want to get some revenge?"

"Yeah, yes!"

"Quiet. What your first name?"

"Luke."

"Okay, Luke. First question. Have you seen any foreigners outside this spot?"

"No, sir."

"Do you have a landline at your house, and does it work?

"Yes. We've not tried Laramie or Cheyenne, but we have talked to some neighbors."

"That's great news. Now, here's what we're going to do. My team of pissed-off special operators need you and any friends you can gather to shoot at the radar trailer and those upright containers. But not until we hear the National Guard counterattack. That will take place around first light. Everyone shoots three rounds from whatever gun they can bring to the fight. Then you haul ass. Do you understand?"

"Yes, sir."

"Good. When the Russians respond to your attack, we will catch them in a crossfire. Remember, three shots, then haul ass. We'll do the cleanup."

"Are you guys green berets?"

"Yeah, some of us. Tell your friends they will be fighting alongside Army Green Berets and Navy SEALS."

Luke's eyes went wide in the starlight.

"Stay here. I'm getting someone to go with you. He needs to use your phone."

The kid nodded so I moved forward to Doc. When I crawled up to him, he whispered, "What's that all about?"

"A kid with a hunting rifle looking for revenge."

"Ah, a kindred spirit."

"Yep. He lost some friends in the ambush so I recruited him to find some buddies to help us and you're going with him," I said, telling him the rest of the plan and to collect any intel that might be useful.

"Roger that. Can I scream, wolverines?"

"What the hell am I going to do with you?" I said, shaking my head. We returned to the kid and I introduced them. "Head home and assemble your crew."

Grinning, the kid motioned to Doc and headed east.

I don't figure they'll pull together more than a couple of guys, but that's all we'll need.

From my position under a fir tree, I took a minute to think the situation through using my "two wolves" process.

"Employ Boomer with his shoulder cannon. He can easily disable, maybe even blow up the missiles and destroy the radar, while you kill everyone else," the black wolf says.

"True, but we need to build a resistance force. Now that we are blind, larger forces will start to arrive. But we can change their mind about Wyoming if we own the missiles," the white wolf says.

Both wolves turn to face me. "Ever think you'd be in an unconventional warfare fight inside the United States?" they say in one voice.

"Hell no, but we practiced enough, didn't we?" I whispered to myself. I was going to thin the herd, but what we really needed was more intel.

***

Ranch S-400 Missile Site
Harmony, Wyoming

Putting my Unconventional Warfare hat on, I reviewed our ability to gather additional resources before the fight started. The houses we spotted west of us were on the other side of the barren land we crossed. *Too risky.* Doc was headed east with Luke to his house. *He's got it.*

All that was left was before me. So, I opted to see if the Russians were keeping hostages and to find items of use. Like propane, gas, or diesel tanks, and any other fun components for improvised explosives.

I started at the main house, then looked for the tornado shelter we hadn't seen yet, and followed up with the barn.

I stayed in the tree line until I was looking at the back of the house. There weren't any lights on in the first or second floors. There was no one within the limits of my NODs or when scanned through my IR-enabled scope.

Their security focus is the missile system, and rightly so.

I checked the corners and I didn't see lights or motion sensors. So, I ran at a crouch for the house. Peeking over the edge of the window frame, I found a living room with the last of a wood fire burning out.

I moved north along the back and discovered a dining room cluttered with Pelican-style cases. Surprisingly, there was no basement.

But I kept moving and stopped under a window, hearing someone with major sleep apnea. They'd stop breathing and then snort and groan before falling quiet for a beat.

When I got to the north end, I found a motion-activated light and strode around the detector arc toward a shed, then stopped at a mound with a hatch, It was locked with a stout padlock.

I put my hand on the hatch to feel for vibrations and got the slightest tingle. I scanned and found what I suspected was the exhaust between some bushes.

I stuck my hand up the pipe and found a screen. I smeared off some of the oily residue and put it to my nose, regretting it immediately.

Crap, something's dead down there.

It was a combination of odors different from the dead and decaying animals I'd come across hunting. It was probably the owners, but we won't know until we've opened it.

Seventy-five feet away was a long shed used as carport. Inside was a Ford Contour and a F-150 pickup with several Chevy Tahoes and Suburbans scattered out front. I put ornamental bushes and trees between me and the cars as I headed to the barn.

There lay three dead horses. A tear worked its way to my chin. I'd ridden since I was a kid and revered horses as my ancestors did. *These assholes have killed everything that might get in the way of their mission.*

I will revisit their lack of compassion.

Looking through a knothole, I made out tables with weapons cleaning material, spam cans of AK ammunition, and boxes of AR-15 rounds, but not much else. I strained to see the sides and the plank creaked.

I dropped to the ground. A flashlight swept the wall from the inside and a pissed off guy grumbled and stomped on his boots. Then walked to the door and exited.

I scuttled to the far side of the dead horses and lay prone, pulling my knife. Ivan had an AK on a loose sling banging his thigh as he walked, swinging a flashlight back and forth as if to scare away an animal.

He was an overweight city-type dressed head to toe in REI's latest. He got to the edge of the barn and coughed. He dropped his rifle to bury his face in the crook of his arm.

I wanted to end him, right then, but needed to delay instant gratification for the larger hurt and win we'd get the next day as a team.

A couple of times in my career, the idea of taking a scalp like my forefathers had crossed my mind. Now it was three times.

The target departed and I waited another fifteen minutes before heading back to the team. I memorized the placement of the fuel tanks and other components, like the Russian MON-50 claymores, that we would use if our primary plan went to shit.

I glanced at my watch. The Russians didn't know it yet, but we were about to take everything from them, including their souls.

***

Nautical Twilight

Ranch S-400 Missile Site

Harmony, Wyoming

Back at the hide site, I gathered up the team to tell them what I found and let them vent.

"It's the Stalin—kill whatever doesn't serve the purpose mindset," Ringer said.

"More like the Ebola virus as it grows, sucking the nourishment out of a cell and then on to the next until it kills the host and eventually itself," Elle said.

I pointed a knife hand at my teammates, deadly serious. "We stop the outbreak here and now. Hell, with the eight remaining missiles, we can secure a large portion of southern Wyoming and norther Colorado."

I continued with the plan of attack and gave them their assignments. "Two mission imperatives. One, kill or capture the Russians and anyone working with them. Two, take control of the remaining missiles. My Russian is a little rusty, but together we can make it work."

"You're not a radar specialist, how will you know friend from foe?" Elle asked.

"The S-400 has radio systems we can use to make contact, and if the IFF pings, it's going to be a Russian plane."

"And if it's not, a Wild Weasel or an F-15 will light up the trailer and put an anti-radiation missile in your lap," Ringer said.

"If I get painted, I'm turning everything off and setting the grass on fire running for the river," I said inside a chuckle.

"Not funny, Wolf. But I do like the idea of downing a few aircraft. It will boost the locals' spirits and their will to fight."

"Boomer, when this kicks off, I want you to be in position to target the ranch house and cover the road. I need you to contain anyone returning to help the support pukes, check?"

"Got it, boss."

"Let's set an example for the rest of Wyoming and any Russians stupid enough to think they can survive invading America. To recap, it's National Guard from the highway, Doc and the civilians from the southeast, and the five of us from the south. We'll handle squirters after we secure the missiles. Roger that?"

Hoorah was the response.

We moved up to a ditch that put us seventy-five yards from the ranch house. The wait was just shy of forty-five minutes. In the distance, the fight kicked off with the beautiful report of a couple of Browning 50-caliber heavy machine guns.

Like yesterday, there was an explosion, but this time the machine guns didn't stop, and I recognized the thumping of a grenade launcher.

The gunfight on the road rose to a crescendo, and I smiled. The National Guard was leaving no doubt who wielded the superior firepower. My ears moved my eyes to the pinging of rounds hitting the radar trailer and the missiles.

I understood they didn't have the armor-piercing rounds to affect either, but it did have the intended effect. Men swarmed out of the house, and we cut five of them down.

The rest took cover and fired in our general area. But our suppressors reduced our visual signatures, and they couldn't locate us.

Where's the giant? I mused.

I crawled over to Boomer on our western flank and told him to hold firing on the house. "I'm going forward to deal with the commander and stop him from calling for reinforcements."

"Probably too late but I'll let everyone else know," he said.

Just then, I recognized the kid and his friends were still firing. Knuckleheads.

"Tell Doc to hold fire."

"Roger that."

I took off west to a spot where the trees around the house hid my advance. I sang an abbreviated version of my death song, asking my spirit guide and the ancestors for strength and courage.

Then I loaded an arrow in my bow and tightened down my sling, so my rifle didn't beat me to death. I ran forward in a combat crouch.

At the fence surrounding the house, I did a quick search for signs of dogs. Not seeing any, I slid over and sprinted to the base of a tree. Just then, the commander stepped out on the porch with a handheld radio, barking orders.

I stood and took the shot.

He must have registered my movement, because he spun to bring a pistol up as the four-bladed broadhead slammed his left shoulder. He dropped the radio and dove into the house.

I waited a beat, fortunate to avoid stepping into a line of AK fire that raked the ground and tree I hid behind. When he shot his last round and dropped the magazine, it clattered on the floor. I sprinted to the porch and knelt at the left side of the sliding glass doors.

The wall above my head exploded in a shower of splinters as the commander fired his AK. I crawled backwards a body length and prepared to enter. His rifle jammed, I'd experienced it myself. He grunted, trying to clear it.

I exploded through the door and rolled behind some containers. When he didn't fire, I caught his reflection in the window. He was bleeding and had broken off most of the arrow shaft.

To my surprise, he dropped the jammed AK and drew a Gerber Mk II fighting knife.

"Let's fight like men," he said in perfect English.

***

Ranch S-400 Missile Site
Harmony, Wyoming

Standing, I dropped my bow and unslung my rifle, dropping it too. "Okay, Ivan. The last Russian I killed with this knife was from Alpha group. Clearly, you're not," I said, retrieving my gleaming blade Randall Model 18.

I blinked as Boomer engaged with his sniper rifle. The Russian must have triggered at my lack of concentration and attacked. He tried to vault the cases and slash at me like a Cossack with a saber. I used his energy and threw him through the plate glass window.

Too bad for him it's not safety glass.

I followed him out as he scrambled to his feet, wincing in pain. "Go ahead, I'll wait."

He groaned as he took hold of a chunk of glass stuck in his thigh. Barry sent another round and I heard a vehicle crash into a tree.

"Being a sleeper for all these years has made you soft."

He grunted as he pulled the shard out. "It has not. Alpha is full of posers as you Americans call them, I am not. I will take your life, then cut up your friends."

"Do you know how many dead assholes have said that."

The Russian circled right, leading with his good arm.

He lunged, I blocked, but as I slid to my right, he slashed the outside of my knife hand. It hurt, but wasn't deep enough to cause me to drop my knife.

He closed again.

Jesus, he's fast considering the broadhead in his shoulder, I thought as our blades sparked.

Our fight devolved into a closely matched battle of wills. I softened my gaze and at an uppercut attack, I registered his stance.

We switched from offense to defense and back. Our steps and lunges cracking the broken glass. Our knives swishing and tinging as we blocked each other's attacks. We continued to circle as we battled with combinations of lunges and kicks.

To my teammates, it probably appeared like a wildcat skirmish. I recognized what my wife was thinking, her green visible light laser dancing on Ivan's side and chest. I wanted to tell her it was okay and to get back in the fight, but I was redlined.

The only thing in my favor so far was the copious amount of blood coming from Ivan's shoulder. I entered to his left and snatched at the arrow, intending to wrench it from his shoulder. It was slick with blood and he jumped away, cursing.

I backed up to create space and time. Then entered a state of no mind to let the path forward reveal itself. A beat later, his stance clicked. I let him enter, defend, then kicked the inside of his right knee, resulting in a satisfying crack.

He screamed and dropped. I hammered his temple with the bronze-pointed butt cap of my knife. Lights out, he fell face first into the glass.

As I flex-cuffed Ivan, rounds snapped by my head.

I cranked the cuffs tight and vaulted back through the broken window, scrabbling to find my rifle.

I grabbed it and put fire on the growing crop of bad guys Barry had pinned on either side of the road into the ranch. I reloaded and stood at the side of the window providing cover from the Russians' view. I whistled. Boomer and Elle scanned for me.

We made eye contact, and I signaled them to move forward to the house.

A round splintered the window frame. I dropped and took a quick peek.

Great, Luke thinks I'm a bad guy. We'll have to discuss the idea of positive identification when this is over.

I left the room and quickly cleared the dining room and kitchen. Between bursts of gunfire, someone thumped down the stairs. I hid, then tripped a younger guy who turned out to be the drone operator. He tumbled and crashed to the floor, sacrificing himself to protect the controller.

I lifted him and pushed my hot suppressor into his chest. He yelped and I gave him my best demonic stare. "What's your name, kid?"

I had a heartbeat of remorse as the kid stuttered, "T-T-T-Tim."

With a quick glance out the backdoor to make sure it was safe, I pushed him into a chair at the kitchen table. *This kid was born and grew up here in America. How the hell did his parents turn him?*

"Tim, you got weapons on your drone?"

He didn't even make eye contact but fidgeted with the controller. "No, surveillance only. Night vision and IR."

From the other side of the house, a voice. "Wolf Pack clear to enter?"

"House is clear," I replied.

My wife and Boomer trotted into the kitchen, and she leaned in and whispered, "We left the rest of the team outside to keep the Russians engaged."

I nodded. "Just asking Tim here if he has weapons on his drone and he lied to me."

Elle didn't skip a beat as she slapped the back of Tim's head. He recoiled, and I kicked his chair.

"Tim, it's not the time to lie. The man you're talking to," she pointed at me, "would rather shoot you than deal with a prisoner."

"I-I-I-I'm not lying. The drone I'm operating is surveillance only."

I unsheathed my bloody Randall knife and waved in it in front of his face. They shook their heads and started to turn away.

"The combat drone is on the roof!" he said, breathless.

I put my knife away. "Can you operate it with this controller, and what's the payload?"

"Yes, a six-pack of grenades."

"Good. You're going to follow his instructions if you want to live," I said, pointing to Boomer. A radio chattered upstairs.

I smiled. "Where are the rest of the radios, Tim?"

"In the pantry," he said.

Elle opened the bi-fold doors. "Pantry, armory, whatever, it works."

There was a pile of radios and most importantly, AK rifles and a couple of RPG-18s. They were based on the US light anti-tank weapon, aka the LAW.

Elle and I each took a radio, an AK, and four mags. I grabbed the RPGs and tossed Boomer a radio.

I turned on the radio and switched channels until I found the Russians calling for Tim.

"I speak Russian. Tell them you are calling the surveillance drone back and deploying the combat drone against the attackers."

Boomer pushed his carbine into Tim's head, and he shakily repeated what I said.

"Switch to channel three," I said, then double-clicked my radio, and they did the same. "Elle and I will let you know when we are set up to the west of the tangos hunkered down at the tree line."

"Roger that. Tim and I will be upstairs."

I checked the area around the door before we slipped out. We ran in a crouch behind the bushes and into the trees.

***

Ranch S-400 Missile Site
Harmony, Wyoming

Working through the woods on the west side of the property allowed me to get a sense of the fighting here and up at the highway. I liked what I was hearing.

Elle and I moved north with a purpose until we slowed one hundred yards away and went into stealth mode. We stopped at fifty yards and found a log to hide behind. They were firing and we caught sight of an occasional muzzle flash but other than that, they were well hidden.

"Boomer, Wolf. Drop the grenades from east to west," I radioed.

"Sorry, brother. Tim resisted, so he's taking a nap."

"Can you get the drone over here?"

"I think so. But I'm not sure how to release just half the payload."

"No worries. Release it all on the east side. We'll take care of the rest. I'll step out in the road when we're clear. Make sure Luke doesn't shoot me."

"Roger that. I've got Doc's attention, he's still with them."

Seconds later, the drone wobbled up the road. The Russians must have seen it. They broke cover, crashing through the brush.

Several ran toward us, and we dropped them using the AKs. We ducked behind the log just before the grenades exploded. The woods filled with screams.

Boomer's sniper rifle barked, then silenced. Standing, Elle and I worked our way to the shot-up SUV. We made sure the three Russians we dropped were dead and found the driver still in his seat with a baseball-sized hole in his chest from the Lapua round.

Four more were dead on the far side of the SUV.

"Are we good?" I radioed to Boomer.

"Yeah, Doc is bringing the partisans forward."

When I walked into the road, Doc stood by Luke with his motley crew. Ant was guarding two civilians next to the radar trailer. I nodded, then spun to Elle.

"Do you hear that?" I asked.

"Yeah, tracks. How we going to contact them without comms?" she asked.

"Very carefully."

Ever since joining the Ranger Regiment, one of my biggest fears had been coming back through friendly lines or contacting another unit in the middle of a fight.

The men and women heading towards us had seen their friends die. And they fought hard to break through a series of IEDs and anti-tank defenses.

"Head back and process the site. Start with the missile command-and-control trailer and have one of the operators make sure it's not on automated intercept," I said.

"I got it. Be careful, they'll be jumpy," she said, staring into my eyes. "Forever plus two."

"Plus two," I said, restating our commitment to each other.

I put my weapons and my uniform top in the woods alongside the road. Then I tied my orange signal panel and a white combat bandage to a stick and walked along the road to the edge of the trees.

I peered around a tree. Two Bradley fighting vehicles advanced down the road with squads of dismounted infantry behind them. I stuck my makeshift flag out and waved it. The formation came to a halt.

A voice called out, "Step out, hands in the air."

And when I did, both Bradley chain guns slew in my direction.

Crap! If someone twitches, there won't be much of me left.

I was told to advance. Without being told, I lay face down in the dusty road. Soldiers rushed over, pinned my arms behind me and flex-cuffed me. Then they picked me up and checked my pockets. They found the radio and the get-out-of-jail card we all carry when on training missions.

A hard-looking captain came from behind the lead Bradley and strode over, grabbing the card.

He tried to speak to me in terrible Russian and I told him we should talk in English.

"Okay, who the hell are you?" he demanded.

"Hakaniyun, huagande," I said, guessing there was some Shoshoni in his bloodline. "I'm Lance Bear Wolf. My team and I were in the Brown's Peak area when the EMP hit. We observed the ICBMs launch and get shot down, so we came to investigate. We also overheard your fight yesterday."

The captain grimaced. "Yeah, we had a gung-ho major race down the road. Those smoldering hulks behind us are all that's left of two hummers and a deuce and a half full of men."

"Sorry for your loss. This morning when you counterattacked, we hit the ranch from the south."

"You look Crow. How many on your team?"

"I am. There are six of us."

The captain frowned. "And you attacked three dozen Russians?"

"More like twenty. We enlisted some locals, and you drew most of them to your counterattack. Did you see the element disengage and head back to the ranch?"

"Yeah."

"They're dead. We control the ranch and the missiles. Have a squad come with me and they can confirm," I said.

"Not happening. Carter, get the drone up," the captain said, talking to a private whose M-4 carbine rattled in his hands.

Four minutes later, Carter reported, "I had Sergeant Paluzek watch the feed with me. We agree, it appears he's telling the truth, sir."

"The next step is yours, Captain."

He spun a finger over his head and the grunts loaded into the Bradleys. I sat on the floor of the lead vehicle as we inched forward. A long, stressful three-plus minutes later, the captain told the driver to push the SUV out of the way and move left.

Crunching ensued, and the other Bradley rolled to a stop on our right. The back hatch opened, and the captain led me out front.

My teammates nodded and Luke's people cheered.

"Welcome to the Wyoming Army of Resistance," I said and snapped my flex-cuffs. "We've got work to do."

The End

Character List

Brigadier General Lance Bear Wolf, Wolf – Special Mission Unit Commander

Elle Parker – Wolf's wife and Intel lead

Chris Bell, Ringer – Special Forces Team Sergeant

Barry Seale, Boomer – US Navy SEAL sniper

Jim Bennett; Ant, short for Antenna – Special Forces Communicator

Brian Hennessy, Doc – Special Forces Medic

ABOUT THE AUTHOR

Steve Stratton

Steve Stratton's first duty station in the US Army was at the White House as a communicator. His next job was at the US Secret Service where he worked physical, electronic, and explosive protection for the President, Vice President, and Presidential candidates. Steve left D.C. for defense contracting and joined 20th Special Forces.

Steve deployed on counter-drug and partner country training missions in South America while working as a contractor supporting USCENT-COM, USSOCOM, DISA, NSA, and the rest of the intelligence community. Retired, Steve now writes, travels, and enjoys the Colorado outdoors.

REMEMBER THE DRIFT

Mark Sibley

Paul stood outside the municipal building in uMhlathuze in the late afternoon. There was a slight breeze coming in from the Indian Ocean. It was rather nice weather with not a cloud in the early January sky. Richard's Bay was just southeast of his location. The deepest port on the African continent and it sat within the confines of uMhlathuze. He held his mobile phone in one hand while he smoked a Marlboro Light with the other, waiting for Rajesh to call. Raj was his second-in-command. Paul was commander of the Quick Reaction Force, the QRF, and he'd chosen Raj to lead it with him when everything went to shit.

He and Raj had been friends for over fifteen years and had absolutely nothing in common with each other except their soul-rending hatred of communists and any other factions that would force their control on people. Here in South Africa, that meant the African National Congress, or ANC, and the Economic Freedom Fighters, or EFF. He and Raj were both in their forties and had fought and patrolled together through some of the worst civil strife South Africa had to offer. Saved each other's hides more than once. They had trained with the British SAS more than once and were employed together multiple times in one of the many private military contractors used as security outfits throughout South Africa. There was no one he trusted more except his older brother. Rick was ten years older and in overall command of the security and defense of Richard's Bay and uMhlathuze. Even as a kid, Rick has his back.

At first, when the war started in the Northern Hemisphere, the civilian leadership of the city stayed and tried to exert their authority. That quickly fell apart and they left late one night over a week ago, leaving the city and port in the hands of the security forces, civilian, police, and what military that stayed. His brother quickly sorted it and set up patrols and perimeters. They had a professional force of over three thousand, augmented by thousands more from the general population that wouldn't be ruled any longer by the ANC or EFF factions. But that wouldn't last long. ANC Cadres and EFF hooligans and highwaymen were pushing further out from Joburg and Pretoria daily.

Raj had gotten a call from his uncle in Dundee, about four hours' drive west of Richard's Bay, two days before. Things were getting tense there. Raj had requested to take a small team to get his uncle and some of his neighbors out. He wouldn't take no for an answer, so Paul allowed it, but he hadn't heard from him since he arrived and was getting worried. He was about to go back inside when his Purge Siren ringtone went off on his phone. He looked at it. Raj. He answered it.

"Raj, man! You okay?"

"Boss! Can you hear me?"

"Loud and clear, man. What's your situation?"

"It's a fucking clusterfuck, boss. Still in fucking Dundee. These EFF fuckers are coming in from the west in big numbers. Recruiting from the townships and shanties. We're okay for the moment."

"Why haven't you left yet?"

"We have a problem, boss. My uncle has more than a few people to get out and we don't have the vehicles for it. Mostly whites and Indians with some blacks and coloreds, a few Asians as well. Families, boss. Can't leave them to what's coming," Raj explained calmly. He was always calm.

"Shit, man. How many?"

"About a hundred or so, give or take. Can't leave these people, boss," Raj said. Paul thought it through.

"Okay. We're coming. Early tomorrow morning. Can you hold until then?"

"We'll hold. We'll be ready. Thanks, boss."

Paul ended the call and pulled another Marlboro Light out and lit it. He took a long pull and thought about what he'd need and what they had. They could do it, but just barely. He flicked the cigarette and walked back into the building to find his brother.

***

Later that night, by Paul's watch, it was 2145 hours, and the Quick Re-action Force was gathered outside the municipal building waiting to go. Paul chain-smoked as he watched his brother, Rick, walk around and chat with Paul's men. It had been a couple of hours of heated debate, first on whether to go, but then once that was decided, how big a force to send and on what routes. The command council was none too pleased, but Paul had made his mind known up front, so they could argue all they wanted. The situation was fluid and frenetic all over South Africa. They had crowded around maps and news reports all evening.

When Europe and America went dark on Christmas, the ANC spent no time starting to consolidate power. Armed ANC Cadres formed up in Pretoria and Joburg and began to work their way outward. Reports of massive traffic flowing to the Western Cape didn't really surprise him, but the speed at which it all went to shit, however, really did. His thoughts were interrupted by a convoy of Armored Personnel Carriers and towed artillery that passed by on their way to where they were being consolidated and re-organized into the Bay's defense force. Military units from the several bases in KwaZulu-Natal Province, of which Richard's Bay was central to, were still arriving.

South Africa was truly a fractured country and well on its way to self-segregating along racial lines as well as tribal and factional lines. Whites and anyone that didn't want to live under the ANC and EFF were moving to the Western Cape, with Cape Town being the center. They were moving rapidly, it seemed, and had been for weeks, since Christmas. Richard's Bay was the Alamo of sorts for the east. A member of the command council ran up to his brother just then and he couldn't hear the animated conversation, but by body language alone he could tell it wasn't great.

"What's going on there, you think?"

Paul jumped, surprised by his third-in-command, Walid. "Jesus, man! Don't sneak."

"Sorry, Reaper. So, that's bad news, eh?" Walid said. No one called him Paul. Raj called him boss. Everyone else used his call sign, Reaper. Walid was a slight man. Egyptian and devoutly Muslim, but like everyone else here, he hated communists and wanted to raise his family freely practicing Islam. He also hated radical Muslims. He had told him that they twisted the Koran to their purposes and that was not Allah's intention. He was a trusted advisor and fighter. Paul flicked his cigarette as his brother approached.

"Your team ready, Paulie?" Rick asked. Only his brother called him Paulie.

"We're ready. What was that all about?"

"It seems that the Americans or someone struck back. Russia and China are both dark. A few cities are gone for good measure. Looks like the Global North is pretty much gone," Rick explained.

"Shit," Paul said.

"Wait, this isn't all bad, is it? I mean all the colonizers are gone, yes?" Walid asked enthusiastically and Rick shook his head.

"What it means, my Egyptian friend, is that there's no big powers left to stop what's going to happen here. Or, at least the threat of stopping it. No world order left, Wally. No one is coming to save us," Reaper explained.

"So, situation is the same as it has always been. Inshallah," Walid replied with a smile.

"Paulie, remember the routes. R34 to R66 to R68 to Dundee. Get 'em. Come back on the southern route, R33. You'll likely be seen. Head on a swivel," Rick said.

"It's like a five-hour trip there and probably a bit longer back. It will be difficult to see us with no headlights on and taillights disconnected. Night vision goggles for the win. I'll see you for breakfast," Reaper said and slapped his older brother on the shoulder and turned to Walid.

"Wally, get 'em loaded. We're leaving. Quietly and dark."

Walid nodded and ran to the groups of men and passed the word and everyone began to mount up.

"Paulie, be careful. We need you here and I can't come get you if you get stuck," Rick said.

"Just send the helo."

"Can't. Pilot left for Durban to see to get his family this afternoon. You are the Quick Reaction Force. There isn't another one."

"You worry too much, man. Make sure there's hot coffee when I get back."

"You got it."

Reaper climbed into the passenger seat of the Mamba, their armored personnel carrier. He had to squeeze in with his gun belt and plate carrier. He had extra magazines in pouches on the front for his AK-47, which was already in the vehicle, muzzle down. He strapped his ballistic helmet on and dropped the night vision goggles to his eyes. Each driver in the convoy had night vision. They would be able to move with stealth, or a measure of it, most of the way. The other Mamba in the convoy was point and started them out to the R34 West.

He watched as a Ratel four-wheeled, infantry fighting vehicle moved out next, followed by six Samil 20 open-air logistics trucks and two transit buses for the people they were picking up. After that came his Mamba, and then a Samil 50 fuel truck. They didn't want to have to stop for fuel on the way back. They'd re-fuel in Dundee as they loaded people. Then came the Casspir, an armored troop carrier with firing ports. It had four large wheels and sat high above the ground and was armored underneath as well. It was the mainstay of South African military and civilian authorities since the '80s. Bringing up the rear was the second Ratel IFV. The Ratels were critical. They both sported a twenty-millimeter cannon. With each fighting vehicle fully loaded and crew and security on each truck and bus, his QRF complement was fifty highly trained fighters, give or take.

He hoped they would have an uneventful trip. However, hope was not a plan. They were armed to the teeth, including with rocket-propelled grenades. A lot of them.

***

The knock on the door startled him awake. It took him a minute to get his bearings. General Mbuso was at his residence in Pretoria. He lived alone and had taken no other wife after the passing of his first and only spouse. He was too old for that anyway. He reached over to where she used to lie. Empty. She had died in an attempt on his life last year. He had been wounded, but she took the brunt of the explosion. He thought about it all the time. When he tried to go to sleep. When he eventually woke up. His simmering anger was always there.

They had eventually found the ones who'd carried out the attack. A faction of the EFF had planned and authorized it. He smiled in the dark, remembering their very slow deaths. General Mbuso was the commander of the ANC's fighting cadres. He had tens of thousands of fighters under his command. He used them in the service of the ANC leadership. Strategically. Not these riot, murder, and plunder tactics the EFF employed. His cadres were professionals, of a sort. Former military and police. Security forces. The ANC used him and his forces for acquisition. Land, industry, mines, the lot.

Another knock. This time more forcefully.

"Come!" he bellowed and the door opened to the light of the hallway outside his bedroom. His trusted aide entered. Aside from the security staff, he was the only person allowed to be near him alone.

"General, you wanted to be awakened with any urgent news."

"Well, what is it."

"There are reports that the Americans have struck back against Russia and China. They employed the same tactics. Electro-magnetic pulse above the earth. All the electrical grids in the Northern Hemisphere have been knocked out. Our intelligence says that most will die within the year."

"So, they've destroyed each other. Leaving the Global South to do what we do. No one will come and in time after most have died off, we will be the ones to colonize what's been left behind. What time is it? What else do you have for me?"

"Eleven in the evening, General. There is one more report."

"Oh, I just got to sleep! I'll never go back to sleep now. What's this other thing?"

"Apparently, the Quick Reaction Force from Richard's Bay left covertly about an hour ago. Several armored vehicles, a fuel truck, and a couple of buses and empty trucks. Lights off. Our eyes in Dundee say that one of their men showed up yesterday and is gathering about a hundred or so whites and others. We think this convoy is meant to retrieve them."

"Well now, that is interesting." Mbuso swiveled out to the edge of the bed and sat up, thinking.

"Do you want to intercept them, General?"

"I do. However, I do not want the cadres to intercept them. We need to save those for our push on Richard's Bay. I want our EFF friends to do it. You have the phone numbers, yes?"

"Yes, General. Although, wouldn't it be more effective to use our forces?" his aide asked.

He chuckled, low and guttural. "Why, of course it would, but that would cost us. The Richard's Bay QRF is highly trained and well-armed. Yes, it would be costly for us. However, using the EFF is free."

"I'll make sure they go out in force, General."

"Yes, do that. Also, let them know to intercept them on the way back from Dundee. They have a couple of hours to set their ambushes. Which way is the QRF traveling to Dundee?"

"They're taking the R34 to R66 and R68."

"Okay. They won't likely take the same route back. I suspect they will take the R33 back to Richard's Bay. Have them set up ambushes well out where it's sparse. Tell them to send as many as they have. This will send a message to Richard's Bay and weaken the EFF while we're at it. Thank you for this. I certainly cannot sleep now. Go make the calls and I'll be down directly. We have some work to do."

His aide left and he sat on the side of his bed and laughed silently to himself for quite a while.

***

They came down into Dundee on the R68 from the North. Reaper glanced at his watch. 0403 hours. It had taken them longer than expected. They had to move more slowly so the buses could keep up. As they came into the center of this town of around thirty-five thousand inhabitants, he scanned relentlessly with his night vision for any movement that could be a threat. The town was fairly dark so his goggles worked well. Load shedding was common from the lone power company in South Africa, Eskom. It would undoubtedly become much worse, and had since the war started. The point vehicle, the other Mamba aside from the one he was in, led them through the town to the rendezvous point Raj had given him. The Dundee Golf Club on the west side of town. It was in a more well-off area, as opposed to the shanties and informal settlements in the southern and eastern parts of Dundee. He would be happy for some fresh air. He had three of his men in the back, and including the driver and him, five dudes that work long shifts on patrol and other activities didn't leave much time for showering. It was pretty rank in the Mamba.

Dundee was predominantly black, but there was a sizeable population of whites, Indians, and other Asians, along with smaller sets of blacks and coloreds, who were mixed races. These smaller demographics lived on the west side, where they were meeting Raj. His uncle lived there, but didn't have a vehicle to get to Richard's Bay and Raj wouldn't leave him out here alone. His uncle was his only living relative. Reaper kept his mobile phone out and checked the signal strength frequently. Not so much because he would need to make a call, but to ensure the signal didn't die suddenly. Even with the power out, the cell towers should have enough backup power to keep them up until the power came back on.

The ANC cadres and EFF forces employed cheap, easy to acquire signal jammers. They didn't have great range, but were effective. One jammer could affect a residence or two if they were close. If many were used simultaneously and spread around a bit, they could deny cell service to a whole area the size of a neighborhood or small town. If his signal died suddenly, it would suggest an imminent threat. He still had one bar as they pulled into the Dundee Golf Club. He could see a mass of people standing and sitting on what he supposed was the eighteenth tee and some in the parking lot. He spotted a waving hand through the goggles, and as they rolled to a stop, he could see it was Raj with an older man standing next to him. He left his rifle in the vehicle as he hopped out and stretched and did a couple of squats to get the blood flowing again as Raj walked up to him.

"Good morning, boss! You made it," Raj said.

"Took longer than expected, but without incident. Is this everyone? We don't want to linger," Reaper replied. The two men clasped right hands and gave each other a hug.

"Everyone's here. Boss, this is my uncle, Venkatesh. Uncle, this is the boss and my good friend!" Raj said and the two men shook hands. His uncle's grip was strong and enthusiastic for a man well into his seventies, from the looks of it through the goggles. He didn't flip them up as he wanted to keep his eyes acclimated, tired as they were.

"It's good to meet you, Venkatesh. He talks about you a lot."

"Thank you for coming," Venkatesh said. "You can call me Venki. Raj is a good man. I have a feeling we're leaving just in time. The communists are everywhere and those EFF fuckers are making a good deal of trouble, more so since the war started."

"Raj, how many and are any of them armed? Are they capable?" Reaper asked.

"So, we have twenty-one Indian families, four white families, and a couple of Asian and colored families. All the fathers are armed and willing to fight to protect everyone. How do you want them? There are one hundred and seven people total. Some of the women are armed as well. They're pretty mad they have to leave their homes, so they'll shoot communists. The rest are children from three years to teens," Raj explained.

"Okay. Good. I want all the women and children on the buses. I want the men to divvy up equally among the open trucks. If we get into anything, they're not to fire unless ordered to by one of us or their drivers. Copy?"

"Roger, boss. I'll get them moving and loaded up. Give me five minutes and we'll be ready to roll," Raj said and went to get everyone moving. Reaper glance at his mobile phone again. It still had two bars. He stepped out onto the fairway of the eighteenth hole away from the quiet but hectic crowd of people loading onto the vehicles. He scanned around and saw no movement out on the course or at the various tree lines around them. He listened intently and heard nothing really except the running engines of his convoy.

"Reaper."

"Jesus Christ, Wally!" he yelled in a whisper. He turned and Walid was standing there. The man was a fucking ghost in his goggles.

"Sorry. Still jumpy. Kind of entertaining," Walid said with a big toothy smile.

"Stop doing that, man. Nearly shit my pants. What?"

"I think we're about ready to go. It's quiet. Should be an uneventful trip back, Inshallah," Walid said and Reaper thought for a minute.

"Look, Wally, pass it around to all vehicles. We're going to avoid any incident or fighting at all costs, eh. Those buses are not armored. If we get into anything, those women and children have zero protection. If we hit anything, we run or we hide. We only fight as a last resort. Make sure everyone knows. You ride point well ahead of the rest of us. Encrypted radios only with call signs. Yeah, it's quiet and that's good, but it'll be dawn soon." He looked at his watch. 0428 hours.

"I'll pass it around. All business now, Reaper."

"We've got an hour until sunrise. Precious cargo on board. Let's not fuck this up, eh. I'm hungry and want coffee."

***

Reaper glanced at his watch and his phone again. It was 0513 hours. One bar. It was very dark on the R33 in what was essentially no-man's-land. Pretty barren. There was no traffic this early. No one wanted to travel even well-paved roads like this one since the war started and the threats of carjacking and roadblocks were becoming ubiquitous. The encrypted radio sat between him and the driver with the volume all the way up. So far it didn't even peep. They had traveled about twenty miles from Dundee when the radio did squawk.

"Reaper Two to Reaper Six." Wally's voice came through the radio from the lead Ratel and in an odd sort of electronic way, more so due to the encryption.

"Go Two, this is Actual," he replied.

"Stop the column and wait for a minute. We went past a SAPS police station on the right and now are sitting still just before a right-hand bend in the road. About one hundred yards ahead is a roadblock with vehicles and burning tires. You may be able to see the glow without night vision. Over."

"Roger, Two. We're coming up on the SAPS station and will wait here. I've been here many times. Station doesn't seem to have any activity or even vehicles parked. Over," Reaper replied. He didn't have to relay the message as everyone in the convoy had a radio and was listening. They slowed the column to a halt and waited.

"Copy. Stand by," came Wally's reply.

Reaper glanced at his mobile phone again. No signal. Shit.

"Reaper Actual to all vehicles. I've lost mobile phone signal. We may be in a no-service area or there may be jammers about. We're going to be cautious. Reaper Three, get that Ratel up here slowly and make this left turn onto this unpaved road. I will follow with the rest of the column. Reaper Two, come back to us and bring up the rear. We're going to hide for a while. Over and out." He finished and waited.

"Reaper, you know what's down that road, eh?" his driver asked, his calm voice tinged with concern.

"I know."

"Fucking hell," came a response from the back seat along with other expletives.

"Guys, it's fucking Rorke's Drift. I know it. We're gonna hide, not circle up and fight off four thousand Zulu," he said as the Ratel moved slowly past them and his driver fell in behind it, making the left turn from paved to unpaved road. They felt it, but it wasn't too bad. The dirt roads were pretty good up here. He watched their progression through his goggles as they went. Everything was different shades of a ghostly green hue, he thought as they drove the roughly seven kilometers to the drift. He'd been here many times and considered what he would do if he had to defend against a larger force there. Many men do. He was no different.

They passed several farms and piecemeal houses and shacks. There were better constructed residences further on near the very small actual town. It took ten or minutes so to get to the drift on the Buffels River. There was a small museum and hotel and other country buildings. The lead Ratel stopped by the lone Zulu monument just before the town. The convoy behind stopped as well. Reaper got out of the Mamba and swirled his hand in the air to call all the drivers and command element to gather on him. In thirty seconds they were all there. The drivers, Raj, Walid, and several others.

"Okay, look, it's nearly dawn. We don't know if they're just throwing up roadblocks randomly or if that was specifically for us. Yes, I know this is Rorke's Drift, guys. I've been here and hiked here many times and thought about what I would have done in their shoes." He looked at all his men looking at him through their goggles. It was a bit comical if it weren't so serious.

"Why don't we just force our way through the roadblock, blasting as we go?" Raj asked.

"Good question. I got the same in the Mamba. Those buses are not armored. We don't know what else is coming up behind the blockade. If we get into knockdown fight, those buses with the women and kids will be shredded. So, I made the call. Here we are. On the raggedy edge. No one is coming from the Bay. We've been monitoring EFF and some ANC forces starting to gather and mobilize on the outskirts and more are coming. They can't come to us. That's the Alamo. So, we hide. But this time, we'll have the high ground." Reaper turned and pointed across the town to the hill that overlooked the river on one side and the town on the other.

"Wally, take one of the Ratels and hit that dirt road over the river. The R68 isn't but ten kilometers or so north. See if that's blocked as well. If it isn't, then this was just a random blockade and we can get out that way. If there are blockades there, then this was most likely for us and we hide. Go quick and report as soon as you can," Reaper said.

"On it." Walid ran to one of the Ratels and mounted up with the crew and sped off across the river.

"Look, guys," Reaper told his men, "if we get contact from Wally, we're gonna get all the vehicles up a bit on that hill as far as the roads will allow. We'll spread out around it. There's a rocky ledge on the southwest side with a fairly large residence above it. Newly constructed. We park the buses in front of it on the ledge and get everyone inside and quiet. Raj, I want you and two men at the very top for all-around views. I want someone with a radio back the way we came. Don't want them sneaking up on us. We won't have the advantage of these goggles in a few minutes, so whatever happens will be in the daylight."

"What do you want us to do until then, boss?" Raj asked.

"Wait, and get that security down the road."

"Roger. You and you, get down the way we came a bit and keep eyes," Raj ordered two of the men that weren't drivers and they ran off quietly. Reaper pulled a pack of Marlboro Lights from his pants pocket and took one out and lit it, inhaling deeply. He turned around and scanned all over the hill overlooking the drift while he exhaled, then looked down past his plate carrier and extra magazines to the ground and his boots.

This could be nothing, he thought, or not.

***

Twenty minutes later, Reaper's radio crackled in his ears, but it was garbled. He was standing at the structure on the southwest side of the hill and scrambled up the slope a bit to get better reception. As he did, the sun made its appearance in the eastern sky. It was still fairly dark, but shadows were starting to march up the hill. As he got to the top, Wally's voice came in clear and he could see dust in the distance to the north.

"Reaper, Wally. Do you copy?"

"Wally, good copy, go."

"Reaper, it's a trap. We're five minutes out. There's dozens of vehicles on the R68 with more arriving. I don't know if they saw us or not, but I put that force in the hundreds. Over."

"Roger, Wally. Get back here quick," Reaper said as Raj scrambled up to where he was.

"Boss, all the people that live here are gone. Some of the guys knocked on doors and went in. All the homes are empty. Looks like they cleared out or were moved out," Raj said.

"Well, shit. Looks like this was all planned. Didn't know the fuckers had it in them."

"What are we gonna do, boss?" Raj asked in a whisper.

"Looks like I chose poorly, Raj, but if it's a fight they want, we'll give it to them. This is the plan. We'll make our base and fall back on the high rocky ledge with the new structure. It's about a hundred meters wide. I want a Ratel at each end to cover our flanks. Put the Casspir right in front of the structure with the buses and trucks for cover and get all the people in or behind the structure. I want half our guys up here on top. Plenty of rocky cover. Tell them to bring more than half of our RPGs up here as well. We're gonna need them. Go."

"On it, boss. Where do you want me?"

"Organize the guys on the southwest ledge and manage the fight there. Tell Wally to report to me up here when he gets here. I want to bloody them bad right from the start. If we fuck them up enough up front, maybe they withdraw and we can get out."

"Roger, Boss. You think we have a chance?"

"As good as the British did here before. But we have better weapons."

"Yeah we do." Raj ran back down the hill to get everyone organized. His uncle, Venky, slinging an AK-47 over his shoulder walked up.

"I can fight. Where do you want me?" the older man said as if to cut off the questioning look Reaper gave him.

"You're with me, Venky," Reaper replied. "Raj would hate me if I let anything happen to you." The sun was shining bright now, shadows mostly gone except for the west side of the hill, and Reaper scanned the full scene in all directions. There was more dust coming from the R68 to the north, meaning trucks.

"All units, there are hundreds of men on foot followed by technicals coming from the direction of the SAPS station where we came from. We're on our way back to you," the voice of his patrol lead said in his earphones. Reaper continued to scan around as about half his force got to the top of the hill and began to find good cover and reinforce their fighting positions with rocks and anything else they could find. He saw the Ratel's take their positions at each end of the rocky ledge below him. The Casspir was already in position. The buses and trucks were in position as well in front of the new structure with all the civilians they brought moving from the buses and trucks to the structure and behind it for the most cover. The fuel truck was abandoned well away from them down in the small town. He'd use that if he could as his patrol came running out of the bush and past the fuel truck.

Okay, everyone's back, he thought. *Now we wait.*

"Reaper to all teams," he said over the net. "They're coming. We let them come in close then hit them hard. I want them to think twice about this. Stay focused. We have the high ground this time. Top of the hill with me is the fallback. I'll see you all on the other side. Reaper out."

The eastern sun was bright and warm on his face. Venky stood with his AK now in his hands. The old man was smiling and gave Reaper a thumbs-up. There was barely any separation from the report of the distant shot and Venky dropping straight to the ground.

"Sniper!" several of his men yelled as Reaper went prone and scrabbled over to the old man. His eyes were open, AK-47 next to him. Reaper felt for a pulse but there wasn't one. He just stared at the man's face. It still had sort of a smile on it. The main reason they were all here was just gone in the blink of an eye. He had no time to ponder as gunfire erupted all around him.

***

Five minutes later, Reaper was surveying the battle picture from a prone position using a rocky outcropping on one side of him and Venky's dead body on the other. It felt like hours to him as incoming rounds from all around ricocheted off the rocks. Every once in a while he felt, rather than heard, a dull thud, signaling to him that Venky had consumed another round for him. He patted the old man's body in thanks. He heard Raj's voice drift up to him from below where the Casspir was and the structure, yelling orders and directing fire. He wondered morbidly what Raj would think of him using his dead uncle's body for cover, until another round thudded into the man and he snapped out of it. He rested his rifle on the body and went back to work, picking targets out to a couple of hundred meters and below him.

As he did so, he thought about the British back at the first battle of Rorke's Drift. Was this what they saw? There were so many targets. But these Zulu weren't throwing spears. He emptied his magazine and rolled on his right side, ejected the mag and pulled another from the front of his plate carrier, inserted it and chambered the first round. Then he traversed on his belly to the rocks on the other side of him, right into Wally.

"Jesus Christ, Wally! Thought I was alone in this spot," Reaper yelled.

Wally poured fire down the other side of the hill, then turned his head and smiled. How the man had gotten up to the top to join him and the other ten men on the summit of the small hill without him noticing or getting shot was some sort of miracle to Reaper.

"Hi, boss! We're surrounded!" Wally yelled at him with a big, goofy grin.

"I fucking know!"

"We're going to send so many commies to meet Marx and Lenin today!" Wally yelled back and kept shooting. Reaper shook his head and joined Wally in shooting the commies attempting to ascend that side of the hill. The writhing masses of the EFF forces seemed like a leviathan. Part of them would surge forward while another part would retreat a bit and then switch. It continued for a good while with them never reaching the summit. There were so many though. The volume of fire coming from their position and from his squad was overwhelming and kept them at bay. For now. He heard the machine guns and cannon from the vehicles also doing work on the sides and by the structure. He also heard the screams. Nothing to be done about that yet. He knew the screams would be there. He went back to work.

About ten minutes after it all started, their attackers pulled back and the incoming rounds stopped abruptly. Reaper got his bearings and raised his head to survey all around the hill.

"Cease fire!" he yelled several times due to his men shooting at the running EFF forces in all directions. Quiet returned to the Drift. Except for the screams. Several of his men were hit or dead up top with him and from the sound of it, more below.

"Why they leave so fast, boss? We had a good defense, but it's odd to me," Wally said quietly now. Reaper rolled onto his back with a sinking feeling and pulled out his phone with one hand while wiping grit and smoke from his eyes with the other. He looked at his phone and he had cell reception again. He immediately called his brother.

"Paulie! You alright?" his brother, Rick, said quickly without a hello.

"We're in a bind, Rick. I made a bad call and we tried to hide at Rorke's Drift on the way back. There were EFF roadblocks and we had too many civilians to fight through. It was a trap and we're stuck in it."

"I'd move heaven and earth to get to you, Paulie. The ANC forces are hitting us with mortars and artillery. There's no way out just yet. Can you hold?"

"Okay. They've retreated for now, but they'll be back. If you can get here, I'm on the summit of the hill at the Drift. We have over a hundred civilians and the QRF. We'll hold or make them remember the Drift."

"Love you, Paulie. Hold." His brother ended the call and Reaper put the phone back in its pocket.

"Boss, they coming?" Wally asked.

"When they can. ANC are at them right now," Reaper said. It was so quiet now. He looked around and his men were all reloading or just breathing and waiting. Then he heard it. Wally heard it too. Buzzing.

"That's why they stopped jamming, Boss. Drones!" Reaper had just enough time to look up and see the first one as it came in over the summit and plunged down, out of sight where the civilians were behind the structure and buses where Raj was, ending in a massive explosion. Reaper and Wally both rolled to their stomachs and covered their heads as two more drones slammed into their vehicles on the down slopes to either side of the summit. Dirt and debris landed on them for a violent minute. Reaper shook his head to clear it and his hearing. He glanced around, raising his head. He couldn't see anything through the smoke and dust, but he heard them.

"They're coming back! Prepare to defend yourselves! Get your grenades ready, boys!" Reaper yelled to his men on the summit to get them focused on what was to come shortly. Some of his men were already firing into the oncoming EFF attackers again. They were spread in a semicircle with the open end toward where the structure and civilians were. Or used to be. There was a sheer drop there, so they wouldn't get up that way. The summit cleared enough for him to get a glance out and they were halfway up the sides. He began firing into them and their renewed attack. Many fell, but there were more behind them. He rolled to his back and pulled three grenades from where they were attached to his plate carrier.

"Grenades ready!" Reaper yelled to his squad. While they all began pulling pins and holding, some men had one in each hand and several more on the ground in front of them, he tossed one of his three over the side. The other two he pulled the pins on and shoved them up between his stomach and plate carrier, holding the handles in place. It was tight. They weren't going anywhere unless he loosened it himself. Or, they took it off his dead body. Now he waited.

"Wally, toss 'em!" Reaper yelled. Wally had two grenades and tossed the first, then let the handle fly on the second and switched hands, tossing the other about to drop back down when a round hit him in the right thigh. That dropped him and he screamed, now on his back. Reaper covered his head with one hand to shield himself from the exploding grenades while grabbing a tourniquet with the other and rolled to Wally. He couldn't tell if it hit the artery or not, but he applied the tourniquet anyway, cinching it tight, with a scream from Wally who was still coherent and firing his rifle through the pain.

There were explosions all around the summit now from tossed grenades. His men were firing, but now taking hits like Wally. It wouldn't be much longer now. As he thought that, they came over the rocks opposite the opening of their horseshoe defensive positions, overwhelming two of his men immediately. The rest of his men were backing away from the sides into the middle, firing as they either rolled or crawled inward. Reaper did the same and dragged a screaming Wally, who was still firing his rifle.

Over the next couple of minutes, EFF bodies piled up all around them. A few more grenades were tossed, adding to the chaos, until the attackers were right on them and dying amongst them and on top of them. Reaper was out of breath. He was sure he'd been hit at least a couple of times. At least grazing shots and there was blood on his hands and something obscuring his left eye.

Then the shooting slowed and stopped. Reaper was literally buried under several EFF bodies. He tried to catch his breath and was able to do so by adjusting the body directly on top of him. Heavy bastard. He heard voices now. They were all yelling, but he couldn't understand them. Then shooting started and he felt rounds hit the dead men on top of him. He turned his head slowly and was rewarded with Wally's goofy grin. He blinked several times, letting Reaper know he was still alive, as another voice, louder and more authoritative than the rest, began barking orders. The shooting stopped.

Things started moving quickly at this point. The weight on Reaper lessened. Bodies were being moved. Then the one directly on top of him was lifted to the side. *Here we go.* Several hands reached down and grabbed him by his arms and yanked him up into the light. The sun was higher now and bright. The smoke and dust had cleared mostly. He was facing who he could only assume was one of EFF commanders, or the commander. He found out quickly.

"Who are you? What is your name? Where are you from?" the man yelled three inches in front of his face. Reaper didn't respond, which resulted in the man striking him with his pistol in the mouth. Reaper's head snapped around and blood flowed. He spit out a tooth along with copious amounts of blood. He turned back to the man and smiled. He realized that they hadn't uncovered the rest of his men yet, including Wally. The two men holding him had him by the upper arms. His hands were free and hanging near the bottom of his plate carrier. The man, the commander of these EFF forces, leaned in to Reaper's face.

"We are going to wipe your kind from South Africa for good. Our people will remember this day, Afrikaner. This is a new world now. It's our world. Our South Africa!" the man yelled and the rest of his men cheered until he held up a hand and they quieted. He leaned in again.

"Today we have avenged our ancestors and won the second battle of Rorke's Drift. Everyone will remember the Drift, Afrikaner." He smiled broadly as he said it and Reaper craned his neck forward, trying to lean into the man's face.

"Aye, everyone will remember this day. I know I will. I will remember the Drift," Reaper said, sneering at the man while grabbing the bottom of his plate carrier and pulling it outward enough that the two grenades dropped to the ground. Reaper quickly kicked at both of them and with all his strength, pulled the two men holding him back into the pile of bodies on top of Wally as the grenades exploded and his world went dark.

ABOUT THE AUTHOR

Mark Sibley

Bio #1: Serious.

Mark Sibley is a corporate crisis manager and war gamer. He's developed and facilitated over a hundred war games for various organizations over the years and managed as many real-world crises for those organizations. This experience, along with a lifelong dream of writing a novel, provided him fertile ground for pulling together all the aspects of his stories. If you tell a war gamer that a particular bad thing can't happen, that war gamer will come up with a plausible scenario to prove you wrong... eventually.

He is a lifelong Virginian and lives in the Commonwealth with his wife, three kids, and pair of female terriers—a Boston Terrier puppy named Phoebe and the ever-ferocious Chewie the Wookie, a five-pound Yorkshire Terrier with one fang.

THE SPARE PARTS CLUB

Brett Allen

LOCATION: CHARLESTON, SOUTH CAROLINA
CHRISTMAS EVE

Once a month, we meet at Fat Frank's Pizzeria and Poolhall. There are six of us tonight if you count each as a whole person. Most aren't. We're all busted, broken, battered, or burnt, either physically or mentally, the wasted refuse of the Global War on Terror. We joke that, between us, we could form one fully functional soldier. Most of us don't have family close, so our annual Christmas Eve gathering is a way of coping with an otherwise lonely holiday. Call it a support group, call it a "got-your-six" group, call it a "don't-kill-yourself" group—call it whatever you'd like—but we've been doing it a long time. We are The Spare Parts Club.

Our de facto rank structure is based on years in the club, not our prior rank in the military. I've been coming for five years now, so I'm pretty low on the totem pole compared to guys like Stumpy who's been here since the beginning. Jack "Stumpy" Mason has no hands. He has no hands because he was an Explosive Ordnance Disposal Technician who got unlucky the only number of times you're allowed to get unlucky as an Explosive Ordnance Disposal Technician. We all have nicknames bestowed onto us by the club, but we're pretty sure Stumpy nicknamed himself to avoid a more creative name like Mr. Sexy Wrists or The Silent Clapper.

My nickname is "Stripper," which requires a little explaining. I lost both legs, knees down, to a pressure plate IED (Improvised Explosive Device) in the Logar Province of Afghanistan. My prosthetics are essentially two aluminum poles. Do you know who else spends their life on metal poles? Strippers. I can thank Stumpy for the connection. I did point out that firemen also use metal poles, but my input was ignored.

Two weeks ago, Stumpy texted our group about the Christmas Eve Party. He said he'd arranged a secret surprise. There was much speculation on the group text thread, including the possibility that Stumpy had finally landed the part of Captain Hook in the Charleston Theater Club's production of Peter Pan. After a good deal of harassment and disparagement, Stumpy finally let slip that our quiet little club would be receiving a visit from the one and only Trigger Nelson.

Jake "Trigger" Nelson is one of us. A veteran, that is. Not disabled. Unless you call a badass scar down the right side of his otherwise perfect face a disability. I don't. Chicks dig scars and chicks definitely dig Trigger Nelson. Aside from the scar, he looks like he belongs in the Greek Pantheon. According to his Wikipedia page and Instagram profile and Facebook and X page and TikTok profile, he's a former Special Forces guy. I've heard he never made it higher than the rank of Specialist, but out here in the civilian world, he's crushing it. After leaving the military he teamed up with a few equally charismatic veterans and they created Foxhole Inc., a veteran-owned supplier of survivalist gear. They started with basic camping gear like knives, hatchets, and Foxhole tactical bags. As their success grew, so did their product line. Lately, they've jumped the shark a bit and started slapping Foxhole on everything from combat coffee filters to tactical toasters.

The one item Foxhole apparently doesn't make is a shirt with sleeves because Trigger is always rocking cutoffs to showcase his huge, tattoo-covered biceps. It's not surprising that Foxhole blew up, considering Trigger's social media presence. The guy has over five million followers on Instagram alone and is a brand in himself. He uses his platform to showcase his workout regiment, provoke liberals, and post outrageous videos of the Foxhole crew doing ridiculous stunts, all while hocking his gear under the hashtag: #GetTriggered. His videos are over the top with guns, gore, and scantily clad women, so naturally, we all love them. Their military theme reminds us of a time when we did cool shit for a living, a time when we were useful and whole. That feels like something to hold on to.

Stumpy and Sloth are playing pool in the back, and I see Stumpy checking the door every few seconds. Trigger is forty-five minutes late. Of all of us, Stumpy is the biggest fanboy by far. Holding the cue precariously in his pincher-hook prosthetics, Stumpy breaks, starting another round. He's damn good for a guy with no hands. Sloth is less good but at least he's a good sport. I've never met anyone with a better attitude that has more reason to be pissed at the world. The way Sloth tells it, he was a half-second slow pulling the trigger on a suicide bomber at a checkpoint outside of Ramadi. The blast shattered his body but the real kicker was the fuel truck they'd been processing through the checkpoint. The resulting fire left burns over ninety percent of his body. A billion plastic surgeries later and he still looks like a melting ice cream cone. It's a miracle he's even here, let alone that he retained a sense of humor. Every year he walks in ten minutes late, just to be sure we're all here when he yells:

"Heyyyyyy youuuuu guyyyyyyyys!"

It's hilarious. Every. Single. Time.

"Hey, Pimpwalk!" I yell from the table in the back. "Get me another slice of pineapple bacon, will ya?"

Pimpwalk is up front ordering a slice from Fat Frank. He looks back at me, smiles, and flips me the bird. Pimpwalk's real name is Jerome Alveres, but he took a Hot-N-Ready delivery of shrapnel to his ass somewhere along the Helmand River in Afghanistan. It took six surgeries and several skin grafts to get him back on his feet. As a result, he walks with a pronounced drag in his left leg, hence the name: Pimpwalk. I came up with it. When I did, he called me a racist, assuming it had to do with him being black.

I called him a reverse racist for insinuating that white people can't pimp. We've been great friends ever since.

"Ten bucks says he doesn't get your pizza," Loredo says, smiling between massive bites of meat-lover's. Chucks of bacon and sausage shed from her slice. Some hit her plate, some hit the table, some hit the floor. It's carnage. Loredo would catch the droppings if she had more than one arm, but Loredo's right arm was sheared off, along with the right side of her Humvee on a distro convoy down Baghdad's Route Irish in 2010. Lisa Loredo is the newest member of our club. She's quite the character and, honestly, probably the best of us. She copes with her disability by being the biggest badass possible. She's an unabashed gym rat and has earned a moderate social media following by posting her impressive one-armed workouts. She can probably clean more weight with one arm than I can with two. Not probably... definitely. She's also an avid hunter and deadly shot with her bow, which she pulls back with her teeth. She's not hard to look at either, except when she's mashing pizza into her skull, which is all the time. If food is fuel, she's burning jet engines. She doesn't have a nickname yet, mostly because she keeps vetoing our suggestions, which is not how it's supposed to work but none of us dare to tell her that.

"He'll bring it," I say with a smile. "He wouldn't dare make *me* walk."

Loredo rolls her eyes and continues chonking away like a starved Rottweiler.

I look around for Evan but he must still be in the bathroom. He's been in there a long time. Evan's real name is Curtis and he has no physical disability that I'm aware of. We call him "Evan," short for "Evanescence," because he's really into that emo shit. He may not have any visible scars but his mental scars seem deep and many. He rarely says more than two words but he shows up every time like a stray cat looking for any shred of comfort.

I'm just about to voice my concern over Evan's lengthy trip to the john when Pimpwalk flops down in the chair next to me with a giant slice of greasy cheese pizza on a floppy paper plate that's already bordering on translucent.

"You didn't get me a slice?"

"Get yer own damn slice," Pimpwalk says. "I wouldn't be caught dead ordering pizza with fruit on it. Pineapple on pizza is an abomination."

"But I ain't got no legs," I say in my best Forrest Gump voice.

Pimpwalk scoffs. "I'm empowering you," he says, then he pokes at my waist. "Looks like you've been eating a few too many fruity pizzas anyway."

"Stop that," I say, slapping his hand away. "Not all of us can hold our pizza as well as Hidden Valley over there." I point to Loredo, who's been mopping her pizza crust through an ocean of ranch dressing.

Her eyes narrow to slits.

"If you guys even *think* of making 'Hidden Valley' my nickname, I'll kill you all," she says between chews.

"Got it."

"I ran fifteen miles this morning," she says. "I'm training for an ultra-marathon and a backcountry elk hunt. I think I can afford to take in the extra calories."

"Why would you want to do that craziness?" Pimpwalk laughs.

"She likes competing with Trigger."

"Shut up," Loredo says and takes another huge bite.

Pimpwalk looks confused.

"Trigger posted a Story on Instagram a week ago about signing up for an ultramarathon race," I explain. "He says he's doing it to raise money for 'wounded warriors.'"

"My frick'n hero," Loredo says with a mouthful. "And I signed up first."

I'm about to go for another slice of fruity pizza when I remember Evan, who's still in the bathroom. I have a sudden flash of concern. Evan has a history of drug abuse. He copes with his old war by fighting a new one. He's been working hard at getting clean but he was particularly morose when he arrived this evening.

"Is Evan still in the bathroom?" I ask no one in particular. "Dude's been in there a long time."

"I'm right here."

"Hell!" I yell, nearly jumping out of my skin. Evan is standing right behind me, his black, greasy hair hanging in long clumps over mascara-lined eyes. His gray tongue flicks at a silver lip ring. There's a toothbrush in his hand. "Dammit, Evan! You're like a damn ninja."

Evan shrugs and pulls out a chair. I'm about to ask about the toothbrush when the lights go out.

"Dammit, Frank!" Stumpy yells as a pool ball thuds dully off the table's bumper.

We can all hear Fat Frank cussing from behind the counter. The pizza parlor is pitch black and that's when I realize the power outage isn't isolated to Fat Frank's Pizza & Pool. Through the big glass windows and the decorative grease paint, we can see there are no lights in the parking lot either. Everyone shuffles their way to the front window, bumping tables and chairs along the way. Farther down, we can see the streetlights are out too, along with the surrounding buildings. The moon and the stars are the only sources of light.

"My phone is dead," Evan mumbles. He's still seated at the table. We all go for our pockets in unison, only to find the same result.

"Frank, your phone working?" Stumpy asks.

"Dead as a doornail," Frank says. From behind the counter, he clicks on a Vietnam-era, Army-issued elbow flashlight. "At least this works. Everybody okay?"

We all nod as the beam of light passes over us.

"No refunds," Frank says.

"Something's not right here," I say.

There's a knock at the front door and everyone jumps.

Fat Frank shines the door, illuminating a silhouette on the frosted glass.

"It's unlocked," Fat Frank yells.

The door pushes open, causing the bell on top to jingle, and in steps Trigger Nelson.

"Well, look at this bunch of broke-dicks," he says, a mischievous grin eating his face.

I don't know why but I'm immediately soured by his greeting. I'm sure he thinks he's being funny but it's too familiar. And he's too pretty. Too healthy. Too whole.

Stumpy laughs as if they're old pals.

"Trigger!" he exclaims, rushing forward. "I'm Jack Mason, the one you've been coordinating with. You can call me Stumpy."

Stumpy throws an arm around Trigger who recoils slightly before allowing it. Introductions are made around the room and for a moment, we forget about the absurdity of the blackout. Trigger makes up for his original faux pas and greets everyone warmly, though he seems a little too warm with Loredo whose response is colder than the slushy machine behind her. Loredo aside, everyone is taken with Trigger. Even Evan mumbles, "Big fan," when they shake hands. Fat Frank seems genuinely excited to have a pseudo-celebrity in his restaurant, which is surprising considering Fat Frank, a former Marine, looks down on all other branches of the military. Like the rest of us, Fat Frank is a combat vet. He carries his own shards of combat-bling deep in his left arm, a gift he received from the Viet Cong outside of Hue City in '68. Fortunately for Fat Frank, he throws dough with his right.

We stand around the front window, capitalizing on the moonlight and trading theories on what happened, what might have knocked out power to literally everything. As former soldiers, our minds lean toward the nefarious and "terrorist attack" becomes the most popular conclusion.

"My truck died about two blocks up the road," Trigger complains. "The damn thing is brand new. I'm gonna shoot that dude at the dealership."

Out the window, cars and trucks have rolled to a halt in the middle of the road, their drivers now shuffling aimlessly about.

"I don't think it's anything to do with *your* truck specifically," I say.

"I bet all of our cars are dead too," Stumpy says.

Sloth groans. He's recently purchased a fancy new pickup truck too, but has an interest rate guaranteed to land him in a bankruptcy law office.

We head out to the parking lot beside the pizzeria and quickly find that Stumpy is right. None of our cars will start. None except Evan's mom's old station wagon, a 1987 Hunk-a-shit with wood paneling and a "Proud Army Mom" sticker on the back window.

"How is this thing still running?" Trigger asks.

"Too old for fancy electronics?" I speculate.

"No, I mean, how is this thing still functional? It's a fossil."

We all look at Evan, who licks at his lip ring like a lizard.

"I fixed it up," Evan mumbles indignantly.

"But why?" Trigger scoffs.

"It's ironic," he says, crossing his arms.

"I guess," Trigger says. "I'm going to need a lift home. It's about two hours from here but I'll cover your gas."

Evan shrugs, which Trigger takes as consent.

"Do you think that's a great idea?" I ask. "We don't know what's going on out there or how far this goes or whether the power will be back on today, tomorrow, or a year from now. Hell, for all we know D.C.'s been nuked and Brits are back for Revolution: Round Two."

"The Brits?" Stumpy asks.

"I'm just saying, none of us have families to head home to. Maybe we should stick together for a bit. At least until we understand what's happening."

Trigger is about to object, but Lisa cuts in.

"I agree with Stripper," she says. "I've got a feeling it's gonna get worse before it gets any better."

As if on cue, we hear a spattering of gunfire. We turn and squint down the road but the night is too dark and the sound too far.

"Scavengers out already?" Sloth asks.

"Sounds like AK fire," Stumpy says.

We all look to Trigger who still seems to be forming an exit strategy when he realizes all eyes are on him.

"Oh, yes," he stammers. "Definitely AK fire."

"Anybody got any—protection?" I ask.

Fat Frank emerges from the pizza parlor with a shotgun leaning against his shoulder. He tilts his head in the direction of the gunfire.

"That ain't good," he says.

"What ain't good?" I ask.

Fat Frank hesitates. "The Charleston Coast Guard base is that direction—and those are definitely AK-47s sounding off."

Trigger scoffs. "So you think somebody is going to war with the Coast Guard? My grandma could go to war with the Coast Guard."

He laughs and looks around for support. Only Sloth flashes an obligatory half-smile, which could also be an involuntary lip spasm.

"Right," Fat Frank says slowly. "Well, aside from the Coast Guard, there are other agencies on the base. I heard from one of my regulars that there's some interagency co-op junk going on. Some real Secret Squirrel stuff people like us ain't supposed to know about. The fella called it Operation—" Frank pauses, raking his memory, "—was a bird or something. Osprey? No! Seahawk. Operation Seahawk."

We all look at each other skeptically. The only thing liberal about Fat Frank is his disbursement of outrageous conspiracy theories. He's more than a bit paranoid and regularly flips off his own closed-circuit surveillance cameras under the assumption he's being monitored by the FBI or NSA or some other three-letter agency. We tell him he should focus more on the FDA and clean the restaurant occasionally.

"So what do we do?" Stumpy asks. His tone infers he's already decided, but everyone looks to Trigger.

"We pop smoke and get the hell out of here," Trigger says, looking around for support. "We take Lip-Ring's station wagon and boogie. Y'all can come to my place." He's almost pleading. "Two hours into the country and well stocked, food and guns. You can hang out there until we get a grip on what's going on."

"It looks pretty obvious what's going on," Stumpy says.

The rest of us nod, even though we really don't know what's going on at all. A part of me wants to agree with Trigger. Whatever is happening down the street is outside of our lane. We're civilians now and broken ones at that. We did our duty, we served our time, and I'm proud of what we did, despite how it turned out, but our time is over. And if I'm being honest, I feel a bit used, discarded by a government that asked us to give up our youth and our health. Now most of us can't even get a VA appointment inside of two months.

The other part of me wants to shove the first part of me in a locker. He says to "suck it up, Buttercup." I knew the hazards when I signed the dotted line. And now, now that the worst-case scenario has played out, I'm going to grouse about things being unfair? Screw that. I'm in charge of my own destiny. And I'm far from useless. I may have metal legs, and Stumpy may have hooks for hands, and Sloth may look like microwaved cheese, and Evan is a sad-face-clown, but we can still hold our guns and we can still get after it. We can still do some good. We can still agitate.

"I'm in," I announce, clearly interrupting some serious debate I missed while I was having my little inner monologue. "Let's go wax some terrorists, like Loredo said."

"What?" Trigger says.

"I didn't—" Loredo starts.

"We don't even know what's happening," Trigger says. "For all we know, they're running a training exercise down there and we'd be interfering. Best just to sit tight and—"

"Listen," I say. "We don't know what's going on, but I think it's our duty to go find out. If we get down there and we're not needed, great. If we get down there and find out Tommy-Turban is stirring the pot, we can lay down the scunion one last time in the name of God and country. I for one am sick of feeling useless. I'm sick of feeling purposeless. I have a master's degree in death and destruction, with no place to use it. Until now. I mean, maybe."

Everyone just stares at me, blinking. There's a slight smile on Fat Frank's lip and that makes me weirdly proud.

"I'm with Stripper," Loredo says again.

"You are?" I ask, surprised.

"Yes," she says with decidedly more resolution. "Running from a fight is not in my wheelhouse."

"Move to the sound of guns," Pimpwalk says resolutely. Everyone nods. Everyone except Trigger Nelson who crosses his arms and shakes his head.

"Are you all listening to yourselves?" he asks. "You've already acknowledged there's some next-level paramilitary bullshit going on down there and you wanna go throw yourselves in the middle? Why don't we cut out the middle man and just shoot ourselves here in Fat Frank's parking lot? Y'all seem like great Americans but you're all busted as hell. You'll make the situation worse. Let the professionals handle it."

I looked over at Stumpy and there's a pained expression on his face. It hurts to find out your heroes aren't who you thought they'd be.

"Who the hell is this Sally Pissy-Pants?" Fat Frank barks. Frank is not the type to have an Instagram account, so he's only vaguely aware of Trigger Nelson's influencer status and what that entails. Even in the dark, I can see Trigger's face redden. "Assuming we're ignoring this pansy," Frank thumbs toward Trigger, "I've got some guns and gear in the back of the pizzeria."

"We'd be surprised if you didn't," I say.

Fat Frank smiles and waves us along.

"Semper Fi," he says.

Frank's "some guns" turns out to be a gross understatement and I walk out of his storeroom amazed that he's never been raided by one of those three-letter agencies he's so paranoid of. Nearly the whole group is outfitted with a rifle, our pockets stuffed with loaded magazines. Frank has clearly donned body armor, as the bulges of a plat-carrier vest can be seen beneath the long black trench coat he's now wearing. Between the nerdy-ass coat, his fedora and rifle, he looks like he's on his way to shoot up a Pokémon convention. He pulls me aside and hands me an old JanSport backpack, weighted down with something heavy. I peek inside and feel a wash of fear and giddiness.

"I've never had an excuse to use it," Frank says with a wink.

Loredo is the only one who doesn't take a rifle, saying she doesn't trust her accuracy with one arm. While we're gearing up, she returns to her car.

"Check out Katniss Everdeen," Pimpwalk says as Loredo returns to the group. She has her bow in hand, with six arrows clipped into a side-mount quiver.

"Nickname me 'Katniss,' 'Everdeen,' or 'Mockingjay' and I'll tear out your spleen and use it as target practice," she says.

"Check, Roger," Pimpwalk says, looking down at his shoes.

Evan refuses a rifle or a sidearm. He mumbles something about being done with guns forever. None of us press the issue. Frank retrieves an old wooden box from his desk drawer and sets it down next to Evan. From inside he pulls a classic Ka-Bar fighting knife, its leather sheath embossed with the eagle, globe, and anchor of the U.S. Marine Corps. Frank holds it with reverence.

"At least take this," he said.

Evan nods, takes the knife with equal care, and secures it to his belt.

Trigger Nelson grumbles endlessly about Frank's gear and brags about all the fancy equipment he has back home, claiming that if he had "this or that" he'd show the terrorist bastards what was up. He'd insisted on picking his weapon first and made a big show of the process, spouting obscure facts about each rifle and each piece of gear. Who knows if any of it's true, but I'm starting to get the feeling the dude just likes to hear himself talk. I'm certain I'm not the only one to notice the appalling number of times he flags us with his rifle barrel while he's running his big mouth.

With my metal legs, Pimpwalk's gimp, and our group carrying a combat load fit for a small army, we decide Evan's mom's car is our best option if only to put us closer to the objective. Just referring to it as "the objective" feels good, like we're back in uniform, back in the game. Evan is apprehensive about taking the car, of course, but I explain that it's safer to keep it close by, lest it be stolen. After all, it has now become a priceless commodity. He concedes and begins moving junk out of the back seat, into the open space in the rear.

"Have you been living in your car?" I ask as he stuffs a sleeping bag over the rear seat.

Evan mutters something about his stepdad and I hear the word "eviction." I make a mental note to circle back on the matter, assuming we survive the night.

It takes some effort to squeeze everyone into the station wagon with all our gear. Fortunately, the front seat is of the old-school bench variety, so we fit three in the front and three in the middle. Given Fat Frank's considerable girth and my ridged lower half, we're relegated to the very back where we sit with our legs and poles hanging out over the bumper, the rear door propped wide open.

"It's like riding 'doors open' in the Hueys back in 'Nam," Fat Frank says as Evan putters down the road.

I nod but doubt there are many similarities.

The sporadic gunfire we'd heard has ebbed away and now there's only the occasional single, purposeful shot of a pistol. No one says it but I'm sure we're all thinking it: executions. It's incredible we can hear the shots given the distance and the rattle of the old car, but with the electrical power went most of the ambient noise.

With every gunshot, I can feel the tension in the car rising, until finally Trigger brakes.

"Stop the car," he hisses. "This is close enough."

Evan acquiesces and pulls the car onto a side street, shutting off the engine. The quiet floods in and we sit motionless for a long moment, listening to the occasional tick-tick of the cooling engine.

"Now what?" Sloth asks.

Everyone looks at Trigger whose face is sallow in the moonlight. He's about to speak when Fat Frank cuts him off.

"We hit 'em hard and hit 'em fast," Fat Frank says. "Element of surprise and all that. Violence of action. Audacity."

"Easy, Rambo," I say. "That's not a real plan and a good way to get us all killed." Everyone but Fat Frank nods. "We have no idea what we're dealing with here. Someone should do a recon before we go in guns blazing."

Everyone looks at Trigger for approval.

"That's fine," he says quietly but then seems to find himself again and straightens up. "Stumpy, I want you to take Stripper and Sloth. When you can see the objective, put Sloth in an overwatch position at the front entrance. Then, you and Stripper do as much perimeter surveillance as you can without drawing attention."

"You're not going?" Stumpy asks.

"Me? N-no," Trigger stutters. "I'll stay here to maintain command and control. I'll lead the Quick Reaction Force should you guys dick everything up and draw fire."

He says this last part in an unflattering, accusatory manner as if we've already 'dicked it up.' I give a brief thought to pistol-whipping him.

Stumpy, Sloth, and I exit the car and move down the alley. We're all unfamiliar with this part of Charleston, save for the pizza parlor, and there are not many alternative routes we can take, so we're stuck using the sidewalk along the main road. We stay low, hoping the lack of light and the occasional abandoned car will provide the cover we need.

"What the hell is Trigger's deal?" Sloth whispers as we crouch behind a Toyota 4Runner, dead in the middle of the road with its doors left wide open.

"I think he's just a little off-balance by the whole situation," Stumpy said. "I'm trying to give him the benefit of the doubt."

"The dude is a phony," I say. The two of them look at me, surprised. "What? You say he's 'off-balance' by all this? He claims to be ex–Special Forces and a survival expert. 'Off-balance' should be his bread and butter. He should be chomping at the bit to get out here and light up some terrorist scumbags."

"I think you're wrong," Stumpy says. "He just needs a minute to wrap his head around the situation. Then he'll be fine."

"I hope you're right," I say.

We figure we're about two hundred yards from the front gate when we start seeing odd-shaped lumps in the road, scattered between deserted cars and across empty patches of sidewalk.

"Bodies," Stumpy whispers. "I guess we know what all that shooting was about."

They're indeed bodies and, as we pass them, their features become more defined. They are not soldiers, which for me would've been morbidly acceptable. They are civilians, people who had been going about their daily lives. A man in a suit still clutches his briefcase. A woman in a bright pink cocktail dress lies in a heap outside her SUV door. A young man in jogging attire is face down on the sidewalk, dead phone still strapped in an armband. The bodies are contorted in unnatural positions; most appear to have been fleeing, only to have been shot in the back.

"What the hell?" Sloth whispers.

"There's gonna be a special place in hell for whoever did this," I say.

Stumpy shushes us and points with the barrel of his rifle. Down the road, we catch movement, barely visible in the moonlight. We stay low and move quickly between cars. Along the east side of the road is a chain-link fence separating the road from an open expanse of well-manicured lawn. Set far back from the fence and the road is a brick building with a small parking lot out front. The building is nothing special, which, in itself, seems out of place. Everything in Charleston is historic, charming, or appears "southernly" in some way, shape, or form, so this brick building, obviously constructed to be unremarkable, has the opposite effect. Its blandness offends the senses. There are only a handful of cars in the parking lot. A bare flagpole stands out front.

Razor wire loops around the top of the fence, giving the compound the feel of a small prison. At the front gate is a guard hut and a mechanical arm, that probably wouldn't stand up to Evan's mom's station wagon. The movement we spotted earlier is a single man, pacing between the guard hut and two blacked-out SUVs idling on the curb along the perimeter fence.

The man is dressed all in black and appears to be wearing body armor under a tactical vest bulging with pouches. We're too far out to tell the make and model of the rifle he carries, but we can see it's tricked out with lasers, scopes, and all the fancy doodads you get if you're in an elite unit. On his head, a pair of night-vision goggles (NVGs) is tipped up on a sleek black helmet. Had he been wearing them, we'd have been spotted already. I guess even elite units have their weakest links, which is probably why he's pulling guard duty. Thank God for small mercies.

From inside the perimeter, up near the brick building, someone shouts in another language. The man near the guard shack dismissively waves his hand and shouts back. Both men sound irritated.

"What language was that?" I ask.

"Maybe Farsi?" Stumpy says. "Never did learn it."

"Not much we can recon," Sloth says. "That fence goes all the way around and I'd bet this is the only point of entry. From the way they've staged the vehicles, I'd say they aren't planning to stick around long or they'd have set up more of a defensive posture."

Stumpy and I nod in agreement.

"I've got a plan," I say. "But if it's gonna work, we gotta be fast."

Back at Evan's mom's station wagon, Fat Frank, Evan, Lisa, and Pimpwalk are pulling three-sixty security off the four corners of the car while Trigger Nelson sits on the tailgate talking way too loud about a photo shoot he'd recently done with Tanner Knight, owner of Knight's Forge Knives, and some B-grade Instagram models I've never heard of. Lisa rolls her eyes hard as Stumpy, Sloth, and I return from our recon.

Trigger drones on as if he hasn't seen us approach.

"Those chicks were blown away to be getting their pics taken with two full-on American war heroes. By the end of it, they were begging—"

"We could hear you from a block away," Stumpy says, the first hints of irritation in his voice. "Maybe try to keep it down a little."

Trigger starts to argue but I cut him off.

"Everybody, bring it in," I say. The group closes, while still maintaining security. Once a soldier, always a soldier, I guess. Even Evan maintained his discipline, though I can see him checking around to make sure everyone else is too.

Stumpy gives a quick brief on our recon findings—what the target building looks like, the perimeter layout, and the lone sentry outside the small guard hut.

"Going into the building would be suicide," Stumpy says. "They have night vision, we don't. At least outside we have the moonlight. Our best bet is an ambush on the street, as they're leaving. With any luck, they'll have their guard down."

"No, our best bet is to get back in this crap-wagon and get gone," Trigger says, pointing to the station wagon. "This isn't our fight. We aren't soldiers anymore. And we don't even know what they're after or if they'll find it—whatever it is. You wanna die for nothing?"

I'm about to light into him when Stumpy cuts me off.

"It's better than *living* for nothing," he hisses. "It's not about what they might be after anymore. We counted no less than twenty bodies on the road down there. That's twenty American bodies, you worthless turd. Twenty people trying to make it back to their families, gunned down by terrorist garbage, and I for one am not gonna let one more American fall on my watch. Not while I have a gun in my hands and breath in my lungs."

"Hooks," Trigger interrupts. "Gun in your *hooks*."

"I hope to God my phone comes back online soon," Stumpy says. His words have a threatening tone and for once Trigger keeps his mouth shut, though I can see he's fuming. There are several moments of awkward silence before Stumpy looks at me and raises his eyebrows as if to say, "Get on with it."

"Right," I say and launch into my plan.

We divide into two fire teams with the understanding that I'll be bouncing between the groups to provide command and control. I'll be the one with my nuts in the breeze later, so it only makes sense that I'm the floater. Loredo is the Alpha Team leader, along with Pimpwalk and Fat Frank, who is acting much too eager to start shooting. Despite not wanting to participate, Trigger Nelson acts put out by Loredo's appointment and demands to be Bravo Team leader. In an effort to save everyone's sanity, I concede but give Stumpy a series of meaningful looks meant to convey that *he* is actually in charge. Their team is rounded out with Sloth and Evan but right before we move out, Evan pulls me aside and spills his guts. His eyes are rimmed red and he appears to be on the verge of a panic attack.

"I-I can't go-go through this shit again," he says in between dry heaves.

I don't know what kind of soul-crushing trauma this kid saw in his war but it must've been bad. He's on the verge of rattling apart like his mom's station wagon. I put my hand on his shoulder and look him in the eyes which he quickly drops to the pavement.

"You're rear guard," I say. "Stay with the car and keep it ready. When we come back, we'll be coming fast. I'm gonna need you to get your Nascar on."

Evan snuffs back some snot.

"Nascar's for hillbillies," he says.

"Spoken like a true emo-bitch," I say softly.

Evan smiles despite himself and holds up the huge Ka-Bar knife to Fat Frank like he's presenting a religious relic.

"Keep it," Fat Frank says. "Just in case."

We move down the road in a bounding overwatch, one fireteam moving up while the other stays behind cover, ready to provide suppressive fire if needed. We're pretty far out to be bounding the whole way but, truth be told, we're all paranoid as hell. We've all been out of the game for a long time and things are getting real.

We make good time despite Trigger Nelson, who halts his team multiple times for no apparent reason. The closer we get to the objective, the more paranoid Trigger becomes and the more paranoid Trigger becomes, the more disruptive he is to the movement, hissing sharp corrections at his teammates when he thinks they're too far ahead, in a bad position, or covering the wrong fields of fire.

Admittedly, my fuse is short because making successive quick sprints and squatting low behind cars isn't exactly conducive to having two prosthetic legs, so I'm probably overreacting when I sprint to Trigger's position and grab him by the shirt collar.

"You're either in this or you're not," I say. "Everybody here knows exactly what they're doing but you. So keep your big mouth shut before you get us all murdered. If I hear one more word out of you, I'll shoot you my damn self."

Without waiting for a reply, I release his shirt and go back to my position.

Each team bounds twice more before I finally thrust my fist into the air, calling for a halt. Everyone stops on command except Trigger, whom Stumpy has to hook by the collar to gain his attention.

The sentry is still out but he's now leaning against the guard shack, fiddling with one of his rifle attachments. His NVGs are still perched uselessly on the top of his head. Carefully, I slip over to the car Loredo is crouched behind. She has her head up and is estimating the distance between her and the enemy.

"You ready?" I whisper.

She nods.

I give a thumbs-up to Stumpy, who tries to return the gesture before realizing he doesn't have thumbs.

Loredo crouches back on her heels. With a practiced motion she lays her bow across her knees, silently removes an arrow from her mounted quiver, and attaches it to the string. She steps forward from the car only slightly and raises the bowstring to her mouth, biting down on a small rubber attachment. With one fluid motion, she extends her arm, pulling back the string. My teeth hurt just watching it. Just as the bow reaches its full draw length, the sentry looks up. There's a brief awkward moment of nothingness and I imagine he's squinting into the darkness, trying to figure out just what in the holy hell he's looking at. He starts to raise his rifle but hesitates a moment too long. There's a soft *thwack* as Loredo releases the string and the arrow finds its mark. If she aimed for the center of his forehead, her shot is a touch low and to the right. The arrow enters directly through the enemy's left eye. No sound escapes his mouth and he crumples to the sidewalk.

Loredo turns and gives me a wink, which is sexually confusing even though I know she's doing it because her only hand is grasping her bow and she can't give a thumbs-up. I get flustered and wink back but not a smooth wink, an over-exaggerated—probably suggestive— wink. She rolls her eyes.

I give Stumpy and Sloth a thumbs-up because, not to brag, I do have two hands. Stumpy and Sloth move forward, leaving Trigger to pull rear security. I move forward with them. Upon reaching the dead sentry, Stumpy swings his rifle behind his back and uses his two prosthetics to hook both shoulder pieces of the dead man's body armor vest. Sloth grabs the legs and together they drag the corpse into the guard shack and prop him up in a lone swivel chair.

Moving past the gate, I make my way to the two black SUVs idling on the curb. Priority number one. Inside the backpack Frank gave me are several blocks, carefully wrapped in brown paper with big letters reading: C4. Next to them is a long spool of wire. In the front pouch, I find a separate case with blasting caps, a wire stripper, a bundle of zip ties, electrical tape, and a 9-volt battery scrounged from Fat Frank's smoke detector.

Frank picked me for the boom-boom backpack, even though it would've made more sense to give it to Stumpy, given his EOD background, but it's hard to rig explosives with hooks for hands. That and Frank knows about my odd personality quark. I like to play with explosives. It's a fascination that developed after my injuries, probably my brain trying to make sense of what happened. Most people would shy away from a thing that almost killed them, but I've embraced it, nerded out over it. I'm fascinated by the building of homemade explosives and how the insurgents in Afghanistan and Iraq could work with so little to wreak so much destruction. My Google history is rife with instructional searches on everything from fertilizer bombs to pipe bombs to good ol' C4. I'm 100% sure I'm red-flagged on all the worst watch lists, but I couldn't care less. It's a way for me to own my trauma.

Finished with the deadman, Stumpy and Sloth take up security positions nearby as I set about rigging the C4 to the gas tank of the lead SUV. My fingers work quickly, recalling all the times I'd practiced at the height of my obsession.

"Hurry, man," Stumpy whispers.

"I'm going as fast as I can with no fricking light," I say. "I'd prefer not to accidentally blow us all to hell. Or worse, touch it off and have nothing happen."

With two blocks of C4 in place, I crawl out from under the SUV, trying not to let my aluminum legs scrape noisily on the asphalt. Once out, I begin unspooling the firing wire, leading it back to a minivan directly across the street from the gate. Several bullet holes are smattered across the side of the van, and I can see the silhouette of the driver slumped over the steering wheel.

Leaving the end of the wire behind the van, I make my way to a car and truck, which are parked cockeyed in their lanes between the gate and the position Trigger is occupying with Bravo Team. Trigger's position is where Stumpy will initiate small arms fire, making the car and truck closest to the gate the most likely spot for the enemy to seek cover and return fire. Whoever they are, these guys are geared up like professionals and, therefore, are likely to react to gunfire by turning quickly into it and establishing fire superiority. "Turn and burn," as they say. My job is to give that natural reaction deadly consequences.

I rig both vehicles with the last two blocks of C4.

As I slide out from under the truck, I can hear voices. They aren't in English.

"Shit."

I slide to the edge of the truck and look back to where Loredo, Fat Frank, and Pimpwalk are set up behind a single Subaru Outback, directly across from the gate. They are motioning for me to stay low. Men are coming from the Seahawk building.

I can't stay here or the plan will go to shit, so I peek around the truck, but in the darkness, I can only make out vague blobs and shadows. Staying low, I move quietly, unspooling wire as I go. I'm ten feet from the minivan when the wire runs out, dropping from the spool and curling back on itself.

"Shit," I hiss again. Murphy's Law is in full effect tonight.

The voices coming from the courtyard are louder. I can make out their forms under the moonlight, as they near the gate. It will only be a matter of seconds before they discover their dead comrade with a carbon-fiber arrow in his eye socket. I leave the wire where it is and scoot the remaining ten feet to the back of the minivan, where I retrieve the end of the first wire and 9-volt battery from the backpack. My fingers are clumsy with adrenaline and the stumps of my knees throb through the prosthetic caps. I lay flat on the ground so I can see the happenings near the gate. Six figures have emerged and are walking toward the SUVs. With luck, they'll reach the vehicles before they realize their buddy isn't following.

I hold my breath.

Suddenly, one of them stops and looks back. He issues a sharp whistle, beckoning the sentry to get moving. The whistle stops three more of them and only two continue to the SUVs. The man who whistled starts walking back toward the guard shack, clearly concerned with the lack of response from his comrade.

"Nothing can be easy," I whisper to myself. I look over to Loredo's firing position and put one finger in the air. I want to ensure the two enemies heading to the SUV are as close as possible.

The whistler reaches the guard shack, just as his two friends reach for the door handles of the SUV.

"Boom," I whisper as I touch the stripped ends of wire to the 9-volt battery's terminals.

The roar and overpressure from the explosion make my skull feel like it's caving in. The two enemies by the SUV doors disappear in a blooming fireball. What remains of their charred carcasses slams back against the chain-link fence before it too is knocked back by high-velocity automobile parts.

The other four fighters are on the ground gathering their wits when Stumpy's team opens up. The fire devouring the SUV provides ample light to shoot by and shoot they do. The enemy does exactly what we predicted. They scurry for the closest cover while returning fire. Within seconds, all four are crouched behind the last two vehicles I've rigged to blow.

I look at the battery in my hand and then to the firing wire lying ten feet away, in the no-man's-land between me and the enemy. At this moment, it occurs to me that we are insurgents. We are the scrappy indigenous population who won't bend the knee, who will fight dirty with lesser weapons, who will use the spare parts of their limited resources to drag every last one of these freedom-infringing bastards to the depths of hell, even if we have to walk them there ourselves.

But that ten feet looks awfully far and the enemy has established fire superiority, as Stumpy, Sloth, and Trigger Nelson hunker behind Swiss-cheese cars, slowly being whittled away.

I turn and give the thumbs-up to Loredo's team. They let loose without a moment's hesitation. Fat Frank laughs maniacally over the steady thrumming of small arms fire. Pimpwalk is cool as a cucumber with his cheek to buttstock, shell casings glinting firelight as they cascade to the ground.

Loredo sends another arrow and sticks an enemy in the shoulder. He screams something in Farsi or Dari or Pashtun or some damn language, as he and another turn to return fire. With two enemies firing on Stumpy's team and two firing on Loredo's, they are distracted enough that I might have a chance. I try not to think about the fact that even if I make the run, I still have to strip the damn wire without being shot.

"I'm hit!"

I look toward Stumpy's team and Trigger Nelson is on the ground writhing in pain, groping at his back. Stumpy and Sloth are busy trying not to die, so they're unable to render first aid. It occurs to me again that if I can blow those last two vehicles, I can end this in an instant. Trigger's life may depend on it.

I feel a pang of guilt as I briefly consider how much Trigger Nelson's life really means to me. This is swept away when I see the enemy with the arrow in his arm take a bullet to his rifle and one to his leg simultaneously, causing both his weapon and his body to clatter to the ground.

It's now or never.

As the wounded enemy crawls back toward the guard shack, I make my move. For a guy with two prosthetics, I can still hustle. I am the wind, swift and invisible. Bullets zip by. I feel untouchable like I'm wrapped in the wings of a guardian angel.

Snap!

The sound registers as my right leg comes down on nothingness. I hit the ground hard and roll to a stop. When I look down, there's an instant of panic as I realize my right leg is gone below the knee but then remember it's been gone for the last decade. My prosthetic has been shot clean off. The fall and the roll have landed me nearly on top of the wire's end. I snatch it and my eyes alternate between my fumbling fingers as they work the wire stripper and the enemy who has me in his scope.

Thwack.

A round cracks past my ear.

Thwack.

A round bites the asphalt near my shoulder, spitting shards of stone into my cheek.

My fingers don't belong to me. They might as well be cooked spaghetti for all they're worth. I drop the wire twice before I can start in earnest. I wait for the bullet I won't hear. But it never comes. Instead, I hear yelling.

"Frank! Don't!"

I look to my right and can't believe my eyes. Fat Frank has shed his trench coat to reveal a bulky body armor vest, its pouches packed with C4, and spewing wires in all directions. His generous gut, born from years of sampling his own stash, is mashed beneath the vest and swings like the pendulum of a grandfather clock as he runs toward the enemy. He is surprisingly fast. Like a silverback gorilla, his stride is choppy and violent. The two rounds that impact his chest plate don't even slow him down. Between gasps, he sounds his battle cry.

"Semper Fi, bitches!"

The enemy turns to run from the inevitable climax of Fat Frank's suicide mission but it's too late. There are several panicked shouts in their unknown language. It occurs to me, briefly, that "oh shit" probably sounds the same in any language.

There is a brilliant flash, followed by a skull-crushing explosion. Where Fat Frank had been, his huge legs trundling him forward toward annihilation, there is now only a brilliant fireball that expands, greedily consuming one enemy after another.

And then, in an instant, there is nothing.

The fire from the SUV illuminates the kill zone and I can make out the bodies of the enemy, or at least where individual body parts lie scattered. Charred globs of Fat Frank dangle from the nearest car's side mirror and the chain-link fence, like cheese dripping from the top of a pizza box. There is silence except for the crackling of the SUV fire.

"What the hell was that?" I hear Stumpy yell through the ringing in my ears.

I can hear faint crying.

"Trigger's hit," Sloth yells. "Does anyone have a first aid kit?"

Within seconds, the group is gathered around Trigger who is openly weeping. I'm the last to reach the circle because I'm hopping on one prosthetic leg. Trigger is still on the ground, squirming too much for Sloth to get an assessment of his wound.

"I can feel the blood," Trigger cries.

"Hold him down," Sloth instructs.

Pimpwalk is quick to limp forward. "I'll hold his ass down."

He's less than gentle when he grabs Trigger's arms. Stumpy kneels on his legs and they stretch him flat.

"Morphine!" Trigger wails.

"Keep it down," Loredo hisses. "There could be more of them out there."

There's a large hole torn into the back of the jacket Trigger is wearing over his plate carrier. The fabric around the hole is dark with liquid. Sloth runs his hands under the jacket and plate carrier, checking for entry wounds. His face is a mixture of concentration and puzzlement, even through his mask of burn scars.

"Shrapnel," Sloth says matter-of-factly.

Trigger groans.

"Probably from the SUV exploding," Sloth continues. "Punctured your bladder."

"Oh, god," Trigger whimpers. "Am I gonna make it?"

"You should," Sloth says, "because I mean that you punctured the bladder of your CamelBak. The liquid you feel is the water from your hydration system—not blood. Your plate carrier stopped the shrapnel. You may have light bruising on your back but even that's unlikely. You're completely fine."

Trigger keeps his face pointed toward the ground. He snuffs back some snot before speaking. "Well, that all sounds like good news." He reassumes his measured, arrogant voice. "Now, can you guys give me some space?"

Pimpwalk shakes his head.

"Man, I wish our phones were working. I'd have live-streamed your hissy fit for the whole world to see."

Murmurs of disgust percolate from the group.

I'm struck by how unfair it is that we've witnessed the real Trigger Nelson. Most of the world will never know their hotshot, ex–Special Forces badass is a big phony. Even if we could tell, who's going to take the word of six broken veterans over a legend like Trigger Nelson? They'd call it friendly fire. They'd call us jealous. They'd call us "blue falcons."

My thoughts are interrupted by an unfamiliar voice speaking unfamiliar words, foreign words. The quick comedown from battle has left me foggy and it takes a moment before I realize what's happening. Everyone in the circle has their arms—or arm, or hooks—raised, except Trigger who's still lying on the ground, arms draped over his head. Everyone's attention is focused behind me. I turn slowly, raising one hand, while keeping the other on Stumpy's shoulder for balance.

The enemy has gotten the drop on us. An arrow protrudes from his shoulder and his pant leg drips blood, but he holds his rifle at the ready all the same. He spits his words and I can tell he's calculating how many of us he can drop before one of us puts him down.

He sweeps his rifle back and forth slowly over the whole group. I mentally kick myself for not clearing the objective and double-checking the enemy dead. We've all failed in this basic combat necessity, and we can only partially blame Trigger Nelson. It must be true; we've lost our killer instincts.

The enemy soldier barks and then dips his barrel down in quick jerks. He seems to want us all to go to our knees.

No one moves.

The enemy shouts louder.

The shouting must stir something in Trigger because he comes to his hands and knees and looks around. He clearly has no idea what is happening.

"What is happening?" he asks.

For a moment the enemy is silent. His rifle drops a little and then he speaks in strained English: "Trigger Nelson?"

"The one and only," Trigger says, flashing a huge grin.

"The hell?" I whisper.

The smile that breaks across the enemy's face rivals Trigger's dumb grin. The man is positively beaming.

"So, you're a fan?" Trigger asks, getting to his feet.

The terrorist cocks his head just slightly and it's clear he doesn't understand. Then he nods and smiles more.

"I am one to kill the infidel, Trigger Nelson," the enemy says. "I am big hero."

Trigger's smile falls away as his hands come up.

"Whoa, whoa, whoa," he says. But the enemy's rifle is on the rise again.

"Get Triggered!" the enemy shouts gleefully. "Get Trig—" His last word is cut short, literally, as a silver blade erupts from his throat. The blade pushes forward and the enemy falls into a heap on the ground.

In his place is Emo Evan, his bloody hands limp at his sides. Either sweat or tears have caused his eyeliner to run and he looks like a young Alice Cooper. The handle of the borrowed Ka-Bar stands like a monument from the dead enemy's neck. Evan pulls it out like Arthur pulling the sword from the stone. He wipes the blood on the enemy's sleeve before trying to hand it back to me.

"You guys missed one," he mutters.

"You—you keep it," I say.

Emo Evan looks down again and it seems like he might cry.

"This is gonna set my therapy back, I think."

Everyone around the circle nods.

"Where's Fat Frank?" Evan asks.

The mood becomes somber and everyone looked to their feet.

"He's all around us," I say.

Our solemn revery is cut short by shouts from the far side of the burning SUV.

"Drop your weapons!"

"Get on the ground."

We comply to nothing, opting to stare numbly at the team of camo-suited commandos rushing toward us in their tailored gear. The fact that they speak unaccented English puts us all at ease.

"Look at these showoffs," Pimpwalk scoffs. "Two arms and two legs on all of 'em."

"I said, 'on the ground,'" their team leader shouts again.

"Get bent," Loredo shouts back.

"If I go to the ground, are you going to help me back up?" I ask, pointing to the knee stump that used to sport a prosthetic.

The team of five commandos approaches on line, weapons at the high-ready. Realizing we have no intention to relinquish our arms, the commandos stop, seeming unsure of how to proceed. It is clear they're used to forced compliance but they've likely never issued orders to their own countrymen. It hits differently.

"Great. Looks like we have a bunch of disabled vets," one grumbles.

"Careful. They can be unstable," another says.

"Who are you all?" the leader asks as he surveys our various states of disassembly. "And what in the name of holy hell happened here?"

Trigger Nelson, normally the first to shoot his mouth, has quietly drifted to the back of our group. Clearly, the presence of real operators has left him feeling self-conscious.

"You first," I say.

"What?" the commando asks, incredulous.

"You first," I repeat. "Who are *you*? It's been a hell of a night. Forgive my lack of trust."

The commando leader sighs and drops his rifle to the low ready. His men follow suit.

"We're members of a Maritime Security Response Team," he says.

His answer is met by dull stares.

"We're the Coast Guard's direct action, counter-terrorism unit," the leader says. "We're the Coast Guard's elite."

I hear Loredo scoff behind me and the leader leans over to appraise her.

"Is the one-armed girl rocking a bow and arrow?" he asks.

"Yes. That's Hood-Rat," I say, combining *Robinhood* and *Gym Rat*.

Pimpwalk suppresses a laugh as Loredo murders me with her eyes.

"Again, who *are* you guys?"

I look around at the blackened cars, the twisted corpses, and the gloopy strands of Fat Frank.

"The Spare Parts Club," I say. "We're an insurgency."

ABOUT THE AUTHOR

Brett Allen

Brett Allen is a writer of humorous fiction and the author of two novels, *Kilroy Was Here* and *Sly Fox Hollow*. Brett is a former U.S. Army Cavalry Officer, who deployed to Afghanistan in 2009 with 3rd Squadron, 71st Cavalry Regiment of the 10th Mountain Division, in support of Operation Enduring Freedom. His experiences, good, bad, and odd, made him uniquely qualified to pen his debut novel, *Kilroy Was Here*, a tongue-in-cheek look at American operations in Afghanistan.

Veering away from the military theme, Brett's most recent novel, *Sly Fox Hollow*, is a cryptid murder mystery comedy/political satire, leaning into the legend of the Michigan Dogman while also lampooning corrupt politics, media fearmongering, and political tribalism. *Sly Fox Hollow* is set in West Michigan where Brett currently resides with his wife, two children, and dogs.

HUDSON HAY

Shirley Johnson

Hudson Hay sat at the heavy oak table in the early darkness of 4 p.m. in mid-January, meticulously chewing the tender stewed rabbit to make it last longer. He rubbed his thick hands together for warmth and rested his elbows on the table as he stared into the fire. The memories of how quickly his world fell apart played behind his blue eyes as he tried to piece the chaos of the past three weeks into some sort of order. Panic skittered on cold feet on the edges of his mind till finally his dry lips parted and he said, "I've done a bad thing."

Hudson's voice sounded papery in the quiet house as the metallic click of the mantel clock ticked on. If the old man praying over his bread and soup in the painting behind him heard, he did not acknowledge this confession.

In the silence, the black marble clock ticked faster, then slower, and then sped up again. Hudson blinked his blue eyes back to life and looked at the old clock and wondered which gear needed fixing. But he was afraid to stop it because how would he ever know what time it was when he started it back up? It was best to let it be. It was the only thing that marked the passage of time besides the beard on his face.

It'd been weeks since he'd said anything out loud and he couldn't remember what those words had been. Something to his wife as she died and he felt sad that he couldn't remember what he'd said. His memory wasn't working right lately. There was the time before she died and then there was the time after, which was now. There was the time before the world stopped and then after. He did the bad thing before she died. He remembered the last words he said before he did the bad thing.

"I think you better get out of here and hide."

***

Christmas Eve, 5 p.m. Illinois time.

Hudson leaned against the computer kiosk at the Farm Depot gun counter, filling out the FFL paperwork for the 11th SCCY pistol of the night for one Jon Travis Jones when everything stopped, the lights went off, and the computer screens blinked and went black.

Eight men and two women were currently lined up and waiting on shifting feet for Hudson and his coworker Chris to do their required stack of paperwork so they could buy their Christmas firearms. All other gun counter employees were either helping unload a late arriving truck or out smoking in their cars in the blizzard. If you smoked, you got as many breaks as you wanted. If you drank coffee and had a 72-year-old prostate, you did not.

"The internet must have gone down," Hudson said quietly into the dark.

But it was more than the internet. It was everything. The Christmas music thankfully shut off. No more whisper-singing from that lispy son of a biscuit whining about giving his heart. But also, all the lights had gone out, as well as the computers. Even the emergency generator lights remained dark. People, however, all turned on and began to scream at once.

Jon Travis Jones grabbed the purple and black pistol and ran, leaving his IDs on the counter.

"He's going to miss those," Hudson said to Chris under the weak glow of the battery powered Christmas lights that hung from the mounted deer heads behind them.

"What do you think is happening?" Chris asked him and the old man heard the wavering fear in the young man's voice and felt angry at him for being scared.

"I don't know, but let's check the Illinois Power website for outages."

Hudson and Chris pulled out their phones but both screens remained black and useless. That was when the old man knew what it was. He looked up at Chris to see if he understood it too but was met with pure panic and fear on a face bathed in the red glare of the twinkling lights. Meanwhile, the alarm and the roar of the chaos around them grew closer and wilder. Hudson wondered when they would stampede the gun counter.

"I think you better get out of here and hide."

Those words would haunt him for as long as he lived, which might prove to not be very long at all. Hudson hated the taste of the lie on his tongue, bitter like funeral coffee in a Styrofoam cup.

"Where should I go?" Chris asked him as he blinked back tears and gripped the edge of the counter for support.

"Get back to the breakroom and lock the door. You'll be safe there."

The lies came easy, one after another, once the first one was spoken.

"Are you sure? What about you? You should come too." Chris was nearly crying now but even though he was breaking down, he had started to walk away from the old man.

"I'll be fine. But I think you better get out of here and hide."

The kid didn't look back. He ran off and left the old man alone in the red glare in the frenzied roar of the dark store.

Hudson watched the young man dart off in the dark store and disappear amongst the screaming mob. What he should have said was, "I think you should get in your car and get out of here."

But he hadn't said that because he wanted Chris's car.

Now Hudson as stood straight and erect as his 72-year-old frame would allow and turned his back to the stampeding masses and pulled the long skeleton key off the hook and unlocked the first gun safe. He always did everything slowly and with precision and now with chaos breaking loose all around him, he only sped up a little.

He knelt down and found Chris's forgotten JanSport backpack and the keys to his '68 Camaro. The backpack was crammed full of bottles of Mountain Dew and salty snacks, but the keys were clipped to the outside zipper loop.

Might as well take everything.

He slung on the backpack and took a breath and looked around in the dark and saw three men standing nearby staring at him in the red blinking glare of the Christmas lights.

"Here!" Hudson called to them and threw a set of keys to them. "Take what you want!" he said and then with the second set of keys, he unlocked the rifle rack closest to where he stood. He took down the Henry Golden Boy 44 mag. If he was stealing a car from his favorite coworker, he might as well steal a rifle from his employer.

He knew exactly where the 44-mag ammo was but first he had to quickly get the trigger lock off with the two-pronged screwdriver and then cut the zip-tie off the lever.

The three men grew impatient trying to unlock the cabinets of pistols and began to kick at them. The mirrors on the inside shattered but the cabinet doors themselves and the glass counters would not break. They were bulletproof.

Hudson shivered and flinched at how angry and violent the men were and he quickly dug three cartridges out of the 44-mag box on the shelf and shoved them in the gate of the rifle without taking his eyes off the men. He hesitated, then shoved in three more and cocked it and started to leave.

The red Christmas lights reflected off the plastic cases of 22 WMR that stood stacked to the left of the register. Those would come in handy too. His favorite rifle at home was a 22-mag Henry, a smaller version of the 44 he was stealing.

He emptied his lunch box of the remanent of his bologna sandwich lunch and the Frito crumbs and he packed it instead with boxes of 22s and then he skittered away from the gun counter as fast as his old legs would go.

Stealing. That was a bad thing, he said to himself as he paused at the fire door.

If it really was an EMP, his own new Honda CRV would not start. But the Camaro would and he was an old man and he needed to get home to Nellie.

***

Stealing those few things wasn't that bad, he told himself as he remembered how it all started. He hadn't really done too bad a thing. Unless of course you counted him forgetting to get Nellie's refills two days before. It had slipped his mind. He hadn't done it on purpose. He had had a lot on his mind such as not losing their home. Not getting behind on the taxes. The long days at the gun shop had him so he didn't know if he was coming or going. Why did he have to remember everything?

He just did. It was his burden to bear; go to work, make extra cash to keep from losing the farm, as they still called it, even though they didn't farm it anymore. Along with going to work, he was the one who did all the grocery shopping and ran all the errands. It was too much to keep track of, especially when you added on paying all the bills and maintaining the house and property.

He was 72, the same as Nellie. She was sick though. He wasn't. He didn't take a single a pill. Not even the little blue ones anymore. They hadn't had sex in years. Almost twenty years. He missed it as much now as he did at 50 when she first stopped having sex with him. When she first stopped letting him kiss her and touch her. The gun store had been a good place to interact with women, to be reminded he was still a man and an attractive one at that. But he should not be thinking of that now. Now he needed to focus and remember. The world had stopped and then it had really stopped when Nellie died. For some reason he believed if he replayed it all, it'd make more sense to him and then he would be able to fix it like he fixed everything in his and Nellie's life. Which was now just his life.

All he could think of at the time was that he needed to get to Chris's car and get out of there.

He left by the fire door, just around the corner from the gun counter, right behind the hunting supplies. He shuddered as he stepped out into the cold wet snowstorm and away from the screaming masses running wild in the dark store. The door slammed shut behind him and in the moonlight, he saw that it did not have a handle on the outside at all. He hoped he didn't need to get back in and he hoped no one followed him out through it and he turned against the wind and waded through the deep fluffy snow in his old Merrell shoes around to the front of the store to find Chris's Camaro in the employee section of the lot.

But it wasn't there.

Ten-year-old Toyotas and a twenty-year-old Mustang with a ripped-up cloth top (in a snowstorm!) sat dead and lumpy under the snow, but he could not find the hulking muscle car. People ran and screamed, carrying bundles of stolen goods in every direction but weren't able to unlock the doors to their cars, much less drive them.

Definitely an EMP.

His own car sat away from the employee cars. He was the only one besides the managers who had a brand-new car. He didn't want a ding on his door. Now he needed to smash out the window and retrieve something from the center console. He looked around at the chaos spinning wildly out of control all around him and weighed the choice of shooting his own car window out and how that would accelerate the lawlessness happening around him.

With no other choice, he shouldered the 44-mag lever rifle and aimed at his driver side window.

He watched the window explode glass out into the cold night air and then he flinched hard as another shot rang out, more of a pop, from twenty-five yards away.

Jon Travis Jones, and the purple and black SCCY pistol he stole, raised his arm and shut one of his eyes and fired another round at Hudson and made the old man run for cover behind the CRV. But as Hudson caught his breath and calmed down, he heard the man cussing under his breath and racking the little pistol again and again because it was jammed.

Hudson heard several clicks before he came out from behind the Honda and shouldered the 44 mag. He put his cheek to the stock and placed the buckhorn sight on top of the blurred image of the overweight man in the Vikings sweatsuit. He kept the sight on him as the man furiously racked the small pistol.

When Jon Travis Jones held the gun up and pointed it once again at Hudson, Hudson squeezed the trigger on the Henry and blasted Jon Travis's head into red misty bits all over the snow on the ground.

Hudson himself splattered partially digested bologna and Fritos all over the side of his own Honda and then coughed several times before standing back up.

"That was a bad thing," Hudson whispered and wiped his mouth on the back of his hand and then added, "but a good shot, if I do say so myself."

He made sure he wasn't going to puke again before opening the car and retrieving the small pistol and the bag of magazines for it from the center console. He closed his eyes a moment because he realized he was panting and felt a dull pain in his chest. He shook off the nausea and rubbed away the dull ache. The surrounding panic and the need to get home pushed him back out into the blizzard. He scanned the parking lot and the madness.

Then he saw the large hunkering hump of Chris's old Camaro parked twenty yards behind the dead man, and he ran as fast as he dared over the slippery snow to the vehicle and his escape from the madness of society breaking down on Christmas Eve in the parking lot. The car roaring to life and the dashboard lighting up was the most comforting thing Hudson could remember in his life. He quickly pushed the lock down on the door, pulled the knob for the windshield wipers to clear a hole to see out, and he put it in gear and peeled out of the lot.

Hudson drove home on the slick country roads in the over-powered muscle car to find Nellie, worried and sitting in the dining room by a cheerful but small fire in the stone fireplace.

"Power's out," she said with a small smile.

The Christmas tree looked fake in the dark to Hudson as he sat down to explain what was happening to his wife.

***

"I have to go into town."

Those were the last words he spoke to his Nellie.

Not, I love you, or, do you need more blankets, but, "I have to go into town."

"It's snowing awfully hard, dear," she said and they both looked out the long bedroom window and onto the sloping field behind their house where snowflakes the size of quarters fell down heavily and piled on top of the seven inches already packed onto the ground.

"That car is dangerous in this weather! Where is the Honda? You should take it!" she warned him as he kissed her forehead, but his mind wasn't on the weather or that powerful and squirrelly muscle car.

No, his mind was on how dangerous and out of control the people of town would be three days after losing power. City water ran off of electric pumps, and by now people would be getting desperate for water as well as food. Hudson had images of wild violent suffering of Biblical proportions, but he knew he had no choice. He had to go get his wife's medicine. She had gone three days without it and was already showing the effects.

He had faith he'd be okay even if he was an old man. He had been a gunsmith and a competitive shooter his entire life. He could take care of himself even if he was old. But he soon found out that these thoughts were arrogant and ignorant.

His arrogance and ignorance and lack of forethought nearly got him killed because he thought he was prepared to head into the lawless city in the stolen Camaro in a blizzard and get Nellie's medicine.

There were hordes of people fighting and looting and running in clusters on North Market Street all around the strip malls and the CVS that he needed to go to.

He was not prepared to see mobs of people moving as if sped up, killing each other, beating each other with anything they could swing, and some randomly shooting into the crowd. For once no one was filming it. Everyone was armed with something; bricks or poles or guns. Not a cellphone in sight.

Of course he had gone armed. But the old 1911 he had in a leather holster on his hip felt laughable with its eight rounds as he drove fast past the crowds and he heard rifle reports that cracked off all around. Of course he had his Smith & Wesson Shield in the center console which he had smartly converted to 357 Sig, but it and the seventeen mags he'd brought for it were no match against someone with an AR-15. Even his favorite rifle, his Henry chambered in 22 WMR, or the stolen 44 mag, would be useless against someone with an AR-15. No wonder they banned them, but yet there were still people with them apparently.

He glanced ahead at the CVS, which now had billowing smoke blooming out of it blackly across the snowflake-filled sky. He could not go in there. He needed to get back home immediately. There would be no medicine. What was he thinking that he could drive into town, park the car, and go in and get what he needed? What he needed was to get away from the mobs of rabid people who had murder in their bulging eyes.

The Camaro's engine roared and gobbled the gas as the back tires screamed for purchase in the snow and on the ice. The fat back-end of the car fishtailed from side to side as Hudson gripped the wheel with his gnarled hands and fought to keep it on the road and out of the snowbank as the mob parted and ran from him.

***

Back at home he found Nellie on the floor in the kitchen with pasta spirals all around her and foam on her lips. Her chalky yellow skin felt firm and cool under his fingers. She wasn't dead but she wasn't really alive either. He didn't leave her side for two days. He slept in the chair next to the bed in the downstairs bedroom that she had started using ten years ago.

He felt forgotten by the world and by God.

When Nellie finally passed after a day of gasping for air and convulsing off and on, Hudson sat unmoving for a long time and reflected on all the things he'd done wrong in his life and which one of them made him deserve watching Nellie suffer and die. He didn't know, but he did know he would not be giving up his own life so easily, even if he had to do more bad things.

***

He sighed now in the dim dining room as his back ached dull and low from dragging the wrapped body of Nellie out behind the lawnmower shed and burying her in the snow. The ground was frozen solid and he would not be able to dig in it for another two or three months. He didn't like to think of what the weather and the animals would do to her body. He shuddered at the thought then he stood up and lit the wicks of the oil lamps that stood tall on either end of the oak table.

Tears welled in the corner of his eyes and he thumbed them away quickly and looked up at the ceiling.

"I'm sorry I forgot your medicine, Nellie," he said with his voice sounding dry. "You wouldn't have wanted to be here. It's cold. And there's not much to eat."

The rabbits were sparse and the squirrels had stopped coming around the feeder after a few loud cracks of the old Henry rifle. The rabbits sometimes popped up near the brush pile one hundred yards from the back porch. This then required Hudson to trudge the length of a football field in the deep snow to retrieve the little body.

He sat down now on the bench near the back door and rubbed the seams of his boots with rabbit fat to seal them against the snow. His stomach growled though he had just eaten a whole rabbit in a watery stew. He glanced out the back window and up the steep hill behind his house and saw a sliver of smoke drifting upward out of the neighbor's chimney. He wondered how they were faring.

Candy the single mom and her ten-year-old son John lived behind him and Nellie. Maybe he should put on his snowshoes and tromp up there and check on them. It would be the good thing to do and maybe a good thing would wipe out the bad things he had done.

Candy was deaf since birth but could read lips and speak in that blunted flat pitch that deaf people spoke in. Her son John could hear fine but was mute. He wrote everything down or signed and grunted. He had one soft-looking black front tooth and his eyes were flat brown and lifeless. Hudson worried the boy had worms and never wanted him around underfoot. He never wanted his dirty, chewed-up fingers to touch him. He shivered at the thought of catching worms now while food was scarce and medicine nonexistent. Maybe he would not go see them. It would be a lot of expended energy and they seemed to have a good fire going. They were fine, he was sure. Maybe even better off than he was. He was hungry.

With the gnawing in his stomach, he went out on the slanted back porch to see if any animals were stirring close by in the moonlit back meadow. The cold white moon seemed to probe his thoughts and make him shudder and he pulled the collar up on his down coat. As he stepped on the slanted edge of the porch, he saw the large black nose and eye of a deer standing in the middle of the snowy field between the house and the brush pile, staring at him. He stepped down on a thin layer of ice, as thick as his fingernail, and felt his weight shift violently. He jerked and gasped and fell backwards. The round backside of his old head connected with the wooden porch with a crunchy *bam*!

Hudson lay there for a couple of moments before reaching to the back of his head with trembling fingers to probe his injury. Just a little sticky blood soaked his short white hair. He turned his head from side to side and he saw the white flag on the backside of the doe as she ran away. Then he rolled over and got up on all fours and crawled inside the house. He kicked the door shut behind him and crawled to the guest room where he passed out on the thick rag rug on the cold floor.

***

Sleet fell from the sky for five hours while a lively and robust fire roared in the stone fireplace and blasted heat into the dining room and down the hall to where Hudson lay, passed out on the rag rug with his mouth halfway open and a patchwork quilt thrown over him. When he woke, stiff and sore with a gnawing empty stomach, he could hear the brittle crackling sounds the ice pellets made against the old windowpanes. He lay there a moment, his mind fuzzy and confused, and then he realized he was warm and covered up.

He jumped up quick and ran to the mudroom and then to the kitchen, looking out the windows as he went. He glanced up the steep snowy hill beyond the propane tank on the edge of his yard. He looked up at the tall old white house up on the ridge. No sign of the deaf woman, Candy, and no sign of John, her mute son.

It was too icy for John to be out playing. That little fart liked to kick his soccer balls down the hill and bounce them off Hudson's propane tank. It infuriated him to hear the wallop of them against the long metal tank all afternoon when he was outside trying to have peace. Then the kid would drive hell-bent down the hill on his ATV, pulling a cart behind him, and retrieve all the balls. If he saw Hudson on the porch or sitting in the yard in a chair, he'd smile that big goofy bucktooth smile with his one dark tooth.

That kid would wave and wave, mute, but excited, until Hudson gave him a two-finger wave back before shaking his newspaper out and going back to reading. Then John would gather up all his soccer balls into his cart and crawl up the steep hill on his ATV and do it all over again. Hudson never told him to stop, but he would wince and curse under his breath every time the soccer ball hit the tank.

Now, it was too quiet.

Was it Candy who came down and built his fire up and then covered him up? Or did she have a boyfriend now who was responsible for it? It spooked Hudson to think someone had been in the house while he was passed out and that they had been watching him to begin with and knew he was hurt. It upset him that they started such a huge fire. He needed to conserve the wood to last all winter or until they got the power turned back on.

Candy meant well, if it was Candy who checked up on him, and she did keep him from getting hypo-...

His thought trailed off as he started to pull the curtain shut against the draft blowing in through the warped windowpane. He pulled the cloth open and looked back out at the ice-covered back porch rails.

Rabbits. Five dead and skinned rabbits tied by their back feet and hung up on twine from his back porch plant hook.

He shivered in fear. Someone was here while he was knocked out and it was definitely *not* Candy. His heart convulsed and he nearly peed himself.

His Henry. His rifle. Where was it? He'd left it in the corner of the mudroom before he stepped out on the porch, before he fell.

It was still there. He cocked it and one little 22 mag arced out and he plucked it out of the air and palmed it before scooping up a handful of rounds out of the candy dish where they used to keep their keys. Then he stepped carefully out on the porch. He tested each spot slowly before putting all his weight down. He scanned the area for a human as he pulled the brass tube out of the rifle and began to fill it with the small bullets. He was prepared to see a man walk up or a man to come by on horse. He was not prepared for the helicopter whose walloping blades chewing through the air made his ears feel plugged. He was not prepared for the oily stink that smudged the clear cold air as it blasted across the blue winter sky above his house.

Hudson jerked back under the roof of the porch and once again lost his traction. But this time he didn't fall. This time he had his rifle with him and he grabbed the end of the barrel and planted the stock onto the porch like a walking stick. He did not fall, which could have been lethal to bang his head again. But he might as well have.

***

The helicopter was not the type you wanted to flag down. It was not a red and white one from the hospital and it was not the blue and white kind from the news. It was not even American. Hudson didn't know who it was from, but it scared him so bad he nearly fell and would have if he hadn't had his trusty favorite rifle to use as a cane.

"I might as well have fell," he muttered once he got his footing.

He had bent the end of the brass tube of his favorite Henry 22 mag rifle. It would not go back in. He could not load it. It was useless.

He spent the rest of the day in the basement.

Hudson sat at the workshop table with this stack of papers between the bright light of the oil lamps he and Nellie had bought down at the Amish shops last summer. On the table between his strong old hands sat the applications for two rifles he'd never built because the ATF said he wasn't supposed to have them. Chris at the shop would have called them SBRs. Short Barreled Rifles.

The parts for them along with the parts for the AR-10, which were recently banned in Illinois, sat on the work mats on the two tables behind him. Hudson liked to be very organized and he did everything by the book, thus the papers from the ATF which he stared at in indecisiveness. The SBRs were banned before and also required tax stamps before. Hudson was torn about whether he should build the three illegal rifles or not. Hudson thought there probably wasn't an ATF anymore; at least not right now. Everything had come to a stop it seemed on Christmas Eve. But *he* still existed. So if he still existed, the ATF probably did too, somewhere, he was sure. So, that meant he needed to do the appropriate paperwork and keep it on file.

He dipped the nib of the fountainpen into the bottle of ink and pulled on the lever of the small bladder of the pen and drew the shiny black ink up into it. Then he assembled the pen back together, meticulously and without smudging ink all over his fingers, and he ceremoniously straightened the stack of papers and began to draw from memory the ATF tax stamp required for NFA items on his SBR application.

He refilled his pen once as the lamps continued to hiss and burn bright in the basement, as he worked silently and locked away in his secret gun vault workshop tucked behind the staircase. Many minutes later he finished his drawing, cleared his throat several times, and stood up and pushed his chair in and admired his work.

He began to hum Beethoven's Pastoral and as his humming became whistling, he picked up the stack of papers that he'd never sent to the ATF, and he threw them in the small tin trashcan at the end of his workbench with a satisfied smile.

Filed.

***

Eight hours and one box of Ritz crackers later, he had built a short-barreled AR-15. He took it upstairs with a green box full of ammo and laid it on the dining room table.

"Sorry, Nellie. Strange times and all call for strange measures," he spoke to the ceiling and then ran back down to the basement to bring up as many magazines as he could carry and blew out the lamps.

"I wish Chris could see this. He'd like this," he said to the empty dining room as he warmed himself in front of the dancing flames in the fireplace.

But Chris was not here. As a matter of fact, for the first time ever, Hudson worried if Chris had made it home okay without his car. Hudson wondered what was happening in town and he shuddered at the thought of people from town making their way out to his place. He didn't have much that would interest anyone except the propane and the well that still worked. He had a pantry full of cans but no can opener. And he had five rabbits, courtesy of someone, stewing in a pot hung over the fire.

If the power company got the power fixed, that'd be good, he said to himself as he grabbed a kitchen towel and lifted the kettle of water from the hook over the fire and took it to the back door.

With the porch cleared of ice, and the steps too, Hudson tromped out into the early evening dusk to try out the first rifle he built. He cobbled a snowman together quickly, near the brush pile, with the SBR slung on his back with the sling from an old Pendleton wool-covered canteen. He hadn't made a snowman in over sixty years and he laughed as he rolled the three balls with his wool mittens and as the fat wet snowflakes caught in his eyelashes.

He heard no more helicopters, thankfully. All he heard was the satisfying crunch and grind of his boots in the new wet snow, on top of a layer of ice. He walked what he thought was twenty-five yards away from the five-foot tall snowman and flipped up the caps of the short Vortex scope. Then Hudson pulled on the shooter's muffs and shouldered the little rifle. It took three shots to zero the scope and by the time he was done, it was dark.

He walked back to the house satisfied, and once inside he pulled all curtains closed and locked all the doors, something he hadn't done in twenty years or more. Then he helped himself to a bowl of rabbit stew and ate it while his new rifle lay on the table next to his 1911. He built up the fire and hung up all his wet clothing in the dining room to dry while he slept. Then he grabbed his weapons and went to bed in his long Johns and his stocking hat and a fresh pair of wool socks. He slept well and woke two hours before sunrise, made his tea, and headed to the basement for another day of work.

This time, after eight hours, he had assembled not just another short-barreled AR-15, but also half of the AR-10, chambered in .308. He took his time and was meticulous about every part of the procedure as he looked through his thick reading glasses to make sure everything was tightened to spec and that he had staked the castle nut correctly.

Again, he built another snowman and again he practiced shooting the short AR-15, but this time there was no scope to zero, only irons that he needed to practice with, which did not take long. He was an excellent shot, even if he'd never owned an AR platform rifle. Rifles were rifles and this one was no different from any bolt actions he'd shot. This one had a beautiful little barrel he'd picked up in Belgium on their last big vacation they'd taken, and it was very accurate. He couldn't wait to try out the FNH barrel tomorrow on the .308.

But now it was dark and late and he tromped back inside and ate the last of the rabbit stew and several little packages of raisins and went to bed tired, cold, and still hungry.

He awoke the next morning to eight trout hanging on his porch and a large stack of seasoned firewood next to his door. Sitting on the very first step was a jar of home canned jelly and, wrapped in two towels and wax paper all tied up with twine, a small round loaf of bread.

Who was visiting him in the night? He saw signs of sled runners in the snow and woman-sized shoe prints. Maybe it was Candy. He ate the entire loaf with the jelly and fried the fish in rabbit fat and thought of what he wouldn't do to have a couple of eggs and coffee instead of the black tea he had.

Still burping the fish, he descended into the basement and finished building the .308. He'd just finished securing the scope on the cantilever mount and making sure the witness marks were well in place on the screws and was clomping up the stairs on numb feet when he heard it. He froze and turned his head at an angle like an altert dog. The sound crawled outside on the road like a millipede at a picnic.

Tires. Many large tires. Engines. Vehicles. Cold fear tingled across his body and he shivered and felt a little pee dampen his underwear. Damn prostate. Then he ran up the stairs and shoved a short fat mag into the heavy black rifle as he ran down the hall to the back door.

Vehicles. Diesel vehicles. He could hear them. He could feel them. He could smell their stink in the fresh air. But he couldn't see them as they roared down the gravel and tar road past his property. He was shielded from the road by three rows of pine trees. He could barely see the long flat trucks roll past. Eight wheels each, he whispered to himself. What were those?

"UHhh!" the blunted cry startled Hudson and he banged his elbow on the doorframe as he raised the AR-10 up fast and pointed it at the little boy standing next to a long sled with a pull rope in his mitten.

"John!" He took his finger off the trigger.

The little boy wore a snowsuit like you'd wear snowmobiling. It zipped all the way up to his chin and said POLARIS on a patch sewed over his heart. He also had on huge snow boots and a stocking hat and mittens. He had a plastic magna-doodle on a sling slung over his shoulder.

"CHINA" he wrote in childish scribble with the plastic pen that hung from the toy. Then the boy waved that Hudson should follow him.

"Wait a second!" Hudson yelled to the boy and ducked back into the house.

He holstered his 1911 and grabbed the SBR with the Vortex scope and slung it over his head.

"UP HOME" John had written on his little board now and he waved frantically for Hudson to follow him.

John grabbed the rope handle on the long toboggan and turned it around and pulled it through the snow across the field and towards steep snowy hill that led up to his house.

"Why are we going to your house?" Hudson called the question to the back of the little boy as he tried to catch up to him.

The rifles weighed him down and the cold wind began to seep into his hands and his knees and made him ache as he fought to take every step in the deep snow. He'd forgotten his parka and his mittens and hat. His ears screamed with the wind blowing against them and his hands were bright red. It was probably around 10F.

John had no time to stop and write an answer on his little board. He pointed with his small finger poking the edge of his knitted mitten upward.

"UH UH!" he insisted. And then he looked over his shoulder and past Hudson and yelled, "OH OH!"

Panic made the little boy's brown eyes bulge and the whites glimmered blue-white in the cold afternoon sun. Hudson turned around to see what scared the boy so bad and could make out the red flags flapping in the cold wind on dark green buses flying past the trees on the blacktop road. They must have been filled with people. With soldiers. Panic squeezed his old man guts and he turned back around to face the snowy hill ahead of him and the little boy leading the way.

On John ran, pulling the toboggan with firewood and supplies strapped to it. A beautiful buck stretched the length of it with a full rack and bright brown eyes. The boy was bringing him a haul of supplies. Hudson gulped and blinked his wet eyes and ran harder; the short AR cracked him in the spine with every step he pounded up the snowy incline. His lungs squeezed the cold air in and out of his body and his nose poured snot down the white beard that covered his chin. He could not wait to stop running up the slippery, steep, snowy hill. Getting over the ridge proved to be the hardest part and for a second, he thought he'd tumble backwards and roll the two hundred yards back down it. But for John grabbing his outstretched frozen hand, he might have.

John's mittened hand felt amazingly warm like a fuzzy little brick and Hudson realized how cold he was even though he was sweating. He knew if he stopped moving long, he'd be even colder. But John wouldn't let him stop moving. He waved him on to a copse of pine trees at the side of the three-storey weatherbeaten white house. At the edge of the pine trees stood an elevated, homemade child's fort with walls, a roof, and open windows.

"Uh!" John urged and he scrambled up the ladder and disappeared into a hatch in the floor. Hudson made to follow but was too weak to raise his body up the ladder with the two rifles. His muscles burned and his joints ached and would not move. He breathed short chunks of frosty air in and out and got nothing of value from it. He felt nauseous.

"UH!" John came back down the ladder and insisted.

"Can't. Out of breath. Can't move."

"Eee!" John yelled and held out his hand and gestured at the AR-10.

"Too heavy for you!"

"EEE!" the boy nearly shrieked and Hudson handed up the long rifle as high as he could and was surprised when the boy yanked it up through the trapdoor in the fort floor.

Finally, Hudson pulled himself up the rungs by pure grit and determination and made it up too. John was ready for him on a stool next to a telescope on a tripod. Thankfully there was an old kitchen chair next to the scope and Hudson gladly plopped down. The child motioned for him to look, his own young brown eyes bright and wet yet fearless and maybe even excited. Hudson peeped through the eyepiece.

"Mee," the child said quietly and showed Hudson his magna-doodle board.

It said, "CHINA" again.

"I know," Hudson dismissed the kid and looked back through the telescope down at his own property. He saw his cheerful house of stone and blue siding with its fat chimney blasting smoke curls up into the sky. He saw the detached two-car garage where he had stored the stolen Camaro. He saw the snowman and the field and the brush pile where the rabbits always were and he saw the long white propane tank blending into the snow at the edge of the field and the base of the steep hill leading up to John's house.

The long flat dark green vehicles with the eight wheels were still rumbling past on the black top road with an occasional green bus with blacked-out windows thrown in the caravan. From up this high, Hudson could see over the tops of the pine trees and he counted twenty vehicles go past. Then came the smaller vehicles. One lagged behind all the others and it slowed to a stop in front of Hudson's long curving gravel drive. Then it turned off the road and crunched its way up his drive as it sniffed its way towards his house.

"Eee? Eee?" the boy asked him.

The child was watching without the telescope. You didn't need that to see the vehicle drive up to Hudson's garage. But with the telescope he could see the faces of the young Chinese soldiers when they got out of the truck and lit up cigarettes. He could see their mouths moving and then he watched, helpless to stop them, when four of them went into his house and the other four of them fanned out on his property.

Hudson pushed the telescope away and instead he took the caps off the scope of the AR-10 and he shouldered it and poked the barrel out the open window of the fort.

"This will be incredibly loud," he told John and hoped he understood.

John held up one finger and jumped up and scurried down through the hatch and down the ladder. Hudson watched the Chinese soldiers through the scope while John was gone. He frowned when he saw one walk around the back of the shed and towards the large mound of snow where Nellie was resting. Hudson licked his lips and slowed his breathing as the young soldier kicked at the bottom edge of her burial mound. The white-haired man took his eye away from the scope to find the safety and flicked the selector to "fire."

The soldier walked away from Nellie's remains and the white mound that covered her body, but Hudson kept the crosshairs on his back all the same and followed him as he walked towards the back porch.

He wondered what those dirty communist bastards were doing in his house. He felt the cargo pockets of his pants and felt two short ten-round magazines for the AR-10 as John emerged from the hatch carrying two pairs of very old shooter's muffs.

The kid put his on over his stocking hat with a large toothy smile and nodded at Hudson to do the same and the old man complied and then shouldered the heavy rifle once more and peered through the scope.

The soldiers were coming out of his house. Three came out and lit up cigarettes. *Well, at least they didn't smoke in his home.* Then the fourth came out. He was smoking already and he was carrying one of Nellie's plaid nightgowns and holding it up in front of himself and laughing and waving the gown around. Hudson hated him and his happy dancing eyes as he twirled around with Nellie's gown pinched between his gloved fingers.

The rifle retort blew its huge BOOM against Hudson and John's ears in the little fort despite wearing the shooter's muffs but John did not wince. He watched with eager attention as the Chinese soldier's face went from grinning and laughing with a cigarette between his clenched teeth, to exploding red mist in a puff against the snow as his body folded like an old shirt.

The little boy looked at Hudson; his face bright with excitement and wonder and he briskly shot the old man a thumbs-up with his mittened hand from where he sat on the stool next to the telescope.

Hudson frowned at the boy and then stupidly he looked for a bolt to rack until he remembered the rifle he'd built shot semi-auto.

He found the next soldier in his crosshairs. One that was staring up the hill towards Hudson and John's hiding spot while all the other Chinese soldiers scrambled for cover.

Hudson shot that one for trying to appear to be brave.

Then he felt the windowsill next to him shake and he looked over and saw John had the short AR-15 and was sitting wide-legged on the stool and looking through the scope.

"You know how to use that?" Hudson asked the kid and got a big smile back and another thumbs-up.

"I don't think it'll shoot two hundred yards," Hudson told him and he looked back down the large hill back at his own property.

The doubt in Hudson's statement didn't keep the kid from trying. He fired off three shots but didn't drop any of the soldiers. Maybe he just didn't know what he was doing with the scope but they needed to conserve ammo and Hudson motioned for him to stop.

That's when Hudson saw the eight-wheeled vehicle pull up his long gravel drive, its gears grinding and growling and belching black smoke as it made its way through the snow.

"We have a big problem now," Hudson said with heavy dread. "Where's your mom?" he asked the kid and looked at him for the answer.

The kid shut his eyes and stuck out his tongue and shook his head. His eyes had been bright and happy and now they took on that soapy dull look he'd always had before. Before the EMP.

"Sorry. But we're going to be dead too if they start firing up here. We need a plan."

John thoughtlessly dropped the AR-15 down on the plank floor and got his magna-doodle board to write his answer for Hudson but the pen was gone. The little orange cord hung loose with no pen attached.

"Wuh! Wuh?" the kid began to panic.

Hudson didn't have time for it. He needed to keep an eye on what the Chinese soldiers were doing. They were spilling out of the long vehicle and there appeared to be fifty of them or more. Every single one looked the same as the one next to him as they lined up behind the propane tank and began to light up cigarettes. Hudson shook his head at how stupid they were and at the notion of the Chinese invading the US while John jumped up and down next to him and yelled, "UH! WUH! OOOH!"

"What are you saying? You need to be quiet! Let me focus here! Help me out, will ya? Get the rifle back up!" the old man grouched at the kid and nodded down at the abandoned rifle the kid had dropped in a puddle of melted snow on the dirty fort floor.

"EWWWM!" the kid yelled and spread his arms wide.

"OOOM?" Hudson asked him.

"OOOM!" John echoed back and jumped up and down and yelled it again before disappearing back into the hatch in the floor.

Hudson could see the little kid run into a shed where the ATV and the cart he always pulled behind it was parked. The cart was full of soccer balls just waiting to be kicked into Hudson's propane tank. John picked one and strained with a boxcutter to cut a jagged slit in it and then he ran inside a large outbuilding.

Hudson watched the Chinese down the hill point up his way from two hundred yards down the steep snowy hill. They couldn't see him but they knew the direction the shots came from. He wondered if they'd shoot an RPG up at them. He wondered if America was at war with the Chinese and what kicked it off.

John interrupted all his doomer thoughts as he ran out of the outbuilding with the soccer ball in his arms with the sliced open hole now patched shut.

"OOM!" John yelled up at Hudson with a large smile. He set the ball down carefully and pointed up at Hudson and said one more time, "OOM!" and then he mimed holding a rifle and pointing it at the ball.

"What's in that ball?" Hudson asked the kid.

"OOM!" the kid yelled and began to laugh.

Hudson did not find it funny at all. As a matter of fact his stomach felt sour and his back felt slick with sweat and fear as he looked through the scope and down at all the Chinese soldiers milling about in his field, near the propane tank. He was going to do another bad thing, but he had to or the Chinese would come up here and kill them.

"Eddy?" the little boy in the too big snowsuit asked him. His face was screwed up in concentration and he appeared very serious now.

"Ready," Hudson answered back as he shouldered the rifle.

He put the scope on the white propane tank and in his peripheral vision he saw John on the ground down below him kick the patched-up old soccer ball with his huge snowboot with a dull *thunk*.

Hudson didn't watch the ball go down the hill but he did see the soccer ball hit the propane tank and when it started to bounce off it, he pulled the trigger.

And pulled the trigger again.

BOOM!

And *BABBBBOOOOOOM!*

THE END

ABOUT THE AUTHOR

Shirley Johnson

As a young girl, Shirley Johnson dreamed of becoming a writer. Born and raised in downstate Illinois where people are pragmatic, her parents encouraged her to get a good education. She majored in Political Science and minored in Russian and, to the absolute glee of her dad, began selling tanks and armored vehicles for a living.

But the urge to write, to braid plots and invent characters, called to her and she once again put pen to page.

She has nine novels available on Amazon, *The Water War* being her most popular series. When she isn't selling firearms, she is working on the fifth installment of that series.

THE CHERENKOV PROTOCOL

COL Mike Bennett

Since the first Reagan administration, there had always been a Warlock. Simply put, the Warlock was a position occupied by a person of special trust and whose name was irrelevant. The Warlock was not in command but had immeasurable power and influence. With that power came equal responsibility, and the position was only filled by someone of unquestionable integrity. More than anything else, the Warlock made plans, plans that were intended to change the course of the world.

His office was just one of many corporate proprietaries that fell under the rubric of the Joint Reconnaissance Task Force. The corporation was merely a wholly owned subsidiary of Allied Signal, and the Warlock's office was located on the backside of the loading docks. A commercial proprietary complete with a Dun & Bradstreet D-U-N-S number, Flight Concepts Division was just building out its hardstand facilities on Ft. Eustis in Virginia.

Additional moneys were appropriated through black funds and vectored through DOD to build a small adjacent facility that would be split into three functions: warehouse space, office space, and a classroom that oftentimes doubled as overflow billeting. A location at Ft. Eustis had a few advantages: legitimizing JRTF's lineage with DOD and forming the basis of a DOD/CIA collaboration found to be lacking after the Iran hostage debacle, along with proximity to staff and the institutional operational knowledge found just down the road at Camp Peary.

The JRTF was a waived, unacknowledged special access program comprised of persons detailed from DOD and national intelligence agencies. JRTF had an extrajudicial charter loosely organized around Title 10 and 50 authorities and was tailored to satisfy intelligence requirements beyond even the covert activities over which Congress had oversight. Outside of its official Crystal City offices, JRTF was known only as 'the firm.'

By the Warlock's authority, which was nearly infinite, Flight Concepts had access to any resource required to facilitate a plan. The Warlock was successful because the plans *were* finite, the plans were scoped to achieve a *single* objective, the plans were *controlled* with no bureaucratic competition. There had never been an overreach by any Warlock; there would never be corruption. Only the current Warlock could choose his or her successor.

And so had Lonny been passed the torch when Ryder Beaton had retired right after 9/11. A veteran of WWII, Ryder had been 75 years old when he stepped down as the Warlock. Lonny had already given well over 35 years of his adult life to serving his country in this nasty, covert world.

Yet, Lonny had heartily taken the mantle of leadership with an eye toward exploiting opportunities for the next era. He assumed the burden of the Warlord's authority, trying his best to navigate finding the right solutions to problems that others wished away.

At the tender age of 65, Lonny Pemberton's journey south had taken a toll, and this was as far south as south goes. To ensure a level of security was kept foremost, he traveled under the alias of Joe Diamond, an account executive for Allied Signal seeking mining contracts to secure raw materials through partnership with private entities in Chile.

Continuing his journey, Lonny departed on a charter plane full of White Continent enthusiasts from Punta Arenas at the southern tip of Chile and flew to King George Island on the Antarctic Peninsula. The plane itself was a BAE-146 with 4 turbo propeller engines and reinforced undercarriage for remote airstrips.

Under the guise of the United States Office of Polar Programs, a military officer linked up with Mr. Diamond and escorted him via a Navy C-130 flying above the Ronne Ice Shelf penetrating deep over the interior and landing at Amundsen–Scott South Pole Station in Antarctica. When he could peer through the November fog to see the land below, 'Joe' only saw white, a world of ceaseless ice and snow.

Exhausted and colder than he had ever been, Lonny was further guided to a billeting space normally allotted as dual-occupancy, the only deference to his position as he passed out onto his cot still fully clothed, his dreams solely dominated by a glaze of an empty and vast expanse of hostile white desert.

***

Dr. Mark Rutherford started the briefing right on time. "Lonny, our paths haven't really crossed. Most of my previous discussions on particle beam theory were compartmented to your predecessor."

Nodding his understanding, Lonny sought clarification while marking his limitations, "Mark, the BEAR project was Ryder's domain—he grasped the science far better than I, but now that I'm in a different role, I'll do my best to keep up. No pun intended, but just bear in mind you'll have to tailor your coaching to a lower level—I don't have the engineering brain to keep up!"

Dr. Lisa Morris chimed in, "Lonny, twenty-five years ago we completed the BEAR neutron saturation particle beam which then led to other, related research. It's important to note that even though BEAR wrought devastation in Chernobyl, that particle beam was based on low-order energies."

"Particle beam theory led to experimental study of the radio signature of showers induced by ultra-high energy cosmic rays," Mark continued. "In crude terms, we graduated from particle beams to particle showers, the implied orders of magnitude involved led to discovering ultrahigh-energy γ radiation."

Lisa interrupted, "Permit me to quote an article by Zhen Cuo titled, 'Ultrahigh-energy photons up to 1.4 petaelectronvolts from 12 γ-ray Galactic sources:'

Charged cosmic rays that impinge on the atmosphere produce particle showers which develop over length scales of several kilometers. Similar showers may be triggered in dense media, such as water ice, by astrophysical neutrinos with energies of the order of petaelectronvolts... These showers are not globally charge neutral and so represent an electric current that leads to the production of electromagnetic radiation—"

Seeing Lonny wince, Mark clarified, "Please let me break that down into the important segments worth noting and remembering. First, cosmic rays assault Earth's atmosphere every second of every day. A recognition of this has led to the term you just heard, 'astrophysical.' Second, a dense medium is needed to capture the particle. The medium of sufficient purity and density of which Antarctica abounds is that of ice. That explains why you are here of all places on this planet!"

"And I was beginning to think this was just a boondoggle," the Warlock quipped.

Lisa smiled and said, "There are two more elements in Zhen Cuo's quote of grave concern. One is the concept of a neutrino. Possessing no electric charge, the particle emitted from an irradiated nucleus is called a neutrino. A neutrino can *conserve* both energy and momentum.

"A neutrino is similar to the neutron particle on which BEAR was based, yet a major difference being in measuring the magnitudes of mass. Secondly, once a neutrino collides with an ice molecule, it creates charged particles known as Cherenkov light that emit blue to ultraviolet light passing through the ice medium."

Mark paused for questions; Lonny indicated he was ready for the punch line.

Mark laconically delivered it. "Expressed as PeV, a single petaelectronvolt exceeds the total energy released by a 20-kiloton nuclear fission device by several orders of magnitude. A very high energy neutrino flux of extraterrestrial origin has been theorized to exceed 2-PeV."

"So, we're talking about capturing or converting gamma radiation that could be weaponized?" Lonny said.

Grimly, Mark remarked, "I'm afraid so. And we are not the only one's aware of that potential. Zhen Cuo is an officer in the Chinese People's Liberation Army Navy."

***

The Warlock absorbed the data as best he could and, pausing to doublecheck his notes, he queried, "My first thought is this environment down here is so isolated and with a tiny population where everyone on station is going to know what everyone is doing. How could we leverage the legitimate science ongoing with a side project that could go unnoticed?"

"We learned so much about tradecraft and misattribution during the BEAR project, but I think we still need that mentoring/coaching that was provided by Max Vachon, the guy from CIA's Directorate of Science and Technology," Lisa said. "Generally speaking, I think we can establish a protocol exploring adjacencies of neutrinos to neutron particle beams, not in terms of weaponization, but in terms of communications, or how it could be utilized in fiber optic networks."

Sighing, Mark said, "I hate to try to bring the band together, but I agree. Lisa and I will need to focus on the science and experimentation. We just won't have the bandwidth to work on the legitimate neutrino work, then a side, covert project, and on top of that, conceal all out efforts from the community down here and at the National Science Foundation in DC. We're gonna need help."

The Warlock glanced upward in recollection. "Well, I happen to know Max retired from the Agency but that is not to say he isn't a contractor somewhere. Whether he is an independent contractor or working at some-place like Raytheon, he probably has kept his clearances. Even that is a wave of the pen. The issue is whether he'll want to join you on this project."

Lisa replied, "I thought you might be reticent because he definitely has prior association with the Agency."

Lonny recognized this was not these two PhDs' first rodeo. "The thought crossed my mind, but with some magic juju we can obscure that. Perfect world, we'll need to fabricate a story that augments his engineering and science resume so he'll fit into the community down here, but at the same time not stick out as a spook.

"Let's table cover for status specifically for Max since he may not be available, but rather focus on what kind of footprint you'll need to conduct your parallel research. Again, it has to fit in with the adjacencies of the BEAR particle beam methodologies. Even that, obviously, we'll have to obfuscate the true purpose."

Dr. Rutherford thought about that, then said, "To be consistent with the particle beam cover for action, I think some of the first things we need to do is move the modified Positron Electron Project. This is our miniaturized version of the 3.2 km long Stanford Linear Accelerator built in 1966. Another main piece of technology we will need to build is a traveling-wave tube amplifier. The 'Tweeta' is a specialized vacuum tube to amplify radio frequency signals in the microwave range. We'll use it to direct and encapsulate the Cherenkov light photons."

Lonny whistled. "The more I think about it, Mark, the more it seems this project has potential for growth and simultaneously needing its own compartmented staff. Now, if I can get Max to sign up, I'll try to bring on board both VooDoo and Cat from the old BEAR team. You all have worked together, so there is some team cohesion that I think is necessary to maximize the opportunity. Agreed?"

"I really was hoping you'd say that," Lisa said, smiling. "We know how each other thinks to a high degree, and we worked well together. I concur and offer my vote!"

"Still, as far as staff at Amundsen, we'll have to limit it to just Max," Mark noted. "Permanent party beyond that will draw too much attention."

The Warlock made his decision. "I think we're all on the same wavelength. I'll make arrangements to house the support staff in Punta Arenas for dispersion, but relative access to Antarctica to push logistic packages. We'll call the project 'OP Cherenkov'."

***

The Warlock called the meeting to order. Around the table were faces he had not seen for many years, each having earned not only their respective retirements, but more than a few gray hairs and wrinkles. But their eyes still burned with the intelligence and intensity that brought them back to once again serve.

"Each of you have probably read our old friend Dr. Rutherford's synopsis of the project," he began. "I'll reiterate that this Special Access

Program is eyes-only for those of us in this room, Mark and I'm sure you'll remember Dr. Lisa Morris. We don't really need much more for introductions.

"With that, I'll be followed by Cat who's the lead operations officer on this effort. She's branched out a bit from just targeting and has found us what I believe is an excellent cover for action for the SAP we will call OP Cherenkov."

Cat Wolden had indeed expanded her skillset as a targeting officer from the BEAR project when she attended a DoD course called Advanced Special Operations Training Level III. ASOT III was DoD's answer to absorb the rapidly ascending requirements for case officers after 9/11. The CIA Directorate of Operations fully endorsed the program of instruction and certified the graduates as collectors at the same level as those who attended the course at Camp Peary. Being a bit of a masochist, she subsequently went through the Camp Peary program years later and had completed her career at CIA by finishing her 20-year stint by working in the cover shop.

Cat started her brief. "I can't say how happy I am about this reunion! The gang's all here! I'll get right down to it; we'll reminisce and catch up socially later. What I have found out is there has been a multi-country effort including the European Southern Observatory, the US National Science Foundation, the Canadian National Research Council, and the National Institutes of Natural Sciences from both Japan and Taiwan.

"This multi-nation effort is called the Atacama Large Millimeter/submillimeter Array, or ALMA. The main ALMA site is being constructed at a 5000m elevation in the Chajnantor plateau of the Atacama Desert in Chile. This international astronomy interferometer facility will be eventually comprised of sixty-six radio telescopes observing electromagnetic radiation at millimeter and submillimeter wavelengths."

Mark whistled. "It's bloody perfect! We can exploit the correlation of the EM radiation with the radio signature of showers induced by ultra-high energy cosmic rays."

Cat tamped down Mark's enthusiasm by turning to the man beside her and saying, "VooDoo, from a logistical point of view, I'm sure that will present some challenges."

"The cover aspect is fine, I got no problems with that, I can make it work," VooDoo said, nodding. "From the point of view of distances and geometries, I'm not gonna lie. This is going to be a pain in the ass if we ever get down to tight schedules."

"VooDoo, you're right. It will be challenging, especially when we throw in weather as a variable." The Warlock clarified, "Timetable is very flexible, not much of a constraint. Operational Security is the most important aspect of execution."

"Cat, is the HQ for this thing in Santiago?" VooDoo asked.

"It is," Cat confirmed. "Easiest thing for us to do is carve out some space at the Very Large Array near Socorro, New Mexico, then establish a foothold in some real estate in Santiago. All packages can start their journey from Socorro, get routed to Santiago, then forwarded down to Punta Arenas and beyond to the Pole. VooDoo, let me know what you need to build out not only the facility but personnel infrastructure."

"Wilco," VooDoo said. "I'm guessing funding is routed through the NSF?"

"That would be best," Mark said. "The line items should be obfuscated, but that is consistent with the actual neutrino work being funded by NSF. As far as they are concerned, our adjacent particle beam work could be all under the larger neutrino umbrella which ultimately will be centered around a collection array called Ice Cube. It all fits."

The Warlock wrapped the meeting up. "I think I can envision from an OPSEC point of view that this project is workable. Cat, run it as you see fit. Mark, as far as the development itself is concerned, we'll all reconvene as you cross technical milestones along the way. I will have many other efforts ongoing, but I'll give you top priority if you encounter problems needing my influence to sweep aside."

***

Dr. Zhen Cuo had been a scientist in the Chinese People's Liberation Army Navy for nearly two decades. He had risen to the rank of colonel, but his reach into anything to do with nuclear developments and plans related more to his prominence as a physicist and researcher. Using a tank holding scintillator to catch antineutrinos generated by nuclear reactors, China's Daya Bay Reactor Neutrino Experiment was his brainchild and legacy.

Zhen Cuo was not only brilliant, but preeminent in the field of neutrinos, antineutrinos, really *anything* to do with particle physics. His range was expansive. Exploring the radioactive decay of Earth's thorium and uranium, he found that geoneutrinos could provide clues to the planet's composition and geophysical processes such as mantle convection. Nothing was beyond the grasp of his under stimulated intellect.

His research differed from Mark Rutherford's in that the neutrino base from which he conducted experiments was derived from eight separate nuclear reactors 53 kilometers away, not charged cosmic rays. He was an unconventional problem solver and other scientists knew his prodigious reach could be tapped even with the most subtle queries. So, unofficially his charter expanded to helping others reach their goals beyond theory, but in the realm of applied science.

A few years back be had been asked to help miniaturize nuclear warheads. The work itself was interesting, but what made it really unique to him was the requirement to prioritize not creating a large blast yield but to optimize electro-magnetic pulse output. He pioneered the use of artificial intelligence to create mathematical models to theorize the different configurations to maximize the EMP output and to focus it on specific frequency spectrums.

As he became more versatile in his sidebar consultancies, he acquired more access to other defense related projects. Eventually, what he found out regarding the application of his work began to disturb him. As he sat alone in his office, he pieced together all the little nuggets of information from which he had amassed a very clear picture: there was nothing peaceful about China's pursuit of this science. Not one damn thing.

Still, his reluctance to continue his efforts was overwhelmed by his desire to increase his network influencing other scientific endeavors. Perhaps he was easily seduced—an offer to participate beyond design to the implementation of his EMP engine under the auspices of an operation rumored to be called Mongol Moon had been dangled. Even though he felt a passing shiver of shame, he greedily accepted.

***

Time had passed since the Warlock had received a brief on OP Cherenkov. He had read several slide decks or white papers detailing milestones, but Dr. Rutherford insisted the best way to convey some of the recent breakthroughs would be to meet in another face-to-face. Since he was nearly continuously swamped with supervising overlapping operations or planning future actions, his time was short. A trip down to Antarctica was out of the question.

Mark had suggested Socorro as perfectly suited, and there is where the meeting took place. Walking in, Warlock said, "Okay, Mark. It sounded fairly urgent. What's up?"

"I know you got the brief on the progress of the DOMS. I'll start there just as a refresher," Dr. Rutherford began. "In 2011, the Ice Cube array was completed and designated as Full Operating Capability. Ice Cube is comprised of dozens of spherical optical sensors called Digital Optical Modules or DOMs, each with a photomultiplier tube and a single-board data acquisition computer. It's a massive undertaking, as you can imagine because each string of DOMs is buried beneath the ice at varying depths. There are eighty-six strings in the array, with sixty DOMs per string.

"That milestone is relevant to us as Ice Cube is what will collect the neutrinos and of course send the measurements for the regular NSF research all the way up to the University of Wisconsin. The neutrinos themselves initially remain in the DOMs and from there we'll take control of them in our own vault."

Raising an eyebrow, the Warlock asked, "Vault. First time you've used that term. Isn't that dangerous? Containing them—and how do you contain a neutrino? I thought they passed through matter pretty indiscriminately."

"That's one of the developments I wanted to apprise you of," Dr. Rutherford explained. "Without getting into all the geeky detail, we have found that neutrinos don't pass through a barrier made of a mix of cobalt and zinc. As such, we have been successful 'caging' at least 90% of neutrinos stored in our vault."

The Warlock was surprised. "Wow. That's incredible!"

Mark couldn't contain his enthusiasm. "It gets even better! It's complicated because there is quantum and particle physics involved, but we've been fairly successful in building the required traveling-wave tube amplifier. As you may recall, the 'Tweeta' is a specialized vacuum tube to amplify radio frequency signals in the microwave range."

The Warlock frowned. "This will be the means to transport the photons or Cherenkov light is what I remember."

"Yes, but a better way to express this is to say 'neutrino-infused photons'," Mark said. "It's a small distinction, but it distinguishes what we are doing, and how we differ from other projects, like those that transport light over a physical medium, like a 'glass' fiber optic cable. Still, what's important is we now have a means to contain and move the payload as well as direct or orient it.

"Now that you are caught up, I need to break some new ground. Two things. One, we need to be able to 'receive' the signal at a precise spot. And two, we have figured out how to weaponize the neutrino infused beam."

The Warlock patiently waited. "Go on."

Mark leaned forward. "I say 'signal' because it is important to remember the Tweeta produces a radio signal that encapsulates the photon beam. That way, we can get our neutrino payload to a specified point. Here is the last big breakthrough, and fortunately we were working with tiny, nearly singular amounts of neutrinos. When the normally neutral neutrinos are bombarded with a positive charge and then interact with an element called Hassium, it causes intensive vibrations."

The Warlock winced. "I'm not familiar with any element called Hassium. Why this element versus the others on the periodic chart?"

"Hassium has the highest known charge, a charge of a positive 8 or +8. The neutrino bombarded with positive charge invokes a destabilization of the Hassium atomic structure. The interaction is so violent that, with a sizable mass of the element, we could induce earthquakes."

The Warlock was stoic, but it was obvious he was internally calculating. "One point, Mark. The whole induce earthquake thing? Keep that close hold to you, me, and Lisa, okay?"

***

Although Cat had not attended the meeting in Socorro to discuss the Tweeta signal to bombard the Hassium mass, the Warlock felt it was time to bring her in to build the personnel end of the infrastructure in the target area. As always, these things took a great deal of time, but he had some ideas on how to solve the problem.

He had returned to his Flight Concepts office and opened a secure line. "Hey, Cat. Just got back from New Mexico. Things on the technical side of OP Cherenkov are progressing nicely, but now it's time to think about implementation.

"You can get a bit more of the science from Mark, but basically what we have to worry about is one, getting a 'box' to receive a signal designed and developed. And, two, getting that box into country."

"Okay," Cat said. "What's the timeline and what's the country?"

"China, for now. I may also want to get a 'box' into Russia, I haven't decided. Timeline is dependent on the development of the larger system. I think the 'box' is a relatively easy lift; that should only take a few months. But getting into China is going to require vetted assets, and I have some ideas."

Cat whistled. "China. That is going to be tough. Hard target. Might take time, and I mean years."

"Perhaps, but perhaps not. The box is not that large. It's essentially a microwave processor with antennas and hitched to direct the stream of neutrinos to a chunk of a metal called Hassium. Should be an easy build; talk to Mark for more info if you like."

Cat smiled. "We ought to call it something other than the 'box.' How about something like Toaster?"

The Warlock waved his hand. "Fine. Now the hard part—personnel we can trust to move the box, or Toaster, and get it to the desired location. Here is my general thought—since it is so hard for us to find people that can penetrate China, maybe we can double-task some folks I have been setting up for Op Boomslang.

"I have a few: a CIA paramilitary officer true name Robert 'Pak Fai' Chan with an identity formed as Wĕi Qí Liu. He is already partnered with a military guy name Jimmy 'Pong' Zhao whose cover identity is Yuàn Bó Zhao. Pong and Pak Fi will transport the package and then flow to their Op Boomslang assignment.

"Lastly, I have a case officer in Macau who was born in Honk Kong. He has a legit job and can probably receive Toaster at the port. I hate to use a diplomatic pouch out of the US Consulate in Hong Kong or Macau, but that would be a last resort contingency. Your call."

Cat brightened considerably. "Having people already inserted with the skills and a seasoned cover story makes things much, much easier. I'll also work on some alternates, but this sounds very promising. Oh, the guy in Macau—what's his name?"

"Oh, yeah. That'd be helpful, wouldn't it? His cover identity is Li Wu Liang, he works at Checkpoint." The Warlock chastised himself for forgetting this detail. In this business, omission of essential operational details could cause failure and cost lives. He regathered his focus. "Let's discuss compartmentation. You'll have to bring VooDoo in as far as the logistics. Toaster will have to get from Macau to an abandoned granite quarry in Hubei province. You'll not discuss the installation location with Mark or Lisa, okay?"

Cat had been madly taking notes and simultaneously calculating distances, personal relationships, documentation requirements and a myriad of other minutia while gathering her thoughts. "Okay. I'll start working on the plan first to infiltrate the package into country using Li as my postman. Second stage will be transporting and installing the item in the quarry. Methods will be up to VooDoo, so we'll need to know the size and weight of the item soonest." She summarized her projections in an attempt to fill gaps, "I'll also need to know a stop date as far as if it would interfere with Op Boomslang or if you'll need to make a decision to abort one operation or the other. Hopefully, we won't cross over and interfere with either timeline."

***

Hank Tierney had dispatched the manufacture of the Toaster device with relative ease. The hardest part was acquiring a 20-kilogram chunk of processed Hassium, but the loggies at DS&T had their sources across the network of university laboratories nationwide. The subterranean microwave antenna array proved to be the most technically challenging aspect and to the overall apparatus he added a means for command and control: an above-ground antenna to receive radar impulses from 'weather' satellites.

The Toaster receiver was enclosed in a concealment device constructed to mimic a Cummins Commercial 5KW Diesel Generator. Due to the battery pack needed to operate the neutrino beam waveguide and the two radio processors, the overall weight matched the Cummins design of 400 pounds. Into a single 10-foot container, Toaster accompanied another actual 5KW generator and was shipped to the embassy in South Africa. The Toaster receiver was enclosed in a concealment device constructed to mimic a

The diplomatic pouch was processed by a State Department mail room drone and after sterilization, eventually was forklifted off the shipping loading bay platform onto a flatbed headed for the quay alongside the bulk iron ore Panamax-sized ship chosen by the Kumba Iron Ore Company. On the dock itself there was the usual pandemonium: cranes, grabs and conveyors seizing ton after ton of the ore that was loaded into the specially ballasted holds, the air thick with dust flung into the wind and coating every surface.

The *Ubuntu Harmony* made its way to the ports of Macau where the chaotic unloading process reversed the choreography of the cranes, grabs, and conveyors seen back in Cape Town. Amongst all that confusion, a single 10-foot container was set onto the backside of the dock and loaded onto a flatbed. The truck moved to a line of other trucks heading to the Customs inspector's shack.

Here, from a vantage point far enough away to create separation if the port were locked down for a security breach, through binoculars Li Wu Liang watched his asset with some trepidation. Li had no idea what was inside the container, he knew only that it had to pass through Customs and trundle on to a small Kumba Iron Ore warehouse that was used to store off-loading machinery and odds and ends.

For now, he held his breath and waited.

***

The Warlock had returned from a fruitless trip to the White House.

The office of the President of the United States was occupied by a man who had spent several long decades in various positions of government as an elected official. His record was very public—even Johnny Carson remarked scathingly in a 1987 monologue regarding plagiarisms of entire political speeches being ripped off. This activity was consistent with a law student barely graduating in the bottom quintile of his class, a law student who had as an undergrad also been nearly expelled for the same offense. Over the decades he had been equally consistent in being wrong on a huge portfolio of foreign policy issues.

The Warlock knew he was not alone in his pessimism of his threat assessments. Via his myriad of sources throughout the intelligence community, he was aware an analyst at the Joint Intelligence Command named Gale Washington had suspicions of North Korean satellite KM-3 and its true purpose. Its odd launch timing and nearly immediate deactivation were red flags, but its specific orbit was even more disconcerting.

Still, the Warlock felt duty bound to try and warn this Administration of the potential that not only had China, Russia, Iran, Turkey, and North Korea formed a very formal Alliance, but they were more than capable of enacting coordinated actions against American interests. He had briefed the President early in his term; he was politely received, and just as politely ignored.

Not seeming to appreciate the value of an offensive weapon in his arsenal, the President had gormlessly dismissed the Warlock with a vacant expression. Not that the Warlock had briefed any specific plans to this savant; for the purpose of this discussion, those were not on the table and proceeded as conceived.

***

When Wěi Qí Liu and Yuàn Bó Zhao traveled alone, as they were now, they could to some degree relax and call each other by their respective code names, Pak Fai and Pong. At any point where they thought they might be overheard, each resolved immediately to snap back into character. They had already ingrained this habit in a pre-deployment train up 'out West' at a special CIA training center in Idaho National Laboratory and then polished it a bit further in another scenario placing them within an indigenous Chinese population in Vancouver to season their cover identities.

For four days, each had taken turns driving the flatbed Isuzu cargo truck along the rustic, curving unimproved roads leading into the heartland of Hubei province. Finally, they had reached the outer rim near their objective: the super-elevated terminal bend of the haul road leading down to an abandoned sandstone quarry. In the lowest level of the floodplain of the Yangtze River and the middle part of the alluvial plain and basin bordered by the eastern extension of the axis of the Qin, Tongbai, and Dabie mountains, therein lay the rotting skeleton of the quarry well, barracks, and mine operations shack.

According to their instructions, down the well they dropped the subterranean antenna array then they buried the connecting coaxial cable in a trench leading to the ops shack. To the shack roof, Pak Fai attached a microstrip patch antenna, the substrate of which was colored to blend in with the roofing shingles and the ground plane tilted to face the anticipated orbit of the weather satellite radar's emission. Inside the shack, Pong used a heavy-duty hand truck to emplace the Toaster concealment device. After Pak Fai routed the roof antenna coax through a hole he had punched in the rafter, he attached both antenna wires to their respective receiver screw terminals. He then grounded each antenna lead at separate points on the chassis.

They had been provided a purpose-made diagnostic device to test the system's connections and viability. At a specified time that matched the satellite's overpass, Pong turned one switch to observe that the satellite's radar pulse had indeed been received at the rooftop antenna and was providing the receiver programming instructions, in this case to activate the battery pack that powered the traveling-wave tube amplifier, the microwave receiver, and the Hassium photon interface. All lights on the diagnostic device indicated all systems were functioning. When the diagnostic device was shut down, Toaster itself shut down and was put into a dormant, stand-by state.

The men looked around the remote activation site to ensure they left nothing behind. As Pong drove away from the quarry, he paused on a bridge that spanned a deep gorge. Pak Fai rolled the window down and tossed out the diagnostic device. Both smiled to have gotten out of the way what they thought was only a vetting operational act; they continued onto their actual operational area vicinity of Urumqi where they would settle in as field workers as cover for status to support the Boomslang operation.

***

The Warlock awoke in the middle of the night to silence.

Not a sound. Dark—eerily dark in his apartment close to Flight Concepts Division; a safe house really, one close enough to walk to his office. The oily, cloying murk ate into his wakening consciousness. Something was wrong.

He reached to his bedside bureau and groped for his Glock; he slid on the Surefire weaponlight to scope the room. He got to the window, turned off the light, and let his eyes adjust. Outside—total blackness. Nothing moved; it seemed no one else was awake.

He made his way to his garage, hit the button to activate the garage door opener. Nothing. Enroute, he had noticed not even the LED clock on the microwave was lit. He tried starting his BMW. Nothing. His cell phone was dead.

He got to the door and opened it to see the street under which the neighborhood normally was emblazoned by the Halon glow of the overhead streetlights. Nothing—but he could hear someone else awake down the street banging his shins in the dark. Hitching his bug-out-bag straps a bit tighter, he started his slog to the office.

At Flight Concepts, there was a little more order. Underground generators had kicked on. Once through the gate, he noted the other resident military personnel on duty had an aura of chaos about them. As the Warlock, his business was not with them, but to his duties in his own little sphere. He was embedded only within the compound where they provided his cover for status, and they knew enough to leave him be.

He had been paranoid enough to harden his facilities and fiber-optics links to an EMP pulse; no expense had been spared in shielding his assets. Still, the endpoints like the data centers in Langley and Herndon to which he was dependent for information were useless now. He settled into his chair and turned to his bank of computer consoles. After an hour of fiddling, and double-checking with what he had at hand, he could only conclude the obvious. Obvious, but unsettlingly disconcerting yet not completely unanticipated.

America was at war.

America had been attacked, and from far-flung places bits of data came in to confirm the Warlock's suspicions. The Alliance had taken the initiative and set forth a long-planned sequence of events. The coordinated attacks were global against targets the Warlock himself also would have chosen—communications links in Australia and Guam and other sensitive nodes to blind American responses.

And on this Christmas Day, he reviewed his options.

***

Alone, the Warlock tensed with his hand poised over the phone handset connecting him to Dr. Rutherford at Amundsen–Scott South Pole Station in Antarctica.

Jack and Xander were managing the triggering and the effects of the Quohog operation. Having been apprised of the status of ten Chinese PLAN ships having entered the constricting throat of the Malaccan Strait, the Warlock made his decision. The time to unleash the potential of the Toaster neutrino-photon infused inciter beam was now. He had left this decision solely to himself, knowing fully the potential of the destruction the earthquake might wreak.

He had severed breadcrumbs linking the target and the overall system; Mark Rutherford and Lisa Morris both knew that enormous energy would be released by bombarding the Hassium mass with the neutrino beam—but they didn't know the target, not even the country for which it was intended; Cat Wolden and Li Wu Liang knew only that a device of some sort would be delivered to Macau; Pak Fi and Pong knew only a device capable of receiving signals from both space and subterranean sources was delivered to and tested at an abandoned quarry in Hubei;

Obl*sk had constructed the targeting algorithm directing the vector of the neutronium beam towards its destination—a geodetic point in space for which separately the Warlock had subcontracted via cutouts with no context.

Only the Warlock knew that all the pieces together enabled a system capable of inducing an earthquake at a particular point on the ground.

He felt the crush of command, the solitude of having the responsibility to take thousands of lives; that, he knew, was inevitable. He had chosen the site in Hubei quite deliberately, and he justified its choice knowing the economic impact would strategically erase China as a competitor for likely decades. He had been clear minded in assessing damage to the Three Gorges Dam would be catastrophic to China's industrial base.

The Three Gorges Dam lies along a seismic zone where far below the Earth's crust, several tectonic plates converge: the Yangtze plate, the Indian plate, and the Eurasian plate. The Indian and Eurasian plates had already collided and resulted in the Sumatra earthquake of 2004 as measured as 9.1 on the Richter scale. Only a gentle nudge would bring the three colossal plates together to grate and clash on a scale evocative of a Titans' grudge match.

The Warlock called Dr. Rutherford and with no preamble spoke one word only, "Now!" Dutifully, Mark Rutherford approached the computer console and entered the code sequence to initiate the transfer of neutrinos from storage in the Vault. The dielectric absorption fully leveraged, far beneath the Antarctic ice the transmitter silently vomited its payload: a stream of neutrinos artificially impregnated with a positive charge that hurtled through the Earth's outer core.

The Tweeta signal pierced the mantle of the Earth, unimpressed by the heat or gravitational forces implied within. Onward it sped, the microwave 'tube' encapsulating the photon beam bending the payload to meet the antenna array suspended below the quarry. In mere milliseconds, its target was reached. Here, the payload was dumped, the 20-kilogram chunk of Hassium receiving the offering, its natural charge engorged.

The Hassium mass was over stimulated, its normal +8 protons super-charged, the atomic excitation reaching an unstable state, all matter within range vibrating, expanding or contracting, a cacophony of chaos where particles were desperately jostling for equalization. These efforts were rendered impossible by the manipulated neutrino bombardment. The realm of quantum physics itself was challenged to retain order and failed.

The intended consequence of proton immersion took flight well beyond the anticipated measure, the deluge of molecular imbalance spun far out of control, beyond the theoretical limits of a terminal cascade of flux distributions or void incompatibilities. On X, Y, and Z axes, the targeted tectonic plates ground out a discordant refrain, where incalculable masses of continental crusts abraded and sent shock waves to the surface.

To the west of Three Gorges Dam, the earth split right along the subterranean fault line bordering the Tongbai mountain range. Into this chasm the Yangtze plummeted, a fume of mist erupting like a whale's blowhole when the fish decided to ascend to the surface and expel the contents of its lungs. Whole towns and villages were engulfed by the rising waters or sucked deep down into the greedy, sucking maw of sinkholes miles across. Buildings crumbled instantly, the dust of cement and bricks thrown high into the air, a plume of pulverized glass and steel hung suspended in an arc of magnificent color.

The dam itself split directly down the exact middle; 403 square miles of pent-up liquid rage spewing through the burgeoning crack like a crazed pressure hose. The crack widened slowly at first, the reinforced concrete striving valiantly to contain the fissure but failing conclusively as the torrent of water propelled by tidal waves probed violently and with vigor. Through the breech, a force many powers of magnitude beyond the tolerance of the structural design was expelled, its violence inexorable and impossibly destructive.

Downstream lay Wuhan and Nunjing, previously vibrant cities where Wuhan was utterly destroyed and Nunjing partially submerged. The Chinese government had taken great care to move the occupants of 13 cities, 140 towns, and 1,350 villages and the entirety of Chongqing Municipality's 31.44 million people to make room for the reservoir's displacement when full. Many of those lives had likely been saved, but millions still fell to the river's wrath.

What the Warlock cared about most was destroying the capacity of the 101.6 TWh of hydroelectric power generated by the Three Gorges Dam. For some context, that output is 20 times more than the Hoover Dam. The over 100 trillion-watt hours of hydroelectricity had powered nearly all the industry in Shanghai, Wuhan, and Nunjing, and now their collective industrial contributions were either obliterated or severely diminished due to permanent power outages and flood damage.

Over time, the Chinese would fire up coal generators in Shanghai to make up for the 32 generators comprising the dam's underground power station that fed the grid. Each of those generators produced 700MW of economy-fueling juice; combined, they were the largest hydroelectric plant in the world. Most coal-fired plants were in the 500 MW range; it would take years of planning to redistribute capacity to make up for the loss of the Three Gorges Dam.

***

The Warlock contemplated his next act, his next foray in this World War. The strike on Three Gorges Dam was merely retaliation, and he recognized that although it was not weak, at the same time it was not nearly sufficient in strength. Clearly, deterrence was over. As he ruminated options, he kept foremost the idea that America would prevail and a post-war paradigm must be constructed.

His thoughts were bent toward influencing this post-Apocalyptic world. As it stood right now, the accounting was thus: the earth was charred by nuclear blasts; violent gusts carried more death downwind where millions more would reap the devastation of intense waves of radiation, its victims' flesh burned scarlet and fissured with seeping boils of blistered pus; entire food sources contaminated, the survivors scrambling for sustenance, more often than not resorting to cannibalism just to survive; millions and millions of people and animals committing these atrocities and more every day.

From ashes wrought from a flawed humanity, a new civilization would form. The Warlock pondered how to find the equilibrium of justice and peace, yet how to deter a future that continued the cycle of madness.

He grimaced. This isn't gonna be easy.

ABOUT THE AUTHOR

COL Mike Bennett

A former military officer and graduate of Ranger School and the Special Forces Qualification Course, COL Mike Bennett deployed to war zones seven times over a span of thirty years. There he witnessed many young (and older) Americans serve with great distinction. Observing firsthand their sacrifice and dedication, he decided to pursue writing to perhaps capture the spirit of a fighting element representing America at its finest hour. He sees his writing journey through the lens of Special Forces' "By, With, and Through" doctrine—a path that may require a recruited indigenous support asset to emplace the collection device or weapon system selected for a specific job. Sometimes the entire process takes years; there is no shortcut.

After Iran held America hostage for 444 days, COL Bennett knew his destiny was to serve—how could he do less? But first: college. At the University of Maine/Orono, enthralled and giddy, an aspiring Honors student sat in a seminar with one Stephen King. And then... Grenada, and the die was cast. While he knew he would write eventually, there were adventures to pursue in the meanwhile. Remnants of those adventures find their way onto his pages; even if they were not his own, they were stories worth telling. The Warlock's journey begins in *Rosehips in June*, travels through the *Spine of the Hindu Kush*, and ends in the upcoming *Soldier Grown Weary*.

THE WORST CASE WAS HIS JOB

Doc Spears

"What's war reserve?" I asked him. "I'm not familiar."

There was a long pause before Jim answered my question about what he did before retirement. I thought maybe he hadn't heard me above the whine of his side-by-side as we rode together up the twisting logging trail to where the dogs had a bear treed. I knew this path up Snowy Mountain well. It was his property but most of the West Virginia legislature were bear hunters and even had he objected, state law lets us follow our radio-collared dogs wherever they go.

I knew Jim only slightly, but hadn't talked to him since recently making Circleville his home. We pulled up his drive to find him working in the front yard with a chain saw. He killed the saw and raised his goggles with a puzzled look. The sight of my hunting rig with the kennels welded to the bed should've told him all he needed to know. He recognized me as I stepped out of the truck and greeted me with a smile. "Hi, Tom. What brings you my way?"

"The hounds have one treed up the mountain." It was only polite to inquire if there were any new gates or tricky fences we needed to know about. Rather than balk at us coming onto his land—like so many of the ignorant newcomers we gleefully educated—he was enthusiastic to join us and I accepted his offer to guide, unnecessary as it was.

I got the sense the old guy was lonely.

I rode beside him up the path as he drove expertly, my brother-in-law Danny and another friend following in my truck. We wanted to get the dogs kenneled and off the mountain quickly and on to another scent before it got dark. I judged Jim to be a healthy 80, his sinewy thin frame telling me he'd once been a heavily muscled man who watched what he ate and stayed fit; like the way he'd been handily trimming the dead tree he'd dropped away from his house. The property looked better than it had in a long time, and Jim's work told me a lot about the kind of neighbor he might actually be.

I'd developed an odd casual acquaintance with him over many years. My sister and I run our small general store, and being so far from anywhere, we carry a little bit of everything. I always assumed he was some sort of fed, but he never produced a badge and asked me if I'd sold explosives to any of the men in the pictures. Whatever business it was that brought Jim in once or twice a year, he never said and I never asked. He was always friendly in a respectful and knowledgeable way when he inquired about the local hunting and fishing. But I never saw him back to partake in any of the activities he seemed so interested in.

We'd all heard he bought the property and moved into the old farmhouse after the McGonagles lost it all from unpaid taxes. They were rich now, but it was still tragic. The farm was huge and in addition to the cattle pastures, the property ran up into the prime hunting grounds of the mountain. That it was an individual and not some corporation that purchased the farm was a minor consolation to the community. It still didn't mean it wasn't waiting to be developed into some kind of getaway condominium complex—the many hills offered spectacular views up and down our mountain valley—but if not that desecration, we wondered what other kind of unwanted baggage the new owner might be dragging along with him.

Our area was becoming infested with escapees from Northern Virginia; retirees fleeing crushing taxes, looking to stretch the wealth they'd accumulated through civil service careers anchored to the D.C. area. They fled the Virginia they'd help turn from red to blue—ready to screw up their new home likewise—but Jim struck me as possibly different from the other newcomers infesting our state. I was curious to know more that might put some meat on the bones of the man I hoped was of a different sort.

When he answered my question about his previous profession—war reserve—it struck me as like the kind of slang Millennials use; simple enough words that when joined together took on a meaning I didn't comprehend. Like, "squad goals" or "it me." I'd spent eight years in the Marines, so war reserve sounded like something I *should* understand, but it meant nothing to me.

We came to the bend where the road was usually mucked from runoff channeling down a sharp rocky draw that often washed out this part of the trail. The piercing bark of my Walker hounds rose from over the next ridgeline, confirming the GPS marker that they were just ahead. It was the first week of a warm December and the dense stands of trees shading the winding path were still quite full. I started searching gaps of leaf-filtered sun for the black fur of a bruin high in the treetops. Jim concentrated on driving us through the tarry mud, the driver's side tires slipping close to the drop -off. The path widened again and then in an offhand and good-natured way, he returned to explaining his prior profession to me.

"Oh, it was mundane sort of stuff. But it kept me traveling a lot. I was responsible for making sure defense stores, prepositioned all over the globe, were stocked with what was supposed to be there and in good condition."

That made sense to me. "Were you military?" I asked, almost certain he had been. One vet just recognizes another.

"I was, but at that point I was a civilian contractor." He named a few acronyms full of STRAT-this, and LOG-that, all of them ending in -COM, meaning Command; titles of the organizations he'd worked for. I recognized them as Department of Defense gobbledygook but ones mysterious to me. There were thousands of them; names of agencies or departments that could have staffs of three people or number into the hundreds. Save to virtually any but those who worked under the auspices of an acronym, their purposes were largely a mystery.

Under his breath he added, "I still do a little bit of work for them, but I don't travel anymore."

"Where'd you serve?" I asked, having an intuition about him.

"Southeast Asia war games. I flew Thuds." He said it in a world-weary sort of way that spoke volumes. I'd placed him at the age to have served in Vietnam—but him flying an F-105 Thunderchief meant he'd been there about the time my dad had. I'd grown up hearing about Lyndon Johnson's control of the Thud jockeys and what they could and could not bomb. And how their micromanagement from halfway across the world exemplified so much about the first war we'd ever lost.

"I'd put my dad there 'bout the same time's you," I said. "Tanker. 9th Marines. Got there in '65."

"Runs in the family, huh?" he said. The Eagle, Globe, and Anchor hung behind the counter of the store and was tattooed on my forearm. "I'm guessing you were an '80s Marine? Beirut. Grenada. Wasn't as quiet a time as the world would like to remember, was it, Tom?"

Jim kept rising in my estimation. "I have a son in the Air Force," I shared with him.

He gave a prideful grunt. "My branch. But I bet that must've been an uncomfortable family conversation."

"Nah. I'm glad he's not a grunt. He's the first officer our family's ever produced. I'm happy for him—relieved he wasn't going to end up on welfare like most of the boys he went to school with. I never could get him off the computer. Now he gets paid to play on that damned thing all the time. He's a cyber warfare specialist."

Jim snorted. "It's a different generation, for sure."

Standing out against the golden-yellow leaves and pale bark, the bear's stout black body wrapped the narrow top of the trunk, its tapered head stretched low to stare down at the hounds directly beneath. It was fifty yards of steep grade to where the hounds circled the base of the tree. I didn't think Jim would want to make the climb, but he set out with me. I kept an eye on him but he moved with care and confidence, matching my own stride.

The best part of the hunt for me was seeing the dogs work. Heads high, their excited high-pitched yowling was a tireless chorus they kept up whenever they had one treed. The boys were right behind us and joined me in leashing the hounds and pulling them back.

I offered my rifle to Jim. "You want to take this one?"

He politely declined. "I appreciate the offer, Tom. Nothing personal, but it's not my thing. Not so much of a challenge. No offense."

"None taken, Jim, but I wanted to offer, especially after you being so nice and all. Don't mean nothing by it, but most of the folks moving in to our neck of the woods aren't so accommodating to our ways."

"Tell me about it," he agreed knowingly, then quickly said, "I did my best to stay out of D.C. all I could."

We let the hounds pull at the dead bear for a bit—their reward—then hefted the kill into the back of his side-by-side. As we rode down the mountain, I asked him to tell me more about his previous line of work.

"Are you familiar at all with contingency planning?" he asked.

Growing up and then serving during the peak of the Cold War, I sorta was. "Like, for when the Russkies would make the push through the Fulda Gap to invade Western Europe? Scenarios like that?"

Jim chuckled. "Ah, the good old days! When things were simple. I was part of the mechanism that took those plans and ensured we had the necessities in place for potential military operations all around the world. I was the steward for a lot of programs started as far back as Eisenhower."

We were no longer the country that won WWII, one that not only used to think about such things but that also dedicated the resources to ensuring we were never caught in the crappers of the world without toilet paper. His work sounded interesting. "So, you made sure our forces had what they would need in whatever potential theater, ready in case the balloon went up?"

Jim seemed pleased by my understanding. "That's right. I had a career in logistics after I left the Air Force. I came on as a contractor to DoD just before Desert Storm. After we burned through the reserves in Diego Garcia and the Middle East, I rebuilt them. And with the fall of the wall, we stayed busy establishing as many reserves throughout the freed Eastern Bloc as we'd ever placed. So, in addition to Asia and the Mid-East, I was busy in Poland, Romania, the Balkans, the Baltics—just about everywhere."

He'd said he traveled a lot for his work.

"I'm betting in recent years, the well's run dry for that sort of thing."

With eyebrows raised, I received another impressed appraisal. "And you'd be correct, Tom. With our political climate being what it's become the last decade, it all tapered off."

I pictured parking lots of M1 Abrams and M-triple-seven artillery pieces. Bunkers of munitions and gas farms of petroleum stores. He'd been responsible for billions of dollars of hardware and expendables. "What happens to it all when the appropriations go away?"

He sighed. "Twenty years of war in West Asia taxed the reserves, but I was able to rebuild them. For a while, anyway. But fortunately, even when the funding to fully restock is eliminated, the titles they're funded under pretty much provide in perpetuity for the maintenance of whatever's in those sites. Some things, not even congress can decapitate."

I wondered what business had brought him to my acquaintance when he'd shown up once or twice a year to dreamily browse the rods and reels. I didn't get the chance to ask. We arrived back at his house, and I thanked him quickly and hurried off to get the dogs working again. Jim returned to his chain saw, and I promised myself I'd look in on him once in a while.

It wasn't until Christmas Eve when everything went dark that I thought about my neighbor again.

***

I blamed the twinkling Christmas lights clipped to the house trim. That none of the breakers had tripped just confirmed for me it was a power outage; rare and highly inconvenient. "Appalachian must be running skeleton shifts for the holidays," I told Cheryl. "Could be awhile before they get it fixed."

My wife made a tiny groan. "Everyone will be over at noon, Tom. I have to start cooking early. If the power's not back up by then, we'll need the generator." She patted the seat next to her and I stoked the wood stove before joining her to curl up on the couch. The red coals and dancing flames through the glass window were better than any TV.

It wasn't until later she fiddled her phone out of her pocket and said with annoyance, "My phone's dead. I wanted to text Janet to see if she was going to have trouble bringing dessert."

I checked mine. It was also dead. I got a tickle in my brain and told Cheryl I was getting a lantern from the shop. My flashlight worked, filling me with hope. The emergency radio sat on the top of dad's machinist tool chest. It was one of those enticements offered for paying the life membership fee of whatever organization it was that hooked me about fifteen years ago. It had sat untouched since the day I first played with it, testing the solar cell and hand crank.

After a few minutes of dedicated cranking, it failed to come to life. I changed the rechargeable batteries for some alkaline ones and tried again. It stayed dark. The tickle was replaced by a knot in my gut. Perhaps some internal circuit board had corroded.

But I knew that wasn't it.

I returned with the lantern and told Cheryl we should go to bed. "First thing in the morning, I'll get the generator running the kitchen circuits. The fridge and freezer'll stay cold with the doors closed until then."

"I already have dough rising. I was going to bake some of the bread tonight," she said.

"That's why we kept the old gas stove. It lights fine manually but if you really want, I'll run the generator now."

"No, that's okay. Lantern light will be fine and I don't need in the fridge for anything."

The oven warmed right up and Cheryl kissed me. "My hero. Go to bed and I'll be up after I get this batch done."

I lay in the dark, wondering how Jim was getting on. I wondered what the man whose profession had been readying for World War 3 was thinking right now about these portends of a war come to our shores. I fell asleep picturing the nuclear explosion at the edge of space that had caused the EMP.

***

We were up before the sun, the smell of bread in the air. I'd inherited Dad's old surplus diesel generator and it cranked on the first try. I made sure the kitchen and well pump were powered, started coffee and stocked the stove with more wood, then grabbed the keys off the hook by the door. I fed the dogs, dreading what I was going to find when I tried the trucks. When neither started, I went to the pole barn.

Other than to park my restored beauty out front of the store in the summers to attract business, I hadn't driven my 1954 Dodge Power Wagon in some time. There'd been an old military Dodge joining the other ancient tracked and armored vehicles that were targets on one of the multi-purpose ranges at Lejeune. It always hurt me a bit when a LAW or a 40mm was launched at it, fantasizing about someday having a Power Wagon for myself. Restoring the rusted-out one I'd bought off an estate sale had been a hobby I'd dreamed about since I was a teenager. I could never hold my own son's interest for very long to teach him what I knew about engines, but Troy was a great kid. Everyone had their own interests, and his were in the realm of the electron and not the mechanical.

It turned over perfectly and I shut her off, feeling a little stouter and more secure. I returned to the kitchen to find a frustrated Cheryl repeatedly running a finger over the microwave controls. It was the only thing in the kitchen with a chip. After experiencing the pocketbook pain when learning they were cheaper to replace than repair, I refused to go through the same by upgrading our other older kitchen necessities just for the sake of it.

"Tom, the microwave's not working." Concern coated her voice. "This isn't just a power outage, is it?"

I didn't yet want to worry her with what I really thought. "Hard to say, sweetie. I'm going to check on your mom. Be right back."

"What about Danny and Janet?"

My brother-in-law had an older Ford he used as a farm truck, and I bet it would still be running. "I'll get your mom first, then swing by their place after I bring her here." I kissed her, and when I stepped outside, press checked my Glock to ensure there was a round chambered and returned it to my holster. I carried every day, everywhere. Though I had the store, it wasn't two-legged threats I worried about. For me, the necessity became crystal clear that day when Troy was little and I heard him screaming outside, the snow splattered in blood, and me, stunned to find two large dogs I'd never seen before in our yard. The feral animals had been tearing up a barn cat, but had it been otherwise, I'd have had nothing more useful than a stick from the woodpile to fight them with. They were long gone by the time I reemerged from the house with a rifle, and I swore I'd never be without again.

On the way to get my mother-in-law, I was planning to make a slight detour up my new neighbor's drive, when, walking in my direction down the middle of the two-lane hardball road, there was Jim. A black military sling ran across his shoulder, attached to an old AR with a triangular handguard. I rolled my window down as I came to a stop.

"I was coming to your place to check on you," Jim said, beating me to it.

"Back atcha," I said. Neither of us spoke for a minute, soaking up each other's trepidation. He knew what I knew.

"Jim, is there anyone else at home with you?" I asked.

"No, Tom. I'm alone." He said it with no sadness. He rode with me to Mom's, then insisted on hopping in the bed to leave room up front for her and her bag. While we waited for her to gather her things, neither of us addressed the circumstances that brought us together on a snowless gray Christmas morning.

We returned to my place to the noise of the generator humming perfectly and to find Danny's primer-painted F-150 in the drive. Everyone was in the kitchen and I introduced Jim to Cheryl and Janet. Danny had met Jim the day he'd accompanied us up the mountain. "If you're hoping to join us on another bear hunt, it don't start up again for a few days," Danny said to him, noticing Jim's AR. "'Course, truth is, we don't pay much attention to the dates around here," Danny admitted with a sheepish gr in.

"You're joining us for Christmas dinner," Cheryl told our guest. It hadn't been a question.

He started to beg off and I intervened. "Not gonna work, Jim. We already feel bad we haven't been more neighborly sooner. There's no fighting it."

Cheryl gave him a polite command. "Put your rifle in the mudroom and hang your coat up by the fire. What do like in your coffee? Can you hold off until lunch or do you need some eggs?"

Jim's eyes glistened a tiny bit. Living alone might be a circumstance he didn't mind, but it was clear being in a woman's kitchen stirred something in him. "Coffee's fine, Cheryl, thank you. Black, please."

We stared into our cups as we sat around the table near the wood stove, listening to the three women as they joyfully divided tasks for the holiday meal. It filled me with a temporary reassurance that the world had not changed for the worse.

Danny broke the silence. "This ain't no simple power outage. So've we been nuked or what?"

Jim offered an alternative I'd forgotten about. "Could be a solar storm."

Troy was home on leave when we'd watched a program about dooms-day scenarios. It was sometimes annoying how smart my son was, and that he often launched into criticisms with long technical explanations about why something was not quite correct. This one time he did not deconstruct the History Channel's science. "Oh, that's a fact, Dad. If the power grid got fried by a solar event, it would put us in the pre-industrial age overnight. 90 percent of the US population would be dead inside a year."

But the way Jim had mentioned the possibility to explain current events, I didn't think he believed that's what had happened. "It was an EMP, though, wasn't it, Jim?"

"Almost certainly, Tom," he said.

"And what d'ya reckon caused it?" Danny asked.

Jim sighed. "A nuclear bomb in the ionosphere producing an EMP wave. One placed over Omaha would kill the entire grid everywhere in the US."

"So we *did* get nuked?" Danny said. "I thought we had all that Star Wars stuff supposed to knock out all them commie missiles. Reagan got us that. So close to D.C., I always figured we're protected 'cause the politicians would cover their own asses and have that hardware parked everywhere around Virginia."

Danny was a good guy. He farmed and ran an excavating business, but never concerned himself with much other than day-to-day matters here in our isolated haven. He'd barely ever left West Virginia. He was my age but had never served, which even in our patriotic neck of the woods was more and more the norm. I was almost the only vet around. Having been in so many of the hot spots of the world during my time in the Corps, whenever some international event made the news, my opinion was always solicited at the store or after church.

Jim gave a cryptic explanation. "THAAD's never really worked."

I didn't savvy the acronym and said so.

"Terminal High Altitude Area Defense. It's the land-based missile defense system that most people think of when they think about what everyone calls Star Wars. Regardless, it's a secret in the open that THAAD doesn't work, or at least, doesn't against more than one or a few missiles at a time. If a large-scale attack was launched on the US, it would be hundreds of missiles coming at us. THAAD wouldn't be of much use. It's a moot point, since they're all stationed overseas, primarily in South Korea."

Danny's eyes shot open. "You gotta be kidding me!"

A corner of Jim's mouth curled. "There's been talk of putting THAAD missile systems on our West Coast to guard against an ICBM attack from China or North Korea, but it's never gotten past just talk."

"What about all the lasers and stuff we're supposed to have?" Danny inquired of the man who seemed to know.

Jim shook his head to say they didn't actually exist in any state of readiness.

"Do you think it's an all-out nuclear war we're in?" I asked, picturing everything associated with that scenario. I'd had lots of nuclear, biologic, and chemical training during my time in the Corps. Doing PT in full MOPP gear had nearly brought me to heatstroke damn near every time. The NBC warrant officer in our regiment gave the lectures, and afterward always shared his honest opinion with his Marines. If we were ever in a full-out exchange of missiles with Russia or China, contrary to much of the doctrine, he felt it would in fact be a doomsday complete with nuclear winter and the end of life on Earth.

"I hope not," Jim said. "It'll be apparent soon enough if that's the case. But the scenario kicked around most often in the seminars was a different one. A satellite, likely one put up by the NORKs, would detonate its payload to blanket us in a super-EMP."

"Impossible," Danny gasped. "How the hell'd the North Koreans sneak a satellite over the US? I've seen the shows. NASA knows where every satellite and nut-and-bolt bit of space junk is and where it came from. Ain't no president would ever let a dang weapon be parked over the country!" I was a little surprised it was something Danny knew.

Jim took a deep breath. "I've been to Redstone Arsenal in Huntsville many times and have friends there in the Missile Defense Command. They know about and track every North Korean 'communications' satellite. It's been confirmed many times over that North Korea got the technology for an EMP weapon from the Russians. That's another secret in the open. There's just never been any will to do anything about it—always fearful any action might spark a mad king scenario where they feel threatened and go ahead and detonate."

The women had been listening for some time while they worked and Janet spoke up. "I don't understand what they'd get out of it. We ship them food."

Jim turned to answer her. "It's not them alone. It's China. Their population is three times our size and they have half the arable land we do. They have an aging population and they've been falling apart for a long time. North Korea's more dependent on China than us, and they'd surely cooperate with them to attack us. It's nearly the only option for them both to survive mass starvation and internal revolution. The prize is our farmland."

"So, no nuclear missiles?" Cheryl asked.

Jim swallowed the last of his cup. "Short-range nukes from ballistic subs likely hit select military and leaderships targets. Or, they used lower yield tactical-sized nukes and dropped them from disguised commercial aircraft. There're so many bad actors in the country who we have no idea who they are—advanced forces could place devices driven overland. Unless the radiologic detectors were specifically searching for them, they'd could be missed. They're all scenarios that've been gamed for a long time. So, no, I don't think it's an all-out nuclear doomsday event. The most likely scenario's always been they want to keep the heartland as ready to exploit as possible. Our farmland's what they want."

"Which means a ground invasion," I said.

"Which means a ground invasion," Jim repeated.

***

At the end of the night, Cheryl fixed him a plate to take with him and sealed it in cling wrap. I insisted on driving Jim home. I didn't want to insult him by saying I couldn't let an eighty-year-old man leave my home on foot in the dark of winter, and convinced him by saying I wanted to talk alone while we drove.

"Jim, I know you haven't had much time to prepare since you moved in. I don't want you to worry. I have a hundred head of cattle. I have three deer and a bear hanging right now, not to mention what's already processed and in the freezers. We'll start putting up a lot more since now we know we need to, and I can help you do the same. But I didn't see but a couple of cords of wood outside your place the other day. That won't get you through winter."

He cringed. "I have the tree I downed in the front yard, too. I was supposed to be getting a full load delivered between the holidays. Pretty unlikely that's going to happen now."

Cheryl had taken me aside after a day spent with Jim in our home. She'd been equally taken by this fine man who'd become our guest. We pulled up the drive and I stopped in front of his rear porch then hit him with our suggestion, one I'd normally never have considered offering to anyone not family.

"You might think about moving in with us at some point, Jim. At least for the winter. My sister and her family are stocked even better than I am and still have boys at home to help. Danny and Janet are full up with enough wood for a year, too. They all have as many cattle as I do. We've got plenty and besides, I think we need to work together very closely for what's coming. I'm not sure anyone else really understands. It'd be good to have another man at our homestead."

By the dim light of the dashboard, I saw Jim place a hand over his chest. "I truly appreciate the offer, Tom. I can't express how much I do. But, no. You have your mother-in-law to add to your household now. I'm an old man, and I'm not going to take food out of someone else's mouth. Especially from one who's properly prepared when I've failed to." His voice choked a bit. "Of all people, especially me. I was getting it all together, but it seems the clock's run out on me."

He cleared his throat. "But I would appreciate some help learning to properly prepare a deer again. And I've got lots of freeze dried on the shelves until then. And then there's—" he stopped himself from finishing the sentence and reached a hand out. "Thank you, neighbor."

I shook his hand and before he got out, I said, "Our door's always open. If I don't see you in the next couple of days, I'll be by. Especially if I hear anything."

"Deal. And Tom—thank you for a fine Christmas."

I watched him go inside, wondering what it was he'd been about to say before he stopped himself. I didn't pull away until I saw the glow of a kerosene lamp.

The next day we got our first real snow—just a regular light winter coating—nothing to indicate the world was ending. A few days later the word of mouth Danny and I sent out to meet at the store had gotten around. The parking lot was full of old trucks and beater cars. When the area in front of the counter in our small store was crowded, everyone looked to me to get things started.

"Grosvenor's got something to share."

Sam Grosvenor was from our church. He ran a short-haul trucking company and had done well for himself, but other than his King Ranch apportioned pickup, showed his wealth in no other way. "One of my men got stranded south of here when it all went down. He made the walk back and got home last night. He talked to people who say they saw for themselves the mushroom cloud over Washington on Christmas Eve."

More and more, Jim's intuition about what had likely happened seemed to be proving correct. When the talk died down, I introduced Jim.

"This is my friend, Jim. He moved into the McGonagle place. He spent a career in the Department of Defense and has a lot of experience in these things. I'd like everyone to listen to what he thinks about this situation."

Someone grumbled, "Carpetbagger." It came from the direction of Dustin McGonagle, the grandson, and I shot him a steely eyed look to behave. He'd purchased an 80,000-dollar one-ton dualie pickup once the sale of the farm had gone through.

"What Tom says is true," Jim said as he moved to stand next to me behind the counter. "I do have a lot of exposure to the kind of planning regarding a disaster like this." He went on to describe the same things he'd discussed with us around my breakfast table earlier this week, and answered many of the same questions we'd asked him.

My sister's husband, Jerry, asked the next question. "So what's next? You expecting us to fight off the invading Mongolian hordes by ourselves? Where's your Marines?" He'd always been a little dismissive about my family's service, and I think jealous of how others viewed me, always crabby whenever I was consulted first on any larger family matter.

"I don't know," I said. "But it would be good to organize. If we could set up a watch to cover both ends of 28 into Circleville—kind of an early warning if there are columns of tanks moving our way—it'd be good to know that."

There were some mumbles but mainly a lot of shocked silence.

"I'd like to apportion out what ammo there is on the shelves," I announced. "There's not much. One box for everyone before you take a second, but it probably won't go that far. If you have a couple of hundred rounds at home, please don't take any. And it should go without saying do NOT take any ammo you don't have a rifle for." Some of these guys were dirt-poor, and free anything was an invitation they couldn't resist.

My sister and I had discussed it, and Julie stepped up. "I want to distribute the canned and dry goods in the store to those that need it." We'd already divided a lot of the backroom stock for our own families, and had thrown out the perishable refrigerated stuff, mainly cream and milk. We didn't stock eggs. The local poultry farm gave away flats of them to anyone who wanted them, odd-looking but perfectly fine eggs that didn't make quality for size and shape. Even we had a fridge full of the imperfectly oval eggs. It kept a lot of poor folks from having only game as a staple.

I thought this was a good place to stop for today. "I think we ought to meet again tomorrow after everyone's had time to digest all this. Tell any neighbors who didn't get the word or couldn't make it and bring them along."

Danny and I distributed the boxes of hunting ammo as everyone filed past and left.

Greg Witherspoon stepped up to me, a pair of small yellow hunting walkie-talkies in hand, another set still sealed in the plastic package they came in. "Tom, these were down in my storm cellar. Still work. Maybe you should take charge of them."

A lot of us had homes built over the original rock-wall basements or had deep cellars walled in field stone that still served to preserve food. Most farm buildings were laid on top of thick stone foundations. The lower level of my shop on the farm was dug deep and had two-foot-thick stone walls at least 150 years old. But like my emergency radio, none of my electronics had survived the EMP. Similar items had been capriciously spared for some folks, while others like me had the same deep places that failed to block the pulse.

"Thank you, Greg. We'll put them to good use with the sentries."

Jim, Danny, and I were all that were left.

"How are people armed, Tom?" Jim asked.

"Most everyone's poor. They have the necessities to put food on the table. A bolt gun or a Thompson Center single shot. Shotguns. Just what they need. A lot have ARs, but likely not much to feed them with."

If they were like me, they had a few cases of surplus 5.56. But if they shot often, they may not. Ammunition had become scarce and difficult to procure for many years now, and prohibitively expensive. I used to reload and even carried components here in the store. But as those supplies became even harder to come by and the prices ever more exorbitant, when they did become available to my distributor, I'd stopped stocking them as no one could afford them. Not even me. When we talked about it, we all grumbled that we just had to wait until the supplies became more plentiful and hopefully more affordable. Someday.

Jim's head was bent, brow furrowed. Then he stood straight, bearing conviction about whatever he'd been deciding.

"Do you and Danny want to take a ride? I need to show you something."

***

On the road headed for Seneca Rocks, Jim guided us off the hardball and onto a gravel access road leading toward the base of the mountain. It was unremarkable in my memory. I winced a little as the untrimmed brush and branches scraped the sides of my show-truck. We broke out into an opening near the base of an excavated rock bluff. There was a ten-foot chain-link fence topped with concertina wire, and a chained gate. It looked like a Division of Highways maintenance yard, but there were no plows or trucks parked in the lot. There was a small sign that warned this was US Government property and threatened fines and prison for trespass.

"What's this place, Jim?" I asked.

He just said, "I need to show you. It'll explain everything about what I used to do."

He got out and turned the individual numbered wheels on the large lock, and opened the gate for us to drive through. He closed the gate behind us and secured the lock again.

"Whatcha think, Tom?" Danny said, excitement and curiosity in his voice.

"I think this is going to help us," I said.

We joined Jim and he said, "We'll need your flashlight, Tom." I grabbed my ancient and heavy D-cell flashlight and followed. He led us to the only structure, a small cinder block building built up against the rock bluff. It could've housed a pump station or a transformer, but there were no power lines leading from it. Recessed into the wall near the lock set of a heavy steel door was a covered key panel—five pins protruding from the face. Tom punched them one at a time, then opened the door. Daylight exposed a barren room. It merely protected the security door on the far wall, another mechanical push-pin lock panel beside it like the one outside.

"May I have the light, please?" Jim said with a hand out, and I passed it to him.

The pins clicked, the door opened easily, and he shined the light ahead. On the other side was a rough rock-walled passage that ended in a vault door. My heart quickened.

He handed me the light and I aimed the beam on the two sets of dial locks. Jim put on his cheaters but without consulting any other aid, slowly rotated the combination of each. The lever resisted him, then he placed a second hand and added some body weight. The dark cave amplified the sound of metal bolts retracting. He pulled the handle with an effort that spoke to the weight of the massive door, and stepped back.

"I lubricate it all every visit," Jim said, "but rust never sleeps."

Crates and crates stacked high and deep. My old flashlight was inadequate to the task, and I searched the space with a slow sweep, trying to discover its limits. The ceiling, floor, and walls were concrete, only ten feet high but forty feet wide. The beam dimly painted the wall at the end of the central aisle.

"It's enough for about 300 men. Meant to arm a home force a little smaller than a regular battalion."

"Why's all this here?" Danny said, his jaw returning to hanging open.

"This is one of many on the east coast. Were America ever invaded, the idea was to have reserves in place to support a guerilla warfare model. It was first laid in during the '50s. The cold war was very hot then. And the men with the foresight to do this knew how to build things. The bed this room rests on diverts and drains away ground water, and I've never found one of the caches to be anything but dry."

"Who knows about this?" I asked, amazed, though the clues Jim had sprinkled about his life's work had me almost certain this is what he was leading us to.

Jim clucked. "There's knowledge, then there's attention. Most of these sites have dropped out of attention. They're on the books, or I should say, numbered items on an Excel spreadsheet that no one looks at. Compared to the billions of dollars budgeted over the decades for war reserve, it's not even a blip. They cost virtually nothing to maintain. I visit them every six months, change the desiccant containers, do an inventory, and maintain the locks and check the physical security measures."

"So no one really knows about this except you?" I said.

He shrugged. "Someone knows. The locations of these caches were of course top secret knowledge, and distributed down to the level of the Army Special Forces Groups. They were the ones expected to be utilizing the contents of these sites, to equip partisan forces when they trained and led them in behind-the-lines warfare here at home. I can't say if the establishment at any level outside our agency has cared about them in a very long time. But it was always a part of my job to maintain them and file reports on the conditions in these old sites."

"That's what brought you here all those times over the years," I said, understanding.

"Yes, Tom. And over all those visits during all those years, I fell in love with the area. I'd been planning to move here, eventually. I'd finally tired of so much travel around the world, and the signal for me to finally do it was when the perfect property on Snowy Mountain became available. They tempted me with the offer of help and a larger salary, and in the end, I took their contract to maintain this site, as it served many of my purposes."

I think I heard what he meant. "Did you ever think this would happen in your lifetime, Jim? That you'd be doing what we're doing now?"

"Never until the last few years, Tom. Let me show you what's here."

The top crate on a stack read, "10 CARBINES. Cal 30 M1," followed by numbers. There were a lot of them.

"What's this?" Danny said. He was standing over a shorter stack of elongated crates too long to be rifles. I hoped they were machine guns, maybe M2 Brownings. I brought the flashlight over. Stenciled on the lid was, "M67, RECOILESS RIFLE, 90MM. ONE EACH." I'd seen it demonstrated once, but had never fired one myself.

Some of this equipment had been manufactured in WWII. Some of it, like the 90s, from later. Jim saw me thinking. "The inventory in the sites was often updated whenever there was a surplus of something newer, but rifles like M16s or M4s were never added. Someone decided that M1 carbines were appropriate tools for backwoods resistance fighters, so here they remained."

I found another stack of crates with different dimensions. I was intrigued at the thought of busting it open to hold an actual Browning

Automatic Rifle. Indeed, M1 carbines and BARs were a lot simpler and required less maintenance than M4s and M249 SAWs. They weren't the worst choice for such a scenario. But like the 90, they were weapons I had not used myself.

I let the light lead my eyes to the stores farther back. There were scores of crates easily recognized as ammunition. The painted stencils indicated cases of magazines, lubricants, soft goods like bandoliers, and many others. Someone who truly knew had selected the contents for this cache. I inspected the markings on another grouping and shied back when I saw a radiation symbol. Jim grunted.

"Those are rations. Irradiated rations. It was an experiment to increase their shelf life. They tried radiation as the answer for a lot back in the atomic age. These are the same C-rations your father and I once ate. We pulled a case once and had it tested. Out of curiosity, I used one of the P-38s and opened a can of fruit cocktail. It smelled sweet and the colors were just as inviting as I remembered, but none of us took the taste test. We sent the case off for analysis, and the report came back as still acceptable for human consumption."

I'd had C-rats very early in the Corps, before MREs. Every box contained a large can that was the main meal, smaller ones, and the little folding can opener. Fruit cocktail or peaches were always a prized find. I was told they once included a package with two cigarettes. That inclusion had gone away before my time in the Marines, over the protests of Phillip Morris and the cancer specialists, I'm certain.

The rations had to be at least fifty years old. I cocked an eyebrow Jim's way.

"They'd be a last option, in my opinion," he said.

"We see eye-to-eye on that," I agreed.

Danny asked the obvious. "Whadda we do with all this stuff?"

I considered. "We can't get it all right now, obviously, but why don't we grab as many crates of the carbines and ammo as we can get in the Power Wagon and lock up. I think tomorrow we start distributing M1s." I imagined the problem of bringing back crates of fragmentation grenades and the outcome if we passed them out. I could guarantee there'd be at least one hillbilly doing something extremely stupid with them.

On the ride back, Danny spoke my own thoughts out loud.

"There's enough in there to keep folks putting game on the table long after all our hunting ammo runs out. But it's a tall order, thinking we could get folks working together like any kind of resistance to fight whatever's coming our way."

I'd had squads and even the honor of running a platoon for a short while as a staff sergeant near the end of my time in the Corps. There was knowledge I carried that had been forever branded on me but without professional help, I thought it was a nearly insurmountable task.

"But I think we have to try," Jim said.

***

We ended up at my place and unloaded the crates into my barn, and Jim joined us for a meal before he insisted on walking home.

I asked Danny to meet everyone who showed up at the store and bring them to my place. The group was not much bigger than it'd been the day before, crowded into as few vehicles as possible to save on gas. Danny showed them into the barn, where Jim and I had begun opening crates. The carbines were all wrapped in brown paper and had generous coatings of Cosmoline grease to preserve them.

"Where'd all this come from?" my brother-in-law Jerry asked.

Jim said, "It's a gift from the US government. There's one for everyone, and more."

Dalton was the same age as my Troy. They'd been buddies and he was a decent kid, but I never judged him as having any ambition. I was always fearful my son would follow Dalton and the other boys' examples, content at doing small jobs during the summer to spend the rest of the year hunting. He unwrapped one of the guns and inspected it carefully. He wiped at the end of the barrel just behind the front sight. "Stamping says 8-43. These were manufactured in August of 1943."

I hadn't known that, and even Jim seemed impressed.

Dalton expertly led a demonstration how to strip the gun in front of six of his peer group, then offered his crew to clean them all. I was pleasantly surprised Dalton was showing usefulness, and I got another group working on cleaning and loading magazines and filling the cloth bandoliers.

"Don't mess with those," I blurted out too late at one of the young men who was busting open a case of the irradiated C-Rations. I hadn't meant to bring any back, but Danny had thrown one in the truck. I'd barely sputtered the warning out when Dalton appeared next to his buddy and said, "Lemme see. I always wanted to try this."

He fished out a matchbook from the box and returned to where his crew diligently cleaned the carbines with kerosene. Curious, I watched him fiddle with a stripped one then deftly reassemble it. While holding the trigger back, he cycled the bolt several times. With the bolt forward, he released the trigger. There was no "click" of the sear resetting. The hammer had traveled forward behind each closing of the bolt, indicating he'd somehow converted the M1 carbine to fully automatic. He cycled the bolt once more without touching the trigger, then pressed it, receiving the audible confirmation the sear had reset and the hammer had fallen. His face broke into a devilish grin.

"It works! Saw a YouTube video on it once, but it got taken down super-quick."

Suddenly, the cleaning crew descended to strip open individual meal boxes to retrieve matchbooks, returning to the stacks of guns. They begged Dalton to show them what he'd done.

I groaned. "Nuh-uh. Knock that off, boys. That is the worst possible thing you could do. You're making the gun unreliable and besides—full-auto fire is plumb stupid."

Dalton's look was a challenge. "If we're going to be fighting filthy commies, it's exactly what we need."

These weren't Marines, and I had no authority over them. They were undisciplined youngsters in their twenties. Of the other two-dozen men gathered in the barn, their ages ran from 40s up to Jim's age. I knew my people well. For all their excellent qualities, they were all men who had strong opinions about what worked and what didn't, and did not like to be told they were wrong. I could not order anyone. I had to persuade them.

"Friends, I don't know what we're going to do as a community. I truly don't. I know everyone has their own ideas, starting with doing what it takes to protect your own families. But what I'm saying is, please think about what you have in your hands as no different from how you'd use the rifles hanging in the backs of your trucks. A well-aimed and well-placed shot is what it takes to bring a deer down. It's no different for a man."

Dalton had been the lead dissenter to my rebuke to not alter the carbines in the haphazard way he had, and his crew looked for his reaction. The sass I expected wasn't there.

"I understand, Tom. But if we're going to shoot 'em, can we at least *try* it out?"

I took the small victory.

I asked Danny to lead the rest of the group to the field I used as a range, and went into the house to tell Cheryl there'd be a lot of shooting and not to worry. "Where's Mom?" I asked her.

"Napping. She's been very tired lately. She told me she wished she could just die and join Daddy."

I hugged her tightly. "It's going to be okay."

She pushed back to look up into my eyes. "Is it really?"

"I'm not going to let anything happen to us." I meant it. Enough so, I hoped she believed me.

The fields were wet with melted snow, but everyone was dressed for the weather. The rear sights were not adjustable and there was a flip aperture meant for probably 100 and 300 yards. I organized us into two relays to shoot at rocks on the hillside as an adequate way to familiarize and test the guns. I was pleased with how accurate mine was, and that the carbine weighing about six pounds with a full magazine had little recoil despite the steel buttplate.

Dalton was polite enough to ask my permission before he quickly broke his gun down and reapplied his matchbook. He seemed to understand short bursts were preferable and in a few, emptied the magazine. He gave me an, "I told you so," look, and I let it go.

"We're all here," one of the older men said. "You're the only person knows anything about military tactics, Tom. Might as well start teaching us."

I looked to Jim, who gave me a confident smile of support. It was what he'd had in mind all along.

Richard Crawford was in his 70s. "Tom, I got to get back home. Becky can't stoke the stove since her stroke. I don't want her to get cold."

"Of course, Dick. We'll have other opportunities to work together. Nothing to worry about."

He thanked me for my understanding and moved off with a limp.

Atop the big hill we'd just used as a shooting backstop was a smooth, rolling field with great views. And high ground was what I had in mind from which to teach them a basic ambush. "Let's unload, then head up to one-tree hill. It's a good spot to start training."

Mud forced us all to either side of the road to walk on the sod, annoying me. Real winter was late coming and the ground hadn't properly frozen yet. We'd only had the one snow and we had a hard rain the night before.

The road ran up and around the backside to reach the hilltop, five acres of pasture that grew lush grass in the spring. Next to the lone tree sat my deer blind, and 400 hundred yards up along the trail to where the mountain began in earnest, hung my deer feeder. A few small does ran off at our appearance. This farm was my heaven.

It was then from the valley floor I heard the rumble of multiple engines.

"The army's finally come to check on us," someone said.

"No," Jim said anxiously. "I don't think so."

"Hunker down!" I said and broke into a crouched dash across the hilltop pasture. I slowed as the barn roof and my house came in view, dropping to a high-crawl and inching forward through the wet brown grass. A column of wheeled armored personnel carriers snaked up the two-lane blacktop. They sparked a reminiscence of the films we were shown in bootcamp of Soviet BTRs shuttling infantry onto the battlefield. Like the rows of huge tires from those memories, these had heavy machineguns protruding from their turrets. On his belly beside me was Jim and to my left crowded Danny. The rest appeared low on the ground beside us, all seeing what we did.

Below us, Dick and Cheryl were tiny figures standing in front of the house, drawn to view the procession. One of the hulking armored vehicles pulled up our drive. I flipped the smaller aperture up on my carbine and rapidly seated a magazine, chambering a round as others did the same.

It all happened fast.

Soldiers in spotted camouflage uniforms spilled from the back with weapons raised. Dick Crawford was simply standing there when they opened up on him, his carbine held low with barrel pointed at the ground, just like he was in the woods. Cheryl recoiled away, shielding her face, but was still standing. Her screams reached my ears a second later. Soldiers spread like cockroaches across my property. I could not take my eyes off Cheryl.

A trio of soldiers were on her. One buttstroked her to the ground then followed his friends into our house. In a flash they returned and raised my cowering wife to her feet and dragged her inside, laughing all the while.

I found myself leaping up, only to have many hands pull me back down.

Shouting broke out below and the crack-crack-crack of small arms fire aimed our way whizzed overhead. A squad of soldiers in the strange spotted camouflage stood in my yard, firing up at us. We started to shoot back, when the bark of the heavy machine gun in the turret let loose.

There was no winning this fight.

I crawled backward through the saturated grass, then pushed myself up to a crouch. "C'mon! We make for the mountain!" Jim had trouble reversing from the overlook. He placed a hand on a knee to raise himself up from a kneel, when he dropped to the sound of a wet schwack, followed by a crack.

I threw myself down and low-crawled to him.

"Jim, Jim!" A large red pool soaked his abdomen and grew as I watched in horror. He grabbed my coat collar.

"I'm sorry, Tom. We just didn't have enough time." He was gone.

Danny was pulling at me. "Let's go!"

The rest were ahead of us in the retreat, dipping below sight as they ran down the backside of the hill. They appeared again on the trail that ran the ridge leading up the mountain. Everyone's destination was the same: the steep tree line and cover.

Terrible thoughts came to me as I ran. Had the noise of our shooting practice made its way down the valley? Had it attracted the invaders as they drove through tiny Circleville, the middle of nowhere? What else would have brought them up the curving asphalt road and into our haven? Had I inadvertently called them to destroy my home? Was Cheryl alive?

Danny and I caught up to the older men. All were slowed to a walk, some stopped and bent with hands on knees, heaving breaths. "Keep moving," I encouraged them, and kept trotting. It wasn't long before Danny and I slowed ourselves, the grade becoming difficult as we left the trail for the slopes. My own breath was ragged and my heart pounded like a bass drum.

I looked back at the narrow view afforded at my hay barn past the road curving down around the pasture hilltop. The deep grumble of an engine warned the armored vehicle was coming up the dirt road.

With hands pushing knees to climb up the brown slope of faded winter grasses, Danny and I collapsed together just into the tree line. Dalton and the younger men were spread low behind deadfall, panting to catch their breaths.

Below us was a short run of open sod, then the drop-off we'd crawled up on hands and knees. Below and to our right was the deer feeder hanging from an old oak above a small flat patch that was usually covered in acorns, the branches thick with squirrel nests. The older men had taken the trail and moved off into the trees beyond the feeder, unable to make the climb to join us.

We waited for the armored death machine to ascend.

The whine of an engine pitched, paused, then repeated. I anticipated the strangely painted vehicle to crest into view at any second. When the high rev of the engine started the pattern again, I knew what had happened. From out of the woods by the feeder one of the old guys appeared, cupping hands toward us and yelling, "They're stuck. It's getting buried to the axles." Just then the heavy machine gun opened up, and he was gone, trees exploding in a barrage of bullets weighing ten times what those in my tiny carbine did.

"We need to go, Tom," Danny said beside me. He pointed to our left. "We can stay in the woods and skirt around the next ridge and make for McCallister's, or go over the mountain. They'll never be able to follow."

From over the ridge at the edge of my property, I heard distant bursts of automatic gunfire coming from the McCallister's.

Shouts in a language I didn't understand came from below. Soldiers spread and moved uphill in rushes, throwing themselves to the ground while others alternated to dash toward us up the slope. Soon they would disappear into the defilade, just below the short open patch where I often threw bait from my corn crib. I rolled to look at Dalton and his friends.

"I don't think I'm going to let these people on our mountain today. Who's got a matchbook?"

There just hadn't been enough time.

Author's Note

I grew up working in a gun store, apprenticed as a junior gunsmith, and was there almost daily from middle school until I joined the Army at 17. It was owned by an accomplished engineer whose family had escaped the fall of the Russian Empire to the Reds, came of age in Vienna, was trained as a military officer, and was forced to escape to the US when the Nazis invaded Austria. He spoke Russian and German fluently—and many other languages—though his English bore no foreign accent whatsoever. I was a poor student of high school German, though he tutored me daily. He was responsible for my love affair with science fiction and bought me my very first Heinlein book, *Tunnel in the Sky*.

The store was a popular social gathering spot for men who also had a great effect on my life. Among my mentors were several who'd been brown water Navy, all Gunner's Mates who ran patrol boats in the rivers of Vietnam. A plethora of other vets and cops made the store a regular hangout. Most of them had served in combat, and all were experts in their knowledge of firearms. They shared countless hours of their experiences, took me with them hunting, and showed care and friendship to a kid whose father had died. I didn't know much, but knew to show respect and appreciation for the considerable time they gave me. All left an indelible impression on my life. I was very fortunate to have had such influences during my adolescence.

Among many of them, there was a commonly agreed upon bit of lore that the M1 Carbine could be field jiggered into full-auto function by the proper placement of a folded C-ration matchbook. One time I pulled an M1 from the rack, stripped it, and asked them to show me. No one could successfully demonstrate how it was done. It was a life lesson for me. Just because someone I respected had the provenance of real-world experience in the realm of war, it did not necessarily mean everything they supposedly knew was valid.

Nonetheless, I always remembered the claim.

Do not attempt to convert any weapon to automatic fire capability. It is a federal crime. Much less, don't waste time trying to do what was described in the story. It served as a vehicle in the plot to entertain, while illustrating the difficulties with such things—whether the story of guerilla warfare and resistance is an American one, or from that of any other culture.

Like much else contained herein, I do not claim anything in the story to be factual.

Doc

ABOUT THE AUTHOR

Doc Spears

John "Doc" Spears is the author of the Dark Operator and Warlord series. He was an operator in the US Army Special Forces—the Green Berets—serving in the 7th Special Forces Group in the Central and South American theater engaged in the United States' mission against communist insurgencies and narco-terrorism.

He is a retired orthopedic spine surgeon and when not writing, works in the defense industry as a contractor serving the Department of Defense and U.S. law enforcement to provide training for assaulters and snipers.

THE "BATTLE" OF DIEGO GARCIA

Mark Sibley

Corporal Wang Dong of the People's Liberation Army Air Force, or PLAAF, stretched his legs in the spacious cargo hold of the Y-20 transport. It had been nearly eight hours since they took off from Fiery Cross Reef in the South China Sea and he had slept little. He was not alone in the cargo bay. There was a company of PLA soldiers with their gear arrayed along both sides of the bay with a couple of pallets of provisions in the middle. This wasn't usually a cargo-carrying aircraft. It was a mid-air refueling plane. Most of the fuel bladders that took up space had been removed for this hop, but not all.

He would have liked to have seen America, but he was stuck on this and other missions on this side of the world. Maybe when they were done here, they'd get a mission to the States. He was twenty-two years old and had his whole life ahead of him in this new world. This new Chinese world. He'd listened in on the intelligence and mission briefings the officers had given to the soldiers. He hadn't really known what was going on until about an hour ago. Two weeks ago, the US and Europe went dark and the war had begun. World War Three. He couldn't believe it. He wanted to prove himself. Prove his worth. But here he was, just a glorified stewardess. Or steward. Taking care of real soldiers on this flight to yet another hot island in the middle of nowhere.

Apparently, when everything started, the PLAAF had dropped nerve gas on Diego Garcia, which was one of the United States' "unsinkable" aircraft carriers—a small island with a large lagoon in the center of it, way out in the middle of the Indian Ocean. They had to wait a couple of weeks for the sun and weather to degrade the nerve agent so it wasn't a danger to them when they landed. There was also a People's Liberation Army Navy or PLAN submarine already on station somewhere around the island to ensure any hostile ships or other submarines were taken care of. It all sounded very boring to him. He wanted action. He was fit. Best shape of his life. Beating all the physical fitness standards by miles. He'd qualified as marksman with the standard-issue rifle and had studied kung fu since he was a child. His father had taught him and been his teacher until his death five years prior. His mother died shortly after of cancer. He had nothing left but his job and his service to his country. He needed something to reach for.

His ears popped, signaling to him that they were descending. Finally. He left his little window and waited for his crew chief to give orders for landing. The intercom came to life throughout the aircraft.

"This is the captain. We're circling Diego Garcia now and descending rapidly to land. Prepare for landing," the pilot said.

His crew chief's booming voice echoed in the bay. "Get ready to land. Corporal Dong, get up here."

Wang made his way forward to where his crew chief was standing with one of the officers.

"How can I help, Chief?" Wang said as he approached the two men, the officer saying something to the chief that he couldn't hear.

"Corporal, I have a job for you. When we land, I need to you exit the plane before everyone else disembarks and do a walk around the aircraft. Look for anything unusual or suspicious, then radio to me with the all-clear." The crew chief handed him a small radio and a pair of binoculars.

Wang hesitated, and the chief reassuringly said, "Don't worry, Corporal, the nerve agent has had enough time to burn off in the elements. We just want you to do a walk around the plane and ensure there are no remaining threats out there. Scan the horizon with the binoculars. It's pretty overcast out there, and the pilots couldn't see through it to identify any ships about. The pilots didn't pick up any radars out there except the ground radar that's still functioning, apparently. Just focus on that and report back so we can disembark and get down to business."

"Yes, Chief. I'll get it done," Wang responded. He turned and walked back down the rows of soldiers who were all staring at him now. That unnerved him.

This is what I get for being the low man in the chain of command, he thought. He got to the rear of the plane and grabbed the handle to the starboard door and lifted it from lock to open, and heard the door come free. He pushed, then pulled the heavy door, wrestling it into its open position. The heat and humidity hit him first. He'd been in the temperature controlled aircraft for hours and this was a shock, but he moved to the edge of the door and jumped to the tarmac, radio in one hand and binoculars in the other.

He looked around and got his bearings. They'd all studied the maps of the tiny island. The plane he had just exited was sitting at the southern end of the runway with its nose pointing southeast. He was on the ocean side of the plane with nothing between him and the Indian Ocean. He looked back at the plane and door. His chief was standing in the doorway. He gave the chief a thumbs-up and began his walk around the plane.

There was little to see. Nothing, really. He walked toward the aircraft's tail, looking all around until he got to the rear of the plane. The American base was laid out before him to the north and northwest. He turned to his right and saw the lagoon, which was quite large and wide from the ground. Off to his right, or east, separated from the main base, was a collection of low buildings and housing units. He remembered the binoculars and put them to his eyes. That's when he saw them.

There were none around the plane, but through his binoculars, he could see bodies everywhere. Next to buildings, on the roads and pathways. He scanned to his right, past the lagoon and onto the main base. There were more bodies. A shiver ran through him. So many. The morning sun burned through the overcast skies and it was hot. That jarred him out of the horrors he was seeing. He made his way to the nose of the plane on the other side and around the nose gear. His radio came alive.

"Corporal, what do you see? Any threats?" The chief's voice was loud.

"No threats, Chief. Just a lot of bodies everywhere, but none near the aircraft," he said.

There was a pause. Then, "How do you feel, Corporal?"

Wang knew it. He was the guinea pig.

"I feel fine, Chief. Good to go," Wang said as he put the binoculars to his eyes one last time and scanned the base. Nothing moved. Nothing out of place except the bodies and what he thought was a chair and umbrella on the roof of one of the buildings. That was odd, but no one was there. He turned and looked out to sea, first south and then slowly to the north, and stopped. He tried to focus the binoculars to get something out there into focus. He wasn't used to these things and it took him a second to get the blob on the horizon to be less blurry.

"Chief, hold one. I have something out to sea on our starboard side. Trying to get a clear look. Stand by," Wang said into the radio.

"Do it quickly, Corporal."

"Working on it," Wang said. He put the radio in his pants pocket and used both hands to steady the glasses and slowly adjusted focus and his eye distance to the glasses. "Holy shit," he said out loud. "That's a ship out there."

Just as he'd said it, there was a puff of white smoke from the front of the ship. Then another and another.

***

Petty Officer Sandeep Singh was on port watch as the INS *Kolkata*, a Stealth Guided-Missile Destroyer of the Indian Navy, approached the island of Diego Garcia from the northwest. Tall and dark-skinned, his beard pitch-black and his turban blue. He was Sikh and proud of his military accomplishments. Young and very fit, he was his parents' joy. His mother doted on him when he had leave and could be home, and he and his father, who had served in his youth, traded stories. That was gone now. He was on flight operations on the helicopter deck. It was overcast, and they had secured all radars as they approached the island. They were running dark except for the towed array sonar scanning for submarines, which the captain had just given the order to secure. Too shallow close to the island. They had gone to battle stations when the bridge lookout had spotted a Chinese transport drop out of the cloud cover and land on the island ten minutes before.

It seemed the captain wanted to get in the game. Get some payback for this shitshow they were in. As he transitioned from watching the island through his glasses and back to the helicopter operations behind him, he thought about his family again. He had lived an idyllic life in Chennai before everything went to shit a few weeks earlier. They still didn't know who launched first, them or the Pakis, but the aftermath was horrific. The Pakis hit them hard, and they lost tens of millions of people, including his whole family in Chennai. Parents, sisters, fiancée. All gone. Luckily for him, he was at sea at the time. But everyone on the *Kolkata* had lost someone. Even though they'd taken terrible losses, Pakistan no longer existed.

That was then. It took a couple of days, but intelligence arrived that the world was at war. What was left of the Indian Armed Forces had joined what was left of the West's militaries as well as Australia and New Zealand and others against Russia and China. Iran had joined their Pakistani allies in hell, and no one knew anything about North Korea, South Korea, or Japan. That's what brought them south to Diego Garcia. America's Footprint of Freedom. Normally, there were communications from the island, but that had all ceased after the war began. Another Indian Navy warship had done a recon of the islands down here a week prior and gotten nothing. Rumor was, China had dropped a nerve agent. Sandeep figured that rumor was true since the Chinese had just landed on the island unopposed.

He was thinking all this as he watched a single person standing on the tarmac. Looking back at Sandeep and the *Kolkata* through his own binoculars. Sandeep was fascinated and focused until movement and sound behind him startled him.

He turned to see one of the two Sea King helos roll out of the hangar. The crew and team of Indian Marines stood aside, waiting for helo ops to get the aircraft ready to launch. He was wondering how this small team would fare against whatever complement of soldiers was on that Chinese transport when the 76-mm deck gun forward started spitting out rounds with white puffs of smoke rolling from bow to stern. He smelled the acrid gunpowder, an amazing smell. Adrenaline surged through him.

He put the glasses to his eyes and focused on the Chinese plane. In seconds, the rounds began falling and exploding near the aircraft. He saw one soldier, tiny through his binoculars, run away from the plane and out of sight. Must have dived to the ground. Several more rounds left the deck gun and began to find their target. The first hit destroyed the tail of the aircraft and then walked up the fuselage until the plane disappeared in a massive explosion. Once the billowing black smoke and fireball dissipated, he saw the remains of the plane, broken and burning in several large pieces and many smaller ones. He pumped his fist in the air.

Klaxons blared throughout the ship, and the deck lurched under him as the ship increased speed. He almost lost his footing and grabbed the gunwale to steady himself. This could only mean one thing. He turned to scan the horizon and seas on the starboard side away from the island. It only took him a minute to see them—two straight lines of bubbles heading directly for the *Kolkata*. Torpedoes.

Brrrrrrrrrrrrrrrrrt screamed the CIWS on the ship's starboard side, and an incoming missile that he didn't see exploded a hundred meters away. Shocked, he then saw that the forward movement of the ship, apparently at flank speed, had moved them enough that the first torpedo passed just aft of them. A streaking wraith under the waves, the torpedo began a slow turn in an arc to come back, but it didn't matter.

The entire ship seemed to rise up out of the water even as the CIWS kept firing at more incoming missiles. The other men all around him on the helo deck had flattened themselves on the deck and he was thrown against the gunwale. His grip on the side of the ship held him fast as he strained to get a look at the superstructure. There was something very wrong. The *Kolkata* wasn't straight any longer. The bow was somehow bending out to port.

Oh shit! The second torpedo broke the ship in two, he thought, as a missile came streaking in to hit the superstructure on the forward half of the ship. They were sinking! Klaxons blared, people screamed, and out to starboard—just skimming along the waves—two more missiles streaked for the rear of the ship where he was. Without thinking, he stood up on the unsteady deck and leaped out into the Indian Ocean.

***

Sandeep didn't know how long he'd been swimming, but every muscle in his body was at its breaking point. It seemed the farther he swam, the farther the beach he was heading toward got. He tried to keep the thought of what was swimming under him at bay. He swam on. Every once in a while, he looked back to where the *Kolkata* had been. Black smoke wafted here and there amongst the debris floating on the surface, but he knew he was the only one left. The ship had gone down so fast. He'd expended a lot of energy getting away from the ship so he wasn't sucked down with it when it went. His blue, green, and white camouflaged BDUs weighed heavily on him. He had taken his boots off, tied them together, and draped them around his neck so he could kick more efficiently. However, nothing seemed to get him closer to the beach.

Something brushed his right foot and he swam harder. As hard as he'd ever swum, but always waiting for the bite. Moments later he seemed to be more propelled forward than his strokes were taking him and realized he was in the surf. One last push and he was gliding into the beach. Finally. He couldn't stand from fatigue even though the sand was beneath him. He let the waves push him as far as they could, then he crawled up to dry sand and put his head down on it, breathing deeply and completely exhausted, but took his boots from around his neck and put them aside weakly.

After a couple of minutes of deep breathing and coughing fits, he rolled over on his back, then sat up, staring out to sea from where he'd come. There was nothing. No *Kolkata*, no men following him to the beach, no friends. He was it. Alone. Or was he, he thought as a breeze brought warm air over him and with it the smell of smoke, fuel, and death. He'd smelled death before, but this was worse. Burnt flesh. He looked around and saw the black smoke over the low, rolling sand dunes followed by tropical foliage that hid the runway from his sight, but the destroyed aircraft was there, he knew. He'd watched the *Kolkata* destroy it. He took a deep breath and stood. Unsteady on wobbly legs and dripping. The sun was out now and felt good, but he'd need shelter.

He bent down and picked up his boots and walked slowly up the beach to where it gave way to green brush and squat trees. He could see the plane now. Still burning. He turned one last time to scan the ocean for other survivors when he heard a scream just behind him. He turned just in time to duck as a Chinese soldier swung a pair of binoculars at him, and he only caught a glancing blow. He kept his footing and swung his boots in return and was rewarded with a direct hit on the soldier's face, knocking him back into the bushes. He knew he was too tired to win a hand-to-hand fight right now and the soldier wasn't armed, otherwise he'd have been shot—so he ran.

As quick as he could—into the brush—wincing each time something stabbed his feet. He should have put his boots on first, but they were his only melee weapon. He ran faster as he exited the scrub and found a concrete tarmac that took him to the end of the runway where the burning aircraft was. He ran past it and down the long runway, glancing back several times. No one was there—until he looked again. There the Chinese soldier stood. Binoculars up, watching him run. Sandeep slowed to a stop and put his hands on his knees, bent over, heaving air and staring at the soldier. Then the throbbing started in earnest. He touched his forehead and felt the cut. His fingers came away red. He looked up and the soldier was still standing there, just in front of the burning plane.

He hated the Chinese. He needed a weapon. This was a military base, after all. He quickly sat and put his boots on. Laced them up fast and stood. The soldiers was moving toward him now in a slow jog.

***

Dong knew this Indian had nowhere to go and that they were alone. He had time. The side of his head hurt where the boots had struck him. He was angry now. He hated Indians. All the weapons were on the plane and he couldn't go near it. Too hot and too horrible. He'd avenge his crew and the rest. This wasn't what he'd imagined combat would be like if he'd ever gotten to it, but it'd do. He'd started jogging when the Indian sat to put his boots on. He wanted to conserve his energy for when he caught up to him. No rush. They were alone here.

He followed the Indian at a decent pace. The man had to be tired from swimming. He seemed to be out of breath, all bent over with his hands on his knees. They were heading north on the island. The plane was at the southern tip, so there was nowhere to go but north. He wasn't really gaining on him as they were both jogging now, but he wasn't getting away. He followed the Indian off the north end of the runway and then they passed the naval base and docks to the right and a dozen or more large, freestanding, circular fuel tanks to the left. They'd been going for ten or fifteen minutes and the sun was higher in the sky now and hot. The overcast had burned off. Dong was sweating, panting with each breath. The Indian had to be worse off than he was and he wasn't struggling.

He watched from a distance as his quarry seemed to stop and look around at things and then keep going. Probably looking for a weapon of some type. He'd do the same thing and probably should. All he had were his binoculars. He wiped sweat from his eyes and picked up the pace a bit. They moved through some sort of support buildings after the fuel tanks and he spotted a road sign and it said "National Highway" on it. The road went all the way to the top of the island and into the main town. He'd need water soon, he thought, as they passed by a large area to the left of what looked like base housing. The smell hit him. He hadn't thought about it until now. He glanced to the left as he jogged by all the mobile home type units and saw the bodies. There weren't groups of them, but they were scattered on the roads and steps. There was one next to a bicycle he was coming up on next to the road. He stopped to get a better look.

It was a woman. She had either fallen off the bike or got off and fallen immediately. She was in pretty advanced stages of decomposition. He choked back the bile rising in his throat as he started running again. Now faster. He saw the Indian veer off to the left suddenly, only about a hundred meters in front of him now, and it didn't take long for him to get there. He stopped. It was a golf course. Not a big one, but here nonetheless. Then he saw why the Indian ran this way. There were bodies out on the course. And golf clubs strewn about.

***

Sandeep ignored the decomposing bodies and picked out a nice driver from the golf bag and looked around spotting a small pond, what they probably called a water trap here, but he ran with the driver to the pond and around the other side, putting it between himself and his company. He put the driver behind his head and rested his other hand on the business end and stretched his back and tried to get his breath back. He watched the soldier sort through the golf bag lying on the ground. He came away with two irons. One for each hand. Shit. He was too busy and excited to find a weapon, he didn't bother to stay at the bag and finish it then. Clubs it was, then. He couldn't run anymore.

He put the driver's head on the ground and leaned on it, holding up his other hand to hopefully signal to the soldier that this was it, but not yet. The Chinese walked slowly, almost sauntering over to the other side of the pond, and stopped. He too was breathing deeply and swung one of the irons in a wide arc and then twirled it in his hand by the wrist.

Fancy, he thought. They stared at each other for a minute and he figured maybe they should introduce each other.

"English?" Sandeep shouted. He figured this soldier didn't speak Hindi and he certainly didn't speak Mandarin, but his English was good.

"Is okay. Yes," he replied. Sandeep already didn't like his voice.

"What... is your name?" he yelled across the water.

"Corporal Wang," the man replied loudly.

"Fuck you, Wang!" Sandeep yelled and Wang pursed his lips and stared at Sandeep.

"Oh! What is name?" Wang shouted back.

"Petty Officer Sandeep Singh!"

"Hey! Sandeep! Fuck you!"

"Your mother fucked a pig to get pregnant with you, Wang!"

"You mother suck thousand dick. Hope she die in nuclear war. I send you meet her, yes?"

"All your ancestors are pigs! If you come over here, I will beat you to death, PGA-style!"

"You want? I come now? You okay, out of air?"

"Come on then! I fuck you bloody with this driver!" Sandeep had worked himself up now, and it looked like his opponent had as well. They started walking toward each other around the pond. He was holding the driver like a sword with two hands while watching Wang spinning an iron in each hand and taking deep breaths. The space closed quickly and when they were within range, Sandeep swung his driver overhead with it coming down on one of the irons with a crack as Wang blocked it. He was in a rage now and struck again. This one managed to get through to Wang's shoulder just as the iron in his other hand struck his left knee. They both screamed in pain. Sandeep collapsed, driver in his right hand, grabbing his left knee with his other. Wang dropped the iron in his left hand. Sandeep saw it hang uselessly by his side, but Wang was now above him and swung the other iron over his head and down. Sandeep just got the driver up in time to parry it to the side and used Wang's momentum against him, grabbing Wang's wrist and twisting it around the soldier's back, forcing him to the ground.

Sandeep raised the driver over his head to smash Wang's skull, but Wang kicked his wounded knee and he went down again. Wang was quickly on top of him. Iron dropped from his good hand and he started punching Sandeep in the face. He covered best he could, but some blows got through.

He tasted blood in his mouth. He kicked up with his right leg in desperation and his knee found Wang's balls. In a quick heave, Sandeep struggled to get on top of Wang, who was still resisting and fighting, but not as hard. Sandeep started pounding with both fists on Wang's face until the man stopped fighting back. He looked to his right and saw one of Wang's irons. He grasped for it and found the handle. He raised it above his head and then felt something bite his neck. It stung horribly and he grabbed at it. He felt nothing. He tried to raise the iron again but couldn't. His arm wasn't acting right.

"You almost had him. Good fight," Sandeep heard a male voice say and saw a hand with a syringe reach down to Wang's neck and stick a needle in.

"Who... what?" was all Sandeep could muster as he fell off Wang and lay on the ground.

"That's enough for today, my new friends," the voice said as he lost consciousness.

***

Wang opened his eyes. He had to blink several times to focus. Why was he so groggy? He tried to raise his hands to his face to rub his eyes, but they wouldn't move. He raised his head a little bit and squinted down his body. He was restrained. Or, his hands were tied to a gurney. He shook his wrists. They weren't tied so much as strapped down. His feet as well were strapped to this bed he was lying in. He took a long breath in and struggled and shook his arms and legs to no avail. Putting his head back on the pillow, he looked around. He was in some sort of hospital room, but larger. There were half a dozen beds like his. Small tables next to each one with lamps and other things. Large window behind him and along the opposite wall. Three beds on his side and three on the other side. A window above each. There were trees blowing in the breeze outside the windows across from him. Ground floor.

He was still in his uniform. Then he felt the pain. Sharp in his shoulder and dull on his face in several places. Actually, his whole face felt swollen now that he thought about it. The Indian! They had fought. With golf clubs. The Indian was on top of him, he recalled, and then he wasn't. Then he couldn't remember anything after that.

"Good morning, Corporal Wang," a voice said to him.

Wang looked around and saw someone in the bed directly across from him. How did he miss that before? He was so tired. Focusing on the man, the Indian appeared in the bed. As he stared at him, it looked like, what was his name?... Sandeep, was also strapped to his bed.

"What's going on, Sandeep? Who did this to us?" Wang asked the Indian.

"I don't know. I just woke up like you. Seems as though we've been captured and restrained," Sandeep replied slowly.

"I'm tired. Like drugged. You?"

"Yes, I remember beating the shit out of you on the golf course and then someone poking a needle in my neck. It all went dark after that."

"I seem to remember crushing your knee with golf club. I would have overcome you. Stupid Indian."

"So, you were just hitting my fists with your face, then? How's your shoulder, pig fucker?" Sandeep asked.

Wang strained with all his might against the straps, but nothing.

"As fun as it is to listen to both of you insult each other, let's not have any undue fuss," a voice said. Sandeep and Dong both looked around the room, searching in vain for the mysterious voice, and both settled their eyes on a door at the end of the room and rows of beds. The light was on and above the door it said "Restroom."

"Hey, who are you? Why are we strapped to these beds?" Sandeep demanded as Wang just stared at the open door.

"Well, first of all, welcome to Diego Garcia. Otherwise known as America's Footprint of Freedom. You're strapped to the beds for your own protection," the voice explained. Sandeep had spent a little time in the United States and the accent of whoever this was seemed like a Southern accent to him, but he wasn't sure.

"What is going to happen to us? Why you not kill us?" Wang asked after a short silence from the restroom.

"We'll get to that soon enough. What you should be asking is how am I still here and alive," the voice said.

"Out with it then!" Sandeep yelled and strained against the straps again.

"You see, Diego Garcia is a tropical paradise. I've been stationed here for eight months or so and I got into the deep-sea fishing we have here. Very early on Christmas morning a couple or few weeks back, I can't remember anymore, me and one of my homies were up before dawn and out on a fishing boat with the best captain around these parts. Fishing for yellow tuna for a Christmas feast later that day. We had been way out and caught a big one. By the time we came back in later that morning, we could tell before pulling into the dock that something was wrong."

"What does this have to do with us? Me in particular. I'm Indian. We're on your side," Sandeep said.

"Patience, Sandeep. Yes, I know your names. Was watching you two introduce yourselves from the brush not twenty feet from where you fought. So, to continue my story, we tied up to the pier and my good friend hopped off the boat and found a sailor lying on the ground. He rushed over to him while I stayed on the boat, tying it up. The captain went with him. I thought it was odd and scanned the rest of the pier and docks. There were more men. All on the ground. I didn't know what it was at the time, but I had a bad feeling in the pit of my stomach. I yelled to them not to touch anything, but they were already touching the man and the ground around them as they knelt. Checking for a pulse and whatnot. My friend was a Corpsman on the island, you see. He would try to help. I stayed on the boat. Not touching anything. They both died right there next to the other man. That's when it hit me. Some sort of nerve agent."

"I have a proposal, whoever you are. You let me free and I'll kill this communist Chinese bastard and get in contact with the Indian Navy and we'll get out of here," Sandeep offered.

"Shut you whore mouth, Indian!" Wang yelled.

"Easy guys. Settle. While that's tempting, gonna be a hard pass for me. See, after spending a week and a half on that boat, I figured the nerve agent had burned off or decomposed enough to be safe. You see, if it's VX, it will slowly break down in the weather and elements like sunlight over a week or so. From what I could tell, it came down from an aircraft in droplet form. Just a pinhead sized amount will kill many, but it wasn't in aerosol form, which is why it didn't get in here and why we're all still alive. For the last week, I figured at some point I'd have visitors. I also had time to listen to the still functioning communications. As you both probably know, the United States and Europe are dark. My home is in the great state of Missouri, where my wife and cats are hopefully still alive. I have friends that will ensure that. However, you all have put her and my cats in danger. And for that, I cannot forgive. I was going to have a lot of fun with you Chinese that landed two days ago, but this will do."

"What do you mean?" Sandeep asked. He had felt some fear of this man before, but that feeling had just doubled.

The toilet in the restroom flushed.

"What are you doing?" Sandeep said.

"Well, firstly, you two are going to have to become friends and quickly. Secondly, I just finished with a glorious bowel movement."

"What is bowel movement?" Wang asked.

"He's taking a shit, you stupid, fucking communist," Sandeep said.

"Fuck you, Sandeep. Shut up," Wang responded.

"Guys, I gotta ask, do you all have bidets where you live? They're the epitome of luxury. This brand in particular, LuxeBidet, is amazing. It's a portable model I had shipped over from the States when I got here. See, you download your software and then you use these knobs on the side here, to squirt soothing, warm water on your booty hole. You can up the pressure to ensure a comprehensive wash. It's amazing, really. You should try it sometime."

"So, you aren't going to kill us then, if we'll be able to use it sometime?" Sandeep asked, hopefully.

"Kill you? No. Not really. If I had wanted you dead, you'd be dead now. You're alive because I deemed it so," Sandeep heard him say and then he walked out of the restroom and stood between the two beds, looking first at Sandeep, then over to Wang.

Wang took him in. He was certainly American. He wore a camou-flaged boonie hat over gray hair. Glasses rested on his nose. He had a full, sort of half beard, as gray as his hair. It was bushy from the ears to his jaw, but was clean shaven beneath his mouth with a bushy moustache. He looked like someone from the old Westerns they would be allowed to watch at times when he was a kid.

Sandeep was also taking stock of the man. He had a Hawaiian shirt on and cargo shorts. A plate carrier with patches on it was worn over the shirt and he had a gun belt on below that, with a pistol on the side. As he turned to go to a workspace near the restroom, Sandeep saw that he had socks pulled up to mid-calf with what he thought was Bugs Bunny on them and hiking boots. When he came back to the beds, he had two syringes in his hand.

"Where are my manners? My name is Rob. You can call me Rob. I'm one of the nurses here on the island. You could say I'm sort of an educated hillbilly. Now, I've done what I could in the short time we've had together to patch up your fighting wounds. Not much I could do for your fucked-up knee, Sandeep. And Wang, your shoulder is pretty messed up as well. So that's why I told y'all you'd have to become besties. You're gonna need each other today. Help each other."

"Rob, what are you talking about? What's in the needles?" Sandeep asked. He was really starting to panic internally now.

"I'm going to give you both some mild happy liquid. It will put you both out for about an hour or so," Rob said and moved to Wang first and hooked the syringe into the IV that ran into his arm and pushed the plunger. Wang struggled some more, but to no avail. Rob patted him on the leg and smiled beneath the big moustache.

"One down. Now you, Sandeep." He repeated the process as Sandeep watched silently and still.

"Whatever you're doing, please don't. We can get out of here and you can get back to your..." Sandeep almost finished the sentence.

"Get some rest, boys. You're gonna need it."

***

Wang opened his eyes and squinted. So bright and hot. He was disoriented and raised his hands to rub and cover his eyes from the light. Wait! He moved his feet and legs. He was free of the straps! He swung his legs to the left and tried to stand and abruptly fell to the ground. He was so weak. But he was outside. He heard a scream and looked up, squinting again. He saw the Indian, Sandeep, on the ground about ten feet from him, rubbing and holding his left knee. Good. Hoped it was painful. Which reminded him of the pain in his shoulder. He was able to move his left arm again, but it was still not one hundred percent.

"Gentlemen! Take it easy! The sedative will fully wear off in a minute or so. It was just enough for me to move you outside and let you free," Rob said as they looked around to see where he was. He smiled and took a sip of the Corona with a lime slice. Eventually, they found him. He was sitting in a folding beach chair under an umbrella on the roof of the medical clinic. He had rolled them out on their gurneys to the middle of the street in front of the clinic.

"What's going on, Rob!" Sandeep yelled up at him.

Wang started to slowly step away from his bed.

"Don't go anywhere yet, Wang." He raised the M-4 rifle with an ACOG scope on it. Wang stopped in his tracks.

"You shoot us now?" Wang asked.

He looked ready to run, Rob thought. Good. Not yet.

"Before we get to the festivities, a little background. The first short story I ever read was in high school for a book report. The title of the story was 'The Most Dangerous Game.' You heard of it?" Rob asked.

They both shook their heads.

"No? I'll give you the Cliff's Notes. Dude falls off a yacht at night and washes up on an island. This island is owned by a rich dude. Rich dude finds him and helps him at first, but then sets him free on the island," Rob explained.

"What does this have to do with anything, Rob? What's the point?" Sandeep asked.

"Well, this rich man had hunted every animal he could, and it held no sport for him any longer. He wanted to hunt something that would challenge him."

"Wait! You going to hunt us?" Wang spat out.

"I told you both you'd have to become friends and work together. You'll have a better chance together," Rob said.

"Oh, come on, Rob! I've told you before, I'm on your side in this whole war. I'm with America and against the Chinese. I'm on your side!" Sandeep was nearly pleading now.

"Sandeep, you don't understand yet. Sides? I'm on no one's side. I'm just here for the violence," Rob said and took another drink from his Corona.

"What do you expect us to do then?"

"Expect?" Rob threw his head back and laughed loudly. "I expect you to run."

ABOUT THE AUTHOR:

Mark Sibley is a micro-celebrity on Twitter (X, whatever) who spends his days at a day job and his early mornings writing... slowly. He's currently, and probably forever, blamed for all the bad things that happen in the world since his books tell the future. His books? Apocalypse and mayhem. Not the titles, but the content. Soon to be in the nonfiction section. Drinker of coffee, poster of doom. Yes, if you ask nicely, he'll kill you in his stories.

LIBREVILLE

Philip Voodoo

The loud banging echoed through the long dark halls and reverberated into the souls of the men inside the building.

It had been going on for three days now. Every few hours the banging would stop and a brief interlude of peace would fall across the compound as men either prepared for the worst or tried to catch up on sleep.

Major Tommy Burton was one of the former. His entire life he had been one of those people who always expected the worst. But unlike so many of his nervous brethren, instead of cowering, he planned. The banging made it hard, but not impossible. If anything, it relayed the urgency of the need for solutions.

He straightened his gray Air Force uniform and put his glasses on. Around the room, civilians and military alike were counting and inventorying the embassy's supplies. He wanted everything counted. Ammunition, food, water, batteries, even pencils. Anything could bean asset in a siege, and that was definitely what this was, a siege.

He looked at the calendar on his desk. Today was the 28th of December. Three days after Christmas and three days since the siege had begun.

Almost as soon as everything had gone black, the embassy's front gate had erupted in gunfire. A vehicle full of security forces from the Chinese embassy had tried to shoot their way into the American compound. The two Marines at the gate had stood their ground. The lance corporal in charge of the guard had pushed a younger private first class inside the small guard shack to get the large metal doors shut. The lance corporal had stayed behind, outside the gates, firing every round he had to buy the private time to get the doors closed.

Both attacker and defender had died together in the burning wreckage of the truck.

Looking around the room, he found the man he was looking for.

"David, I'm going down to walk the perimeter; let me know when the inventory is done."

David looked up from his clipboard and pushed his eyeglasses higher on his face.

David had come to the embassy two years before as a cultural attaché. He was neither diplomat nor soldier. He was a career civil servant. Now he was the acting supply officer.

It wasn't fair to the young man, but nothing was, Major Burton thought as he walked through the door and out into the dark hallway. The banging got louder as he got closer to the gate. He was a Missile Officer by trade, a man who had begun his career sitting under ground in the ICBM silos. Now here he was, defending a castle under siege.

The ambassador wasn't even here to look to. He had gone on vacation for Christmas to Aruba or some place, not that the man who had been given the job as a reward for fundraising would have offered much in the way of leadership.

The banging abruptly stopped and Burton heard footsteps behind him. He turned to see Staff Sergeant Fernando Diaz and Captain Andrew Anderson walking towards him from down the dark corridor.

Both Marines were giants and absolute physical specimens, the types of soldiers and people that Tommy had avoided his entire life. Both were infantrymen. Anderson was a graduate of the Naval Academy and had nearly been offered an NFL contract after graduation. He had never brought up that he had graduated from a Service Academy and Burton had gone to Fresno State, but Tommy could feel it simmering there. That he stood a full head shorter than both Anderson and Diaz was not something that helped, either.

Jocks, he thought to himself, but despite two Marines making no secret of their distaste at his being in charge, Tommy was glad there were some jocks around now.

"Captain, Sergeant," Burton greeted them as they walked up. "Shall we?" he asked before holding open the heavy door that led to the embassy's large two-story foyer and the courtyard outside.

"Sir." Captain Anderson nodded, and walked through the door ahead of a silent Staff Sergeant Diaz. Sergeant Diaz, a tall and lanky man, was the non-commissioned officer in charge of the embassy's Marine security detail. He had been in Gabon almost three years now. Diaz was a runner, tall and skinny; he looked like he would never tire.

Captain Anderson, on the other hand, had been in Gabon around a week. He had flown in early to acclimatize before a joint exercise. His presence was welcome, considering the circumstances.

Burton trailed the two down the long stairway and into the large foyer. The tables and chairs that had once been scattered through the lobby had been removed. Sergeant Diaz had explained that they needed a clear field of fire should the people outside the compound's walls get in.

That had made sense to Burton. Despite being an Air Force officer, he had barely fired a weapon, let alone understood the type of tactics the sergeant was describing. His deployment to Iraq had been spent in a trailer, coordinating drone flight paths. Now he was the defense attaché at the embassy, which meant he was responsible for being the military liaison to the ambassador and Gabon's military. It wasn't a terribly complex relationship or busy assignment.

"The Marine guard mounts at the security posts are squared away. "Diaz paused before adding a "Sir" and continued. "The embassy personnel who have been assigned as runners, CCTV observers, and ammunition loaders need motivation."

Diaz finished his report without another "sir," and Burton nodded as they reached the two Marines standing at the front gate. The Marines came to attention and saluted.

The salute was silly, Burton thought, here at the edges of the world. Nevertheless he returned it and turned back to his companions. "They have a learning curve, Sergeant. They are not Marines. But keep communicating the expectations and they'll meet them."

The two Marines stood at a pile of bricks, lumber, and metal that had been heaped behind the gate. The gate was tall, maybe fifteen feet, and made up of two giant pieces of iron that swung outwards toward the street. The wall around it was slightly higher here, and it made sense that the Chinese would try to breach at this spot despite the apparent strength of the position.

High walls worked both ways, Burton had learned. While they kept the besiegers on the other side, it also prevented the besieged from seeing them and shooting back.

They had a dozen Marines, another two dozen staff for the embassy, and barely enough weapons and ammunition to go around.

"I trust you two are good?" Burton asked the Marines at the gate who both responded by looking first at one another, then the Marines standing behind Burton.

A Marine with red hair and freckles answered first. "Sir, uh, yessir, we are good." He nodded.

"Good, good, let us know if you need anything," Burton said and turned to walk away. Leading troops was new to him, and he hated it. He had a friend working down in Zambia who would have loved this. The man was a pure officer and could make even a private at the gate feel important, even as he made joke about enlisted men.

He had tried to channel some of his friend into this new challenge, but then remembered what the tall Army officer had once told him over a few beers. *They will know if your leadership style isn't authentic. Be yourself, whatever that is.*

The banging resumed, causing both guards and the major to jump.

Burton played it off with a smile and started walking the grounds with Diaz and Anderson.

The embassy compound was a large rectangle about the size of three football fields, with a large white wall surrounding the entire perimeter. The main gate was in the south-west corner where the main building was located.

Burton had decided to gather everyone and everything they might need and consolidate it in the main building. If anything happened, he wanted everyone together to respond. Completing their walk, the trio quickly approached the main building, and were greeted by a breathless embassy worker running out of the lobby.

"We, we have a problem," he gasped.

***

The group stood around the large thousand-gallon diesel tank just outside of the embassy's garage and listened to the embassy worker try and explain.

"I... I don't know, we had almost a full tank, it was refilled last week, but it looks like... I don't know," he mumbled, flustered at delivering bad news to the men in uniform. "We came todo the inventory, and we are at like an eighth of the tank full."

Burton looked at both Anderson and Diaz and frowned. This was a disaster. With the external electrical connections cut, the only thing keeping electricity flowing was a large diesel backup generator. The electricity ran the CCTV systems, charged the guard's radio batteries, and hopefully would run the communications systems when they came back online.

Without the diesel, they had none of that, and no hope of holding out for rescue. Looking down at the ground beneath him, Burton traced a line from the bottom of the tank, first to a layer of sand and rock immediately below to catch small spills, and then to a larger drain. Had it been left open, no one would have noticed.

"I don't see how this could have been an accident... we can use one of the civilians on this guard post. Let's get an inventory setup. Every time we change guard, they measure the fuel."

Turning back to the young civilian, Burton continued, "Could you please get with Dembe and find out how long the fuel we have left will last us?"

Dembe was the embassy's locally hired maintenance supervisor. He had been at the embassy since before it was built, and was a fixture there.

Anderson broke the silence. "This should settle it. We need to discuss a breakout," he said, and Diaz nodded behind him.

"And go where?" Sighing, Burton shook his head. "We have enough vehicles, but where would we go? We can't shoot our way across Africa with a dozen Marines and minivans filled with civilians. We need to find a way to get our communications back online and get into contact with anybody at all."

"Let me take the Marines out and see if we can't push the Chinese out there back," Anderson said, standing taller. His attempt to intimidate the major was transparent as the direness of their situation. "There can't be that many. My Marines can do it."

The banging started again and Burton sighed, closing his eyes. "As a last resort only. If it gets worse, we will talk about it again. It's almost dark. Let's get everyone ready for the night."

Anderson and Diaz looked at each other for a moment. Burton saw their glance and wondered if they were considering doing it anyway.

"Yes, sir," Anderson said, and headed back towards the embassy's main building.

***

Night settled on the embassy like a dark hood. They were only a few hundred yards from the Atlantic Ocean, and the upper-class houses that lined the beachfront property in this part of town had all of the comforts of modern life.

Lights shone brightly, music played, and loud voices could be heard, yet the embassy of the most powerful nation on earth stood dark and cut off from the rest of the world.

Burton walked into the small security room and looked at the sixscreens that lined the walls. The security system was on a closed circuit, which meant as long as the power kept going, they could at least see the areas they didn't have enough manpower to cover.

Their CCTV system was the only thing that worked. They could see what was happening inside the embassy, but the cameras covering the street outside the embassy's walls had been knocked out. Everything else: cell phones, landlines, even the power, had been shut off by the people waiting outside. They were on their own.

Staff Sergeant Diaz came into the small room behind Burton and the young staffer watching the monitors. He looked at the staffer and picked up the radio that sat on the table. "This radio isn't even on. What the fuck," the Marine swore, his voice rising quickly.

"I didn't know," the young man protested, looking up at the hovering Diaz. "It was like that when I got here."

"The radio is your responsibility. You are in charge of this post. How will you communicate with the guards out there if you see something? We are counting on you to be our eyes and ears, and without a radio, you aren't worth a bucket of warm piss."

"I... I didn't, even know how to use it," the young man said, starting to quiver beneath the sergeant's fury.

"Watch." Diaz held up the radio in front of the young man's face. "This is the on switch. Here, see?" Diaz turned a small dial on the green radio. "This is your frequency. Check your notes. What frequency are we supposed to be on?"

As Diaz continued his instruction, Burton, who had also been watching, noticed something move on one of the screens and he turned back to the monitors on the wall.

"You might benefit from this too, sir," Diaz said.

But Burton ignored the sergeant. He was busy watching the figure move on the monitor from shadow to shadow. "What is that?" the major asked both men, who were still focused on the radio in Diaz's hand. "Is that one of ours?"

"Probably just one of those embassy workers having a smoke," Diaz said. The figure had been crouching behind a wall of one of the buildings, and as two Marines walked by, had run out towards the next building and the row of vehicles parked behind it.

"Holy shit!" Burton exclaimed, and started to run for the door.

The embassy's fleet of vehicles, their only means of escape, were parked behind the building the figure had been moving towards. As Burton ran through the dark corridors, he checked the pistol on his hip.

He had barely ever fired one, but whoever was out there was not thereto be friends.

He could hear Diaz yelling behind him as he grabbed what Marines there were. But there wasn't time. He ran down the steps through the empty foyer and into the dark courtyard. Pistol in hand, he ran towards the large parking area where they had last seen the figure.

Burton breathed heavily before slowing as he approached the row of vehicles. Running wasn't his thing either. He spent most of his day, and career, behind a desk.

"Whoever you are, identify yourself!" Burton demanded. It could still have been one of his people, who knew, but Burton could feel the danger in his soul. He pulled the pistol up, making sure to switch off the safety.

The banging from the gate added to the stress, and covered up the sound of footsteps behind the major.

The blow landed on his outstretched arm first, knocking his pistol from his hand. A second, heavier blow drove him into the side of one of the vehicles with a loud bang and knocked the wind out of him.

Burton tried desperately to find the pistol on the ground as his attacker turned to run back towards the embassy wall. Burton could hear the voices of the QRF and realized in the dark they wouldn't be able to tell one shape from the other.

At the last moment, he reached out and tripped his assailant, who landed on the pavement with a loud crash. Burton could hear the telltale clatter of a rifle hitting the pavement as well. It was a race. He just needed to keep this man on the ground until the QRF arrived. But the man was faster, and back on his feet in a moment.

He stood over Burton, a dark shape in the dim moonlight, but the major could see the dark outline of a man was bringing a rifle up to his shoulder. Burton stared down the barrel of the rifle then closed his eyes, as a loud crack rang out.

The man fell on top of the kneeling Burton in a heap. Burton opened his eyes and saw Staff Sergeant Diaz out front on a knee, lowering his rifle. The rest of the Marines ran past their kneeling sergeant and dragged the dead intruder's body off of the major.

Diaz stepped up and extended his hand to the major who by now was soaked in the dead man's blood, which was still pumping out of the man's wound.

"We don't go into battle alone in the Marine Corps, Major," the sergeant said, helping his commander to his feet. "Ramirez, search the casualty," he continued without waiting for acknowledgment or thanks from the Air Force officer. "Harris, you take a flashlight and see what he was up to."

" Aye, Sergeant," both Marines said in unison, and got about their work.

"I... thank you, Sergeant," Burton said feebly.

"I would have done the same for any man," the Marine sergeant replied, not looking away from the two men searching. "We are in this fight together."

"Here, sir," one of the Marines said, handing Burton the pistol he had dropped at the beginning of the fight.

Burton took the weapon wordlessly and began walking back to the main building, his anxious mind racing.

How had that man gotten over the wall... and what was he doing here?

***

"Mining explosives," said Thomas Placher, a geologist working for one of the American companies in the region, as a Marine dropped a satchel on the long conference table in the middle of the meeting room.

He had been at the embassy to get his passport renewed when the attack had come and now he was stuck.

"Why would a Chinese soldier be carrying mining explosives into the motor pool?" Captain Anderson asked, looking at Placher. He knew the geologist didn't have the answers, but he needed to get the question out somehow.

The banging picked up again at the front gate. Burton closed his eyes, and inside, screamed.

Placher looked in the satchel. Wearing a pair of khakis and a University of California–Santa Barbara T-shirt, he was exceedingly average in build and temperament.

"This isn't enough to cause a huge problem, but, in the motor pool, it definitely would have destroyed those vehicles," he said, dropping the bag.

"Can we use it?" Major Burton asked, knowing anything at this point would be helpful.

"Did you find any detonators?" Placher asked, looking at the Marine, who produced a small bag of them. "Then yes."

"He also had a radio and an earpiece. We listened for a few minutes, but it was just silent," Private First Class Ramirez offered.

"Thanks, Marine," Major Burton said, taking a long breath, trying to clear his head. "Okay. We are going to need to beef up security—"

"Sir, a moment," Captain Anderson said. "That is enemy communications equipment. We should not be talking with it in the room. Private, take it down into the inventory room. Take these explosives, and the detonators separately, and put them in with the ammunition."

As the young Marine marched off, Burton looked back at the small group made up of the Marine captain, the geologist, and David the cultural attaché who had been elected to represent the civilian staff.

"We have a problem," he soberly said. "I don't know how deep it goes, but we need to up security, asap."

" We are already maxed out," Anderson said. "We will need to start arming the embassy staff and using them as the second guard. That way each guard post will have at least one Marine, and we can do twice as many."

" We... uh," David started, straightening his glasses as he stood. "We don't know how to use weapons, really. We are not soldiers."

" Neither are we," Anderson said, staring at the young diplomat. "We are Marines. I can't make you soldiers, and I sure as shit can't make you Marines, but what I can make you is awake, and put you with one with my Marines. Do you think your people can stay awake and walk around?"

"I think we can do that," David replied nervously.

Placher stood up from the other side of the table and cleared his throat. "Despite being from California, I can use a rifle," he said without a trace of hubris or pride in his voice. Only a deadpan reporting of the facts.

"How well?" Anderson asked the geologist.

"I probably won't drop it," he said. Burton couldn't tell if it was a knock on him dropping his pistol or some sort of understatement, so he let it go.

Hesitating, t he tall captain looked at David. "Why don't you go down and talk to your people, tell them what is happening, and get with Sergeant Diaz to see who is going first and where."

David nodded and walked out, realizing that while technically the Marine had no authority over him, it hadn't been a suggestion from the giant standing on the other side of the table.

"You said you don't know how deep it goes. What were you talking about, Major?" Placher asked, his voice still deadpan.

"First the fuel, then someone snuck over the wall and was trying toblow up our only option for escape? I can't square that circle. "Burton paused, letting his statement sink in. The number of American sin the embassy was ridiculously small. To accuse one of them of helping their besiegers sounded crazy.

"It isn't just Americans here," Placher said, looking at the two officers. "What do we know about the local guards and workers?"

The man was right. In addition to the Americans, the embassy had nearly a dozen locals of Libreville employed as either security, translators, or cleaning and maintenance crews.

"We don't know anything about anyone," Major Burton said, lowering his voice. "But I want the three of us, plus Sergeant Diaz, to be observant, to keep an eye on everyone and bring any suspicions back to this group."

He needed this to end. He was in way over his head, but he wasn't going to give up and he wasn't going to run.

***

The banging at the gate woke Major Burton from his troubled sleep. It had been going on most of the night, but something seemed different now. He looked down at his blood-covered uniform and the emotions from the previous night came pouring back into him. The blood, the smell, the fear, and the weight of the dead man raced through his brain again. His brain swam and soon the room started to join it. Grabbing the trash can by the door, he held it to his face and vomited.

"You alright?" Captain Anderson's voice came from the doorway. The Marine captain was wearing just his short silk PT shorts and T-shirt, neither of which did anything to obscure the Infantry officer's giant muscles. The captain wore his academy ring and on one thigh Burton saw what looked like a large scar. Not long and thin like a scalpel would make, but wide and gnarly, like fire makes.

"I, uh... yeah, I'll be fine." Burton spat more bile into the can.

"It gets easier," the infantryman answered. "Someday. I hope."

Burton nodded, then listened again. "Do you hear that? It's getting faster."

The banging had grown faster, and more intense, and was getting more so with each passing second. Before Burton could turn and grab his gear, Anderson was already running down the hallway, half dressed, rifle in hand.

By the time Major Burton made it down the hall, he saw Sergeant Diaz had already set up what able bodies they had into defensive positions.

At Diaz's urging, they had set up several different defense contingency plans. One was for if the besiegers broke through the front gate. It involved getting men in the second-floor windows of the main embassy building and firing at the Chinese as they poured through.

Every rifle the Americans could muster was now pointed at the gate, waiting for whatever came. They assembled on the second floor of the embassy, which featured a large open design with lots of windows.

Not everyone behind those rifles were Marines. Burton saw a handful of embassy staff at the windows. Even Placher, wearing his UCSBT-shirt, was there, checking his rifle.

The banging came nearly every second now, with such force that some of the scrap metal reinforcing the gate was shaking loose.

Sergeant Diaz was pacing behind the men kneeling behind the windows. "Eyes on your sector, no distractions," the sergeant said to his ragtag force. "Get ready— they are coming from in front of you. Steady."

Burton headed towards the other side of the large open room that faced away from the main gate, trying to think. Putting his fingers to his temples, he steadied his breathing.

And, looking out the window, he froze.

Two men had slithered over the wall, quickly followed by two more. The first two had been local, the second two unmistakably Chinese. Burton might not be an expert at infantry tactics, but he could tell the difference between an African and an Asian. Another pair of heads popped over the wall, as the four men inside the compound took a knee behind some shrubs at the wall's base.

While everyone was staring at the shaking main gate, the enemy was sliding over the wall behind them.

Burton wanted to yell, but what should he say? As the two heads peering over the wall turned into torsos, then legs, Burton grab bed his pistol and fired.

He didn't hit anything. The intruders were about fifty meters from where he stood, and even for an expert pistol shot, which Burton was not, that was a tall order.

But while the bullets from the 9mm didn't have any effect on the battle that was unfolding, their crack did. Placher was the first to turn, seeing the major standing by the rear window, his pistol in one outstretched hand like some Olympic air pistol shooter. The geologist ran over to the back window, M16 in hand.

"By the bushes, they are behind us!" Burton cried.

" No shit," Placher said, lifting the rifle to his shoulder and opening fire as the last two men cleared the wall.

He hit both as they swung their legs over. Burton saw the face of one disappear into a cloud of red and pink, and his body collapsed back over the wall he had just climbed.

The second was hit in the chest and stomach, and fell forward in a life less heap. Nearly landing on top of the four men kneeling by the bushes.

Anderson ran up to Burton's left. "How many got over?" he yelled at the major.

"I saw four—they are still down there. I don't know. There maybe more."

"Roger," Anderson said, handing Placher one of his extra rifle magazines. "Diaz, give me one Marine!" he yelled back to his sergeant still staring at the front gate.

Diaz looked back, hesitating, then grabbed the nearest Marine—Atkins, a scrawny private from Idaho—and shoved him towards the captain.

Atkins ran, a giant smile on his face as he slid in the open window next to Placher and let loose with his rifle into the bushes at the base of the wall.

He had his rifle on the three-round burst setting, and very audibly screamed "Die, Commies!" as he emptied the magazine.

Anderson smacked him on the back. "Get your rate of fire under control, Private."

"Aye, sir," Atkins said, frowning as he switched the magazine out. A pair of flashes emanated from the bushes and the window above Placher exploded.

"Oh fuck!" Burton shouted and hit the floor. Anderson too took cover, but he kneeled behind Placher and Atkins more gracefully than Burton had done.

"I want you to alternate—Atkins, you fire two, then Placher," the captain said over the incoming rounds. "I'll shoot while you two reload."

Placher went first, firing a pair, and pausing for Atkins to pick it up. The rhythm of the gunfight that was developing was something Burton had not expected. Yes, it was chaos, but watching Captain Anderson control the chaos was like nothing he had ever seen.

The intruders, on the other hand, had no such discipline and sprayed rounds wildly at the building.

"They're going to make a break for it—they have no cover," Placher said, and no sooner had the oddness of this comment crept into Major Burton's mind, he saw one of the Africans attempt to run from behind the bush towards the north. Deeper into the compound. If he disappeared, they would have to go room by room to dig him out.

The African was running for his life, but since he was a boy, Private First Class Atkins had been hunting game with rifles far worse than the one he held now.

"I don't think so, motherfucker!" he said, turning towards the fleeing man and firing. The man half spun, crumpled to the ground, and lay still.

Burton turned his attention back towards the men at the base of the wall, and saw two of them trying to scurry back up the smooth whitewall. They were still taking fire from the bushes, which meant that the intruders had left one man behind to try to cover the escape. The wall was about eight feet there, and they had no chance. But their options were to die behind the shrubs or take the tiny chance they could get free.

The Chinese soldiers tried to climb as their African ally covered them, and Burton could see a pair of hands and a head pop over the wall to help. Placher saw it too, and as quickly as they popped up, he took a shot, forcing them back down.

But they didn't give up. The first Chinese soldier ran towards the wall, stepped on his countryman's back, and leapt hard. The hands returned and caught him, and slowly began to pull him to safety. "Reloading!" Placher yelled, and a pair of rounds cracked out, as Captain Anderson stepped into the fight. The men were 50 meters away. A tap-in for an expert with a rifle, and the captain did not miss. He hit the dangling man in the spine, and he crumpled back down to the ground. The last Chinese soldier panicked and ran towards the building, screaming and firing, but in his rage he ran in front of the African who had been trying to cover their escape.

The group of Americans watched, nearly in slow motion, as the Chinese soldier pitched forward and fell, his back shredded by the AK-47 he had just run in front of.

"Shit," Placher said, followed by a "—the fuck" from Atkins.

The gunfire from the bushes stopped, and so did the banging. From behind the bushes, a rifle appeared, then got tossed to the cement. It was followed by a pair of black hands raised in surrender.

Burton looked at the scene before him. There were four dead and another surrendered, all lying in heaps.

"Sergeant Diaz!" Major Burton yelled. There was work to do.

***

The banging hadn't started up again since the attempt to scale the wall that morning. The half dozen hours of quiet and calm had been a relief. The prisoner had been of no help. He was a worker at a local mine. The Chinese who ran the mine had brought him here and given him a gun. That was it.

Burton believed him; the fear in the man's eyes hid no lie. He had taken a job as a security guard, and suddenly found himself trying to scale a wall under fire. The major could empathize.

The last body was being lifted and transported when a loud voice rang out over a speaker from outside the compound. It was in English, but heavily accented Chinese-English.

"Americans inside the Embassy. What are you doing? Surrender. There is no hope for you. If you surrender, we return you home to Texas, and Virginia, and Santa Barbara. Why do you fight when you know it is pointless? Surrender. "

Everyone froze as the voice droned on.

"We will take you prisoner for a short time, but in the end, you will be released."

"Fuck you, commie!" one of the Marines yelled out from the court-yard. His fellow Marines laughed, but there were nervous looks exchanged between the embassy staff.

The voice carried on for another moment, and then started playing music. A Chinese song that sounded like something you would hear in a restaurant or while getting a massage.

But there was something that didn't sit well with him. Something about the message bothered him, but he couldn't put his finger on it. He added it to the list of things that had been bothering him for days, but right now he needed to see what everyone's status was.

He walked over to the main office where the leadership was waiting. Anderson and Diaz were standing. David, the embassy representative, was sitting at the long table, pouring over a large piece of paper, and Placher was in the corner reading a book.

No one moved as Burton walked in, which didn't bother him. "Okay, Andy, where are we at?" he asked Captain Anderson.

"Perimeter is secure; no one else got in. We have five more rifles now, and ammunition to go with them, so that is a plus," the captain reported.

"Thanks," he said, then turned to the man pouring over the spreadsheets. "David?"

"We have maybe three days of fuel at our current levels, and six if we reduce to just bare minimums. Water is about the same."

"Okay. Any news on communications?"

David straightened his glasses and shook his head no.

Placher put his book down, and sat up. "I, uh... well, since we aren't getting your system fixed anytime soon, I thought I'd mention that I have a satellite phone in my car."

The group turned their eyes to the geologist in disbelief. The embassy had two satellite phones normally, for use in case of emergency. They were stored in the ambassador's office; both had been missing since the blackout.

Placher having a third was a game changer. They could call anyone, anywhere with it. Then it would only be a matter of time before the US Military arrived to save them.

"But it's parked across the street at the Moroccan embassy," Placher told them.

"That means someone would have to run out and get it. It's toorisky," Diaz chimed in. "We don't have the manpower to spare."

"We'll send Dembe," Burton said. "He knows the area, he knowsboth embassies, and I can trust him."

"Are you sure?" Diaz replied. "He is... African."

"Exactly why he is the only one who can do it."

"Cool," Placher said, getting up to head out. "I'll have him grab some of my clothes from the car too."

As the man walked by Major Burton, his brain connected what had been bothering him. "Stop—come here," he told the geologist. "Your shirt." He looked down at the man's T-shirt. "UCSB...University of California, Santa Barbara."

"Yeah, it's a good school," Placher said, looking puzzled.

Burton frowned. "The message said, Texas, Virginia, and... Santa Barbara."

"What, so what?" Sergeant Diaz asked.

"That is random. Texas—okay, everyone knows Texas. Virginia, same... but Santa Barbara. Why would a guy from China say Santa Barbara?" Burton said, the words tumbling out.

"They're just naming cities," Diaz said

"No." Burton ran his fingers across his scalp. "They've been a step ahead of us for days. Remember the guy last night? He had a radio."

"Of course. Soldiers have radios," Diaz replied, not humored by this Air Force Major suddenly playing detective.

Then Placher connected the dots first. "You only carry a radio if need to know where to go... and the only way they could tell you where to go, is if they could see you."

Burton ran out the door towards the CCTV room. Nearly breaking down the door, he dove behind the desk, tearing at the cables, shocking the young woman who was on duty monitoring the screens.

Anderson, Diaz, and Placher followed him and were watching from the doorway as the major dug through the pile of wires beneath the desk.

"Found it!" Burton cried. "Look at this." He scooted back, and the men leaned under the table.

"It's... a Wi-Fi router," Anderson said.

"Right. But who makes it?" Burton asked as he reached for the box, pulling it forward. " Huawei," he told the group, pointing at the name of the Chinese telecommunications company on the router's label.

"Yeah, but there's lots of stuff here, and none if it is communicating," Diaz said, the nerdiness of the major's glee starting to get to him.

"Yes, but look." Burton held up the box and turned it around. A row of three green lights glowed steadily. The symbol for "power" above one. The second light had a USB logo to show it was connected to the computers, and the third was a satellite icon. And it was glowing green as well.

"They are watching our live CCTV streams," Burton told them quietly.

"Holy shit!" the girl at the desk, all but forgotten, blurted out.

Placher looked at the router in the major's hand. "They are."

"Unplug that shit right now!" Diaz yelled angrily.

Burton smiled, happy they wouldn't be sending Dembe over a wall into the waiting arms of the Chinese Army tonight.

Maybe now they had a chance.

***

The sun had set and risen again on the embassy, and there was still no word from the outside world. As he listened to the Chinese music that floated across the morning air, he wondered if Dembe had just abandoned them, or even worse, had sold them out. Burton looked at his cell phone. No signal. The same as it had been for days.

"I think there is a spy," Captain Anderson said from the doorway. "I think you are right."

"Is it you?" Burton asked.

"No, it isn't me."

Burton smiled and nodded. "Well, it isn't me either, so that's two down."

Sliding his feet into his boots, the music suddenly stopped and the voice came back.

"Major Burton, you have a visitor at your front gate. Major Burton, please come to the front gate. You will not be harmed, Major Burton. Save your men."

Burton froze. Had they just said his name? That the Chinese would know the names of the Americans working in the embassy was not a surprise, but this was unsettling.

Still. As bad of an idea as this was, it was at least a way to get something they haven't had in days. Answers.

Next to the main gate was a smaller personnel door. It had been used for embassy personnel to come in and out of a small guard post on the interior, but it had been blocked up since Christmas Eve.

"If you need us to come out and get you, sir, just holler," the young private told him as the major stepped through the small door, out of the frying pan and into the fire.

He was greeted by two Chinese men who quickly took the major by the arm and pulled him onto the street in front of the embassy. A small group waited on the street and behind them, maybe a hundred more were there, all armed. This was an assault force if Burton had ever seen one.

The group on the street consisted of one short and stocky Chinese man in his mid-30s, a taller white man whom Burton recognized from the various international delegations as working at the Russian consulate, and Dembe.

It only took Burton's brain a moment to realize Dembe had not betrayed them. He was handcuffed, bleeding, and hung his head. Behind him stood two Chinese guards.

It was the Chinese man who broke the silence first. "You surrender. You surrender now."

So much for pleasantries, Burton thought. "Why? And surrender what? We are the United States, we aren't surrendering anything," he replied.

"You surrender or you die," the Chinese man demanded.

"Why don't we start off with introductions?" the Russian said, shaking his head ever so slightly. His English was fantastic, and had a hint of British to it.

"Absolutely, my name is Major Thomas Burton, US Air Force."

The Russian stood erect, almost regal, and smiled. "Pleased to meet you, Major Burton. My name is Colonel Alexey Kaledin, Russian Ground Forces." The colonel extended his hand, which Burton took.

"And my colleague here is Mr. Yuan from the Chinese Consulate. I'm afraid his English is as limited as his manners," the colonel said, releasing Burton's hand. "And I think you are already acquainted with... Dembe, is it?"

"I don't know who this is," Burton lied.

"You lie, you send him!" Yuan blurted out angrily.

"Come now, Major, I appreciate your loyalty to your man, but Dembe has already told us a great many things," Colonel Kaledin said as he turned to face Dembe. "Haven't you, old sport?"

Dembe shied away from the Russian's glance, and trembled in fear. Rage filled Burton. He had sent this man over the wall, and he had been tortured as a result. Fresh blood mixed with dried on the man's face and arms. He had been through hell.

Yuan stepped forward and shouted again, "You surrender, you live! You resist, you die. You surrender now, or he die!" He pointed at Dembe.

"Colonel." Burton looked at the Russian, choosing to ignore the Chinese civilian. "An attack on an embassy is a declaration of war. Do either of your countries know you are declaring war on the United States of America?" He emphasized the last words, hoping to invoke at least a little bit of fear at the name in the hearts of these men.

"They are aware, Major," the colonel said, looking over at the Chinese man. "It would be better for everyone if you just surrendered honorably. Then you will be returned home, safe and sound."

Burton couldn't believe his ears, and a black pit of negative expectations grew inside him. These men weren't concerned about a US retribution at all. What on earth was going on?

He decided to buy some time. "Kaledin?" Burton looked at the colonel. "Are you by chance a relation to..."

The Russian colonel's posture grew even straighter. "Why yes, Major, I am. The general was my great-grandfather. I am surprised an American knows of him."

The colonel was right; few Americans knew of one of the Czar's favorite Cossack cavalry generals, who had stayed loyal to his czar during the Russian Revolution at the cost of his own life. But Burton did. There was a lot of time in a missile silo, and reading was his thing.

"He was a great cavalryman and a loyal leader," Burton added.

"Enough! You surrender, you give it to us," Yuan blurted out.

Burton could see a faint hint of anger in the Russian's eyes.

"We will give you one hour, Major," the colonel finally said, after taking a moment to collect himself. "You have my word as an officer that you will not be harmed."

Burton nodded and headed back. A Marine had the gate open, waiting for the major to return. Burton had just reached it when he heard Yuan call out from behind him.

Yuan had Dembe on his knees, still restrained and bleeding. "You surrender!" Yuan yelled one final time, before saying something in hurried Chinese to one of the guards.

The guard nodded, lifted his rifle, and fired one round into the back of Dembe's head.

Rage ran through Burton as the African fell to the street. He reached for his pistol—but a pair of hands grabbed him from behind and dragged him back inside the gate. Burton struggled, but whoever had him would not give up. He saw the gate shut behind him, and recognized Anderson's voice speaking to him.

"—no point. He's dead. We need you." Anderson wrestled his commander back, and one of the Marines took the pistol out of the holster on Burton's hip. "We got a communication, and... we found the spy."

***

Burton stood in the dark room in the basement of the embassy. Standing next to him was Captain Anderson. Zip-tied to a chair was young Private Atkins. Burton stared at the piece of paper in his hand, then reread the message.

> *Major Burton,*
>
> *It seems like once more our nations will march into the breach together. We have combined our small garrison with the French. They have coordinated with one of their air bases in Mali and are expecting an extraction flight tomorrow. If you are able to make it through, we will bring you with us. The French have secured the airfield, but I'm afraid we won't be much help to you where you are.*
>
> *It seems like only yesterday we shared that bottle of Douglas Laing XOP on the veranda at your Independence Day Party.*
>
> *God save the Queen, and may God bless America,*
>
> *Lucius Cary*
>
> > *Viscount Falkland*
> > *Captain, British Army*
> > *3rd Battalion, Royal Regiment of Scotland*
> > *The Black Watch*

Burton had no idea what the first part meant, but he knew Captain Cary, and the letter dripped with the man's good-natured blueblood. His last line had also been a test. They had once discussed Douglas Laing at an embassy function, but never drank it.

"Why did you do it?" he asked the young man. His voice trembled with rage, barely holding it together.

"I just... I didn't think it was a big deal, I texted her before, why not now?" The young man from Idaho shook, nearly yelling from the chair he was in.

Burton frowned. "Is that what it was, a honey pot?"

"No sir. I, I never told her anything, just... just... I love her," the kid said. Anderson handed the man's phone to Burton.

He scrolled through a few messages and past the occasional nude pic. The messages went back months, thousands of them.

"I don't see anything in here of value. Where are you messaging her? In a gaming app?" Burton asked. Texts and messaging services were easy to scan. It was an old technique.

"I'm not, I fucking swear!" Atkins blurted out, finally realizing what the officers were accusing him of.

"How come your phone works and no one else's does?" Burton asked.

"Every day, at 0430 and 1640, it works. I don't know why. It is just... working," he said. "For, like, five minutes. No messages, just a Wi-Fi signal. There isn't even a password."

Anderson and Burton stepped back from the private, out of earshot.

"Sir, this is the stupidest fucking thing I have ever seen, and that's why I believe him," Anderson whispered.

"Keep him here, post a guard," Burton told the captain.

If it wasn't Atkins, that meant someone else. Someone was selling the Americans out. Someone who knew enough about what was happening.

All of this troubled Burton—the letter, the situation, and the spy. But what wouldn't leave him was something the Chinese leader had said.

"*Give it to us.*"

As he walked up the stairs and into the foyer, he found the outlier. Placher.

"Shame about the phone," Placher said, "and shame about Dembe."

Burton just nodded, before stopping and looking at the man. This was a segue. *Be yourself, Tommy.* "If you parked at the Moroccan embassy across the street, that means you walked over here, because you didn't want someone to see your car enter our embassy. Do you want to tell me why?"

"Took you long enough," Placher said, and led Major Burton to one of the meeting rooms behind the lobby foyer. Shutting the door behind them, Placher looked towards the window as he spoke. "I was supposed to meet the Chief of Station here the day after Christmas, but obviously... well..."

Burton looked at the man and shook his head. He should have known. They shared a CIA Chief of Station with a few of the smaller countries in the region, and he had never made it to Libreville.

"Why?"

"I have some imagery, and some documents about the lithium mines inthe Congo to give him."

"Where are they?"

Placher laughed. "Sitting in my trunk under the satellite phone."

"It has been out there the whole time and all they had to do waslook?"

"Yeah, pretty much."

"How are we going to get to it?" Burton asked the man.

"We don't need to. I know what it says. I have an idea, but you'll have to trust me."

***

It was just past 4 a.m.

Anderson had been with the drivers and the backup drivers, rehearsing the route to the airport. It was two turns, but he had drilled them to the point where they could do it in their sleep.

Diaz had been busy reinforcing the vehicles' doors with whatever scrap metal they could find. They had emptied the seats out of a pair of the eighteen-passenger vans, and were bringing two of the embassy's official sedans.

The plan was simple. They would cause a distraction at the north wall to make it look like they were escaping on foot that way. The tiny convoy would then dash out the front gate and cover the mile to the airfield. It was a terrible plan, but the best they had.

Captain Anderson had insisted on riding in the first vehicle, Diaz would take the last, and Burton would be in the first of the vans sandwiched between the Marines.

The Chinese music had continued to play over the loudspeakers all day and all night. It was playing now, droning through the African night. Burton sighed, and looked at David. The young embassy worker was sitting nervously by one of the walls of the motor pool.

"Who do you think has the best playlist here?" Burton asked him.

"Playlist?"

"Yeah, music. They can play it, so can we. We still have enough generator power to run the PA system at the gate, right?"

The embassy had installed a PA system around the complex. It had cost the US government almost a million dollars to install. Burton wanted to see what that money could buy.

"Well, I, uh, I have a pretty good EDM playlist. Some festival stuff, a little trance," David replied, brightening up.

"Fuckin' nerd," one of the Marines, a blond from San Diego, replied. "If you don't have Public Enemy and DMX, then you are missing out."

Burton laughed. "Do you have 'Welcome to the Terrordome,'Private?"

The kid's eyes lit up. "Oh fuck yes, sir!"

"Let's hear it. Get one of the embassy people to show you how."

A few minutes later, Chuck D's voice blasted out of the speaker sand began to drown out the Chinese folk music.

The Chinese responded, trying to increase the volume, but it was pointless. The American rap, older than almost everyone in the embassy, was winning.

Burton turned towards the group, and motioned Anderson, Placher, Diaz, and David over. Burton led the men into the darkened embassy foyer and up into the office that had doubled as their command center next to the CCTV room.

"Everything in place?" Burton asked.

"We have everything ready. Five-minute drive, walk in the park. Hopefully the French at the airport don't shoot us as we drive up," Anderson reported.

Burton nodded and looked at Placher. "Ready?"

"Let's do it."

"Okay. Instead of the diversion at the north wall, we are actually using that wall to escape." Diaz and Anderson looked at him as if he was growing a third arm.

"Sir! This is not the plan, this is not what we rehearsed, this is not wise, on foot we are as good as dead," Diaz blurted out.

"This—this isn't going to work." Anderson shook his head.

"We have to change the plan; it will keep the Chinese guessing. We caught their spy, but who knows what else they have," Burton explained.

He looked at his watch. 0425.

"Andy, get everyone stacked up by the north gate—Marines upfront; Sergeant Diaz, you in the rear to push any stragglers."

Sergeant Diaz looked at Captain Anderson to see if the Marine would put his foot down and take charge.

Burton looked at Anderson, wondering the exact same thing. It was a decision point, to see if he had earned the man's loyalty. Anderson raised his eyes and looked at Major Burton.

"Trust me, Andy," was all Burton said.

"Get moving, Diaz. David, I want all of the civilians together, everyone with a buddy. If they fall behind, they're getting left behind."

The major's heart leapt. *Thank God*, he thought.

Burton looked up to see Diaz checking his watch. "I'm going to make one last sweep to make sure all the communications gear is gathered so we can burn it when we leave," the Marine sergeant told them and walked out into the hallway.

He walked down the dark hallway, reached into his pocket, and pulled out his phone. 4:29. He looked at the screen, and typed quickly.

He hit send and turned back down the hallway back towards the group. He walked into the meeting room and saw the group staring directly at him.

"What?" he said, suddenly realizing Placher, Anderson, and Burton all had pistols in their hands.

Anderson spoke first. "Show us your phone, Staff Sergeant."

"The hell are you talking about, sir?" Diaz asked incredulously. He looked behind the captain and saw they had turned the CCTV cameras back on. One had been facing just down the hallway Diaz had just walked.

"Put your rifle on the table, Staff Sergeant, and show us your phone."

"No, it doesn't even work, I was checking the time."

"To make sure it was 4:30?" Burton asked.

Diaz's heart sank, and his face betrayed his guilt.

"It was you who came into the CCTV room to distract the person watching the screens when the intruder came. You were on guard duty when Placher walked in before the blackout. It was you who suggested we all defend the gate when they tried to sneak in the back, it was you who had access to the fuel, and it was you... who knew we were sending Dembe out." The major hissed this last line at the Marine. "It was you, this entire time."

"It isn't what it looks like," Diaz pled, trembling.

"Show us your phone, Staff Sergeant," Anderson replied coldly.

He turned and ran. He didn't even make it all the way into the hallway before Anderson grabbed him and dragged him to the floor. Burton watched as the two Marines fought. Placher flew in to help the giant captain, but he wasn't needed. Diaz had been nearly knocked out by the force of Anderson's tackle and was lying like a sack of potatoes on the floor.

Anderson and Placher secured his hands and gagged him.

"Take him to the North Gate. Let's get mounted," Burton said and walked down towards the waiting vehicles.

Stopping for a moment, Burton turned back to Placher and asked, "Did you set up their housewarming present?"

He could see the man's smile in the dark. "They brought the explosives in; we might as well give them back."

Burton knew the explosives would be hard to find, and were strewn allover the compound, tied to tripwires and other booby traps for the Chinese when they inevitably came to take over the embassy. They just needed to wait for Diaz's message to be read, and the Chinese to shift to the North Gate.

They didn't have to wait long. Anderson had told the remaining locals that it had been Diaz who told the Chinese that Dembe was coming, and they had been more than happy to push the gagged Diaz out the North Gate as their last act in the employ of the United States of America.

Everyone in the group heard the hail of gunfire from the north, and the large metal gates in front of them flew open. It was a race now. The four American vehicles came screaming out of the embassy. They passed a few Chinese soldiers, who had been too shocked to react at the convoy of Marines with ghetto armor bearing down on them.

They had slunk into the African night as the American vehicles made the turn and down the side street towards the Airport Road.

There was a car parked under a streetlight as they drove down the back road. Burton could see from the window there was a man standing by it smoking a cigarette. As the vehicles passed him, the man raised his arm and waved. Burton stared in disbelief as he passed. It was Colonel Kaledin.

For a moment the men's eyes met, Kaledin smiled, and turned back towards the car and away from the Americans.

They made the turn onto the main airport road. *Almost there, half a mile*, Burton thought as they drove. He could see headlights behind him coming towards them. *No, they're too late*, he said to himself over and over. *We are going to make it.*

Yellow flashes broke up the outlines of the white lights, and Burton saw tracers fly by the vehicle. *Oh shit, they are shooting.* The vehicles sped up, faster than their armored vans—they were gaining on them. Burton closed his eyes and exhaled. *Come on, come on.* Suddenly an explosion ripped through the night and Burton's eyes flew open.

The Chinese were still firing behind him, but there was fire coming in front of him too. Tracer bullets streaked by his window and flew towards the Chinese trailing them. One of their vehicles was on fire, and another swerved into a building.

Anderson's vehicle swung into the gate of the airport, followed by the rest of the fleeing Americans. The British and French machine-gunfire continued behind him as the Chinese broke away. Burton could see a French C-160 parked on the runway, its props spinning. He saw Placher climb out of the sedan behind Anderson and talk to one of the British civilians.

He nearly fell out of his seat in the van, and was caught by one of the soldiers guarding the airport's gate. Major Burton looked up at the man in the French uniform and noticed the man was wearing the white Kepi of the Foreign Legion.

"Welcome to the party, Major," the man said with a south Texas accent. "You wouldn't want to miss World War 3, now, would ya?"

ABOUT THE AUTHOR

Philip Voodoo

In Inyanga's shade, where shadows blend with light,
Lives Voodoo the author, fierce and grand;
A veteran of war, embracing the fight—
His heart beats freedom's rhythm, his command.

With iron fist he reigns o'er HOA's court,
Where gardens bloom and rules form sturdy chain;
Yet in this realm of order he finds support
With shawarma scents that tease him to remain.

In whiskey's warmth he savors every sip,
Astales unfurl from Aztec pipes of lore;
From Proust's deep ink he takes a thoughtful trip—
Each line unfolds like waves upon a shore.

Great American spirit in each word penned,
Voodoo wields stories that shall never end.

RETURN TO THE BEGINNING OF WORLD WAR III

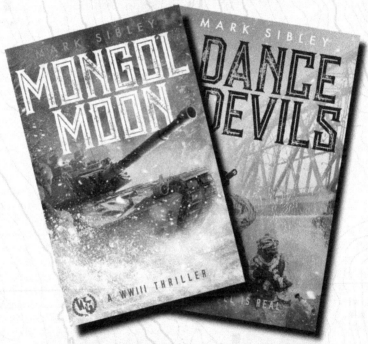

MONGOL MOON

Printed in the USA
CPSIA information can be obtained
at www.ICGtesting.com
LVHW052335071224
798538LV00001B/1

* 9 7 9 8 8 8 9 2 2 0 8 4 8 *